VOODOO DOLL

Also by Leah Giarratano

Vodka Doesn't Freeze

For Joshua and the rabbit:
we forever run together through
every page of this book.

Thanks to our Aussie diggers – our defence forces
and emergency services. When it feels like nobody
cares, remember there are millions of us in silent salute.

'. . . in a real dark night of the soul, it is always three o'clock in the morning . . .'

F. Scott Fitzgerald, *The Crack-Up*

Prologue

FACE MASHED INTO the carpet, Joss concentrated on breathing. If he kept his chin tucked into his neck, it reduced some of the pressure from the boot pressing down onto his cheek. Swallowing was out – his bottom lip was crushed flat against the rug, preventing him from closing his mouth. He let some more saliva trickle out; a wet patch had already formed under his cheek.

He angled his eyes to the left. He'd seen only three of them, all in balaclavas – the gorilla now standing on his head, the small, wiry one guarding the front entrance, and the fuckwit terrorising the women in the loungeroom. But he knew there were four: he could hear the screams of his host, Andy Wu, coming from the back of the house. Each scream was preceded by a dull thwack, a sound Joss already knew he would never forget.

He searched for an option; knew he had none. Not yet anyway. He tried to ignore the point of the machete, inches from his forehead, and focused again on his breathing.

Andy's wails were fading. From the room next door, Joss heard his wife, Isobel, her voice trying for calm, reasoning. Andy's wife, Lucy, was moaning, a low, animal keening. He'd heard nothing from the children upstairs. They had to still be asleep. God, he thought, please let them stay asleep.

All sounds suddenly stopped.

A pair of black combat boots appeared in the doorway and walked towards Joss. Each step upon the polished floorboards left a red imprint. Horrified, mesmerised, Joss watched the boots draw closer. They stopped in front of his face. The blood on the boots filled all of his senses. He could taste it.

'Watches, wallets, phones, jewellery. Get them all.' Boots spoke to the man above Joss.

The gorilla removed his foot from Joss's face. 'Did he open the safe?'

'Now what do you think?' Boots answered. 'We're ready to go. Go and make sure everything's okay in there.'

Joss felt the attention of the man in the boots shift downwards. His head free, Joss was able to incline his face upwards a little. When his eyes reached the dripping machete above him, he dropped them back to the carpet.

A boot nudged his shoulder.

'That your wife in there? Isobel? Is that her name?'

Joss considered the weave in the rug beneath his face.

The boot cracked into his head. Joss felt his left cheek-bone snap.

'Nah,' Joss managed, pain gyrating through his head. 'Met her here tonight.'

'Nice.'

'Um, thanks?'

'Smartarse, aren't you?'

Shit, Joss thought. 'Look. I just want this over.' He rode a wave of pain with each word he spoke. 'We just want to be safe. You came here for money.' He kept his eyes down; this guy was just waiting for a reason.

'Hmm. So give me your wallet, phone and watch.'

Sixteen minutes earlier, Joss had been helping Andy Wu, his wife's boss, clear away the remains of the barbecued dinner Andy had served them in his courtyard. The Wus' two children and his own little angel had been carried upstairs, leaden weights, sound asleep.

When Andy, on his way back into the kitchen, had dropped a ceramic platter onto the concrete, the crack was like a gunshot, and Joss had automatically hit the ground, rolling off the path. Reactions like that usually embarrassed the fuck out of him. Tonight, it had given him ten seconds to take in the sight of Lucy Wu with a fifty-centimetre blade held to her throat, a black mask behind her emerging like a piece of the night. Joss had scrabbled through his pockets. With an awkward twist of his arm, he had managed to throw his wallet into the bush behind him.

Lucy's eyes had bulged, silently screaming. While the intruder had motioned Andy to his knees, Joss had carefully taken his mobile phone from his shirt pocket and palmed it. He had been about to throw it to join his wallet when another pair of eyes and a glint of steel materialised in the night. Joss had dropped the phone onto the lawn. When he'd stood, signalled to rise by the machete, he had stepped on the mobile, and pressed it lightly with his toe into the night-wet grass.

Now, face down on the floor, he carefully lifted his wrist to show his watch to the man above him. Moving slowly, he unclipped the heavy silver band and lay the watch next to him on the floor.

'I don't carry a wallet,' Joss said.

'Sure you do.'

'I don't need one. I've got a company card. I didn't bring a wallet tonight.'

'Your phone then.' The voice was flinty.

Joss felt the man above him tensing. From the corner of his eye, he saw the blade leaving his line of vision. This guy was not going to accept that Joss had nothing at all on him; he was going to use this as an excuse for more blood. Joss inwardly tightened, preparing himself to roll.

'*Công an!*'

Joss knew the Vietnamese words from his childhood – *police, danger*! It came from the skinny one at the front door.

He heard the man above him exhale. He sounded disappointed. His voice flat, Boots directed the other men. 'Out the back.'

To Joss, he said, 'None of you will move from this house for thirty minutes. I may not have your ID, smartarse, but I can find you through these people. If you go to the cops we will be back.' He paused. 'Hell, maybe I'll come find you anyway.'

Anger overriding his training, Joss could not stop himself from raising his face to meet the man's eyes.

All the air left the room when their eyes locked. A millisecond later, Joss prayed he had been able to mask his shock of instant recognition, but he knew the intruder would have heard his gasp, seen his pupils dilate.

The man above him laughed when Joss dropped his eyes back to the ground.

Over the roar of blood in his ears, he barely heard the men leave the house. He hoped that the man in the boots would take his reaction for fear; that he hadn't noticed the non-verbal cues that indicated recall, identification.

The problem was, Joss could recognise those cues, and his hammering heart told him he'd seen them mirrored in the other man's face.

1

'GODDAMN IT!' JILL Jackson's toe caught the edge of a metal filing cabinet. She hurled the half-packed archive box across the room, coloured manila folders and white sheets of paper trailing an arc through the air behind it. 'Ow. Shit. *Ow*!' Clutching her bare foot, she hopped through the room, her face a warning.

Scotty knew better than to say anything, but his eyes danced.

Jill dropped into a chair, cradling her foot. 'I think I broke my fucking toe.' She rocked backwards and forwards in her seat, biting her bottom lip and grimacing.

Scotty waited a few moments then approached cautiously. 'Give us a look.'

'Don't touch it! It's broken!' Jill waved her hand in front of her, motioning him away.

'Oh, you'll be right, Jackson,' he said doubtfully, watching darkness already suffusing the white skin on the top of Jill's foot.

She looked up at the man towering above her, and to her horror, her eyes filled with tears.

'Oh come on, Jill, it's going to be okay.' Scotty reached out to touch her, then stopped. He moved his hand up to run it through his hair, then finally shoved it in his pocket.

'It's not.'

'Are we still talking about your toe?'

'I don't want to go.' She swiped viciously at a tear before it spilled from her lashes.

'It's a big promotion, Jackson. Think of the pay rise. Shit, I wish it was me going.'

'No you don't. And I don't care about the money. I was just starting to feel . . . ' She wanted to say 'safe', but Jill didn't disclose that sort of thing so easily, even to her partner, who was closer to her than her own brother.

'Yeah, I know,' said Scotty. 'But what else can you do? Anyway, it's only a secondment. You'll probably be back here with me and Elvis and the gang in a couple of months.'

They both knew that was unlikely. Job rotations within the New South Wales Police Force were not often reversed, and Jill's new seniority meant there would be little scope for her to easily rejoin the Maroubra detectives.

They stared at one another for a moment. Then silently they resumed packing.

It was a Sunday in late September, and the first day in five months that the temperature had climbed above thirty degrees. Jill and Scotty both wore thongs, crusty with sand from the beach down the road. The morning sun glowing through the dirty windows managed to paint even the dung-coloured walls of the detectives' office in an optimistic light; dust motes danced in the sunbeams. It was gorgeous out there. No way would anyone be in here unless they had to be. Jill needed to pack up, but Scotty didn't have to be there.

Jill swallowed the sob in her throat. She had never cried so much as over the past few months, which surprised her, given that she hadn't felt this secure for twenty years. The previous April, she'd ended the life of the man who had abducted and raped her at the age of twelve, and since then the dread that had nested in her gut had diminished significantly.

The past months had not all been tear-filled, though. Jill had also found herself laughing more than before, and on waking, some days, she had experienced sensations that had taken her a full morning to identify: spontaneity, joy, hope.

And then she'd been promoted. Again. Her rapid rise through the force had never previously thrilled or dismayed her. She'd accepted accolades with the same numbness with which she ignored the jibes of those she passed over. Twelve years ago, coinciding with her graduation from the academy, the force had implemented a merit-over-seniority promotion system. Many rising through the ranks had found the harassment and abuse of the dinosaurs being left behind too much to bear, but Jill thought little of it. She had not been wounded by the rumours – that she gave the best head in Sydney; that she had a cousin sleeping with the commissioner; that she was the token female, advanced only for political reasons. The lies never breached the Teflon cocoon she had spun around herself in adolescence.

But it felt different now. Since the death of the man who had abducted her, she was beginning to feel again. She'd even been on a holiday. For most people, a trip away signalled nothing of major importance, but it had been Jill's first trip away. It was a vacation from her fear and rigidity.

But a new job meant a new partner, and a new partner would mean new risks. The next team would want her to socialise, drink with them. Of course, her reputation for avoiding such activities would have preceded her, but cops always liked to find out these things for themselves. Her armour felt rusty: she wasn't sure she could fit into it anymore.

'So where are they basing the taskforce?' Scotty asked her.

'Liverpool.'

'No shit.' It was hardly the eastern suburbs. 'So you're going to bust the home invasion gang too now? You going to leave some of these crews for the rest of us?'

Jill had once busted an outlaw motorcycle group cooking meth down the coast. It was how she'd made sergeant. With the recent clean-out of a local paedophile ring, her superiors had acknowledged her gang experience with this secondment.

'Yeah, well if you blokes would get off your arses, I wouldn't have to do it all for you,' she said, smiling as Scotty feigned being shot through the heart. They'd closed the paedophile case together.

She sighed and put the lid on the last archive box.

'Looks like we're pretty much done here.' Scotty's voice sounded tight. He'd caught her change in mood. It was time to leave.

Jill tested her sore foot on the floor; it took her weight. It seemed her toe was just bruised. She glanced sideways at Scotty, feeling suddenly awkward.

'Thanks for helping, Scott.'

'Yeah, no worries.' He brushed his sandy fringe from his eyes and shifted from one foot to the other, staring at her. It seemed like he had something else to say.

'What?' said Jill.

'What?' he replied.

'Why're you acting like that?'

Instead of answering, he reached into his pocket and withdrew a package.

'I don't want it,' Jill said, backing away, shaking her head.

'I got you something.'

'I said I don't want it.'

He stood there, self-conscious, his hand stretched out. Jill knew she was being childish and cruel, but she felt unable to be gracious. She hated surprises. She hated endings. The rock in her chest pushed its way up towards her throat. Why couldn't things stay the same for just a while in her life?

The tissue-paper wrapping of the parcel rustled as Scotty's hand shook a little. Jill hugged her arms around her waist to stop herself moving towards him. She wanted to hold him, or punch him.

'You look like a wanker,' she said.

'This wasn't how I saw this going, Jackson. Shouldn't you be squealing and hugging me right now?'

'Oh give it here then,' she muttered. 'I don't squeal.'

Jill knew that when she moved from Maroubra police station she and Scotty would remain friends, but it wouldn't be the same when they were no longer working together every day. This gift symbolised something ending. She kept her eyes on his hand and took the package.

'What is it?' she asked.

Scotty just waited.

Jill picked carefully at the ribbon holding the package together, hoping to delay this. Her fingers became more forceful when the bow knotted, and finally she scrabbled at the tissue.

'Careful,' he said.

The soft paper fell away, and in her hand sat a heavy pendant on a chain. It looked old: a butterfly, studded with yellow and amber stones, its wings licks of green glass. It perched atop a small clear circle, studded around with the same glowing stones. Jill drew in a breath and stared at Scotty.

'It's a, um, magnifying glass,' he said. 'And a butterfly. It's meant to mean that you're beautiful and smart.' He said the last part in a rush, his eyes on the floor.

'You did not make that up.' Jill was incredulous.

'Nah,' he agreed, grinning, 'My sister did. It's nice though, eh?'

'Yeah. Ta. Now let's get the rest of this crap into the car so we've still got some weekend left.' Her cheeks hot, she shoved the necklace into the pocket of her boardshorts, grabbed a box and left the room.

Favouring her foot, a box under each arm, Jill stood in the hallway outside her unit, leaning her head against the door.

'Need a hand there, Jill?'

Mrs Williamson from next door. Jill had lived here for two years and had learned her neighbour's name only in the past three months. Another change.

'Thanks, no. I'm right, Margaret,' said Jill, putting the boxes down and fishing in her bag for her keys.

This was the final trip. Scotty had hauled the majority of

her belongings up in one load. It would have taken her at least three trips. He'd left her reluctantly, but she'd known he'd bail when she told him she wasn't interested in lunch. It took a lot of food to keep Scotty going.

She pushed the boxes inside with her good foot, and dumped her bag next to the others inside the front door. She scowled at their intrusion in her otherwise uncluttered apartment. Grabbing a remote from the dining table, she buzzed open the motorised blinds, and walked straight onto the balcony, slipping through before the blinds were fully open. She tasted the smell of the sea.

Her niece, Lily, last time she'd visited, had said the white-capped waves looked like cream on blue jelly.

Maroubra beach was a carnival today. Spring rendered Sydneysiders a little manic, the warm breezes blowing in some kind of magic – promises of holidays, Christmas, pool parties, heat. It seemed there were babies everywhere, and in every park, pairs of ducks hovered around ducklings struggling through the grass.

However, with the rise in the temperature came a corresponding increase in violence. The new season's energy triggered hysteria in some. Sunshine on the weekend was as good an excuse as any to crack a beer at ten a.m., instead of waiting until four. In homes without air-conditioning, tempers were tinder, the heat combustible, alcohol fuel. The flames ignited when the residents realised that the promises whispered on the winds of spring would not be kept.

At least they've given me a couple of days before starting the new job, Jill thought, moving back into the unit, her eyes blinking, adjusting from the sun on the balcony. Time to try to get used to everything. She didn't think she'd ever even been to Liverpool, although she'd seen the signs off the motorway when travelling out to her parents' home in Camden. Liverpool was fifty minutes' drive southwest from Maroubra, Scotty reckoned. For the first time, a departmental vehicle was parked in the small garage under her unit block. She'd had to sell her old gym-set to get it in.

Jill squatted down with the boxes on the floor. Where did all this stuff come from? Newspaper cuttings, personal files, downloaded articles related to past cases: these could all go, she decided. None of this information had been important enough to leave with the departmental files. She sat cross-legged with the paperwork, creating a pile she could take back down to the garage, to drop off later at her parents' home to be burned. She stopped when she came across a framed photograph. Jerome Sanders and his family smiled up at her. Jerome's mum had sent this, with two dozen roses, last May after Jill had rescued him from the same man who'd abducted her two decades earlier. She moved the photo over to a small pile of things she would keep. With a sigh, she flipped onto the same pile the clippings related to the current Sydney home invasion spree. In its clear, sealed folder, this morning's newspaper article landed face up.

Police Establish Home Invasion Taskforce
Doctors at Liverpool Hospital advise that the latest victim of the crime gang terrorising residents of the western suburbs remains in a serious, but stable, condition. The 52-year-old Green Valley man suffered massive injuries to both his legs during the vicious knife attack yesterday evening. His family remains at his bedside.
Local Area Commander Lawrence Last this morning

8

announced the establishment of a taskforce to capture the gang believed responsible for at least five brutal home invasions over the past two months.

'The violence is escalating,' commented Superintendent Last, 'and our priority is to catch these offenders as quickly as possible.'

Superintendent Last admitted that police have few leads as to the identity of the crime gang, who clothe themselves completely in black, wearing full-face balaclavas.

For the residents of Sydney's west, the decision to dedicate an investigations team to the invasions is welcome, but overdue.

'We can't sleep at night,' commented Kay, a Bonnyrigg resident, who did not wish to be further identified. 'I bet they'd have caught these people by now if this was happening on the North Shore.'

Jill realised she could barely see the newsprint in the gathering afternoon gloom. She snapped on a light and stretched her neck. Too tight. How long had it been since she'd last worked out? No more than a couple of days, surely?

Until five months ago, she had hardly missed a day's training since she was fifteen. When she'd taken her holiday, however, she'd given herself a break from her punishing weights and kickboxing routine. Trouble was, when she'd come home, she'd found it surprisingly difficult to start up her routine again. She really should get back into it right now. But she was hungry, she realised, and she needed a shower. She rubbed her hands, grubby from the clean-up, across her stomach, then stripped off her tee-shirt and walked into her bedroom.

When she dropped her boardshorts to the floor, the butterfly pendant dropped from the pocket and skidded across the granite floor tiles; it hid somewhere under her bed. She frowned in its direction, tempted to leave it there. Eventually, she bent to retrieve it, suddenly worried for the glass and stones. She held it up to the light, where it spun in her hand. Perfect. Nothing like her. Where would she ever wear this? She rarely wore jewellery, lived in tee-shirts and jeans whenever possible.

She held it to her throat in the mirror, scowled at the dainty prisms juxtaposed against the scales-of-justice tattoo on her shoulder, and the scars on her nipples, inflicted before she'd even developed breasts. She'd give it to Lily.

She knew she wouldn't.

She mentally relived Scotty watching her accept the pendant, his whole body a question. Already, she regretted her brusque acceptance of his gift. She wished she could explain to him that kindness from others felt like a threat. She'd like to have told him that her fleeting feelings of warmth towards him were blasted ice-solid before she could even identify them. Although she was beginning to realise that these defence reactions might now be unnecessary in her life, she could no more control them than articulate them. It only made it harder that Scotty seemed to know these things without her having to say anything.

Jill tucked the pendant into her underwear drawer, nestled it in. She shook her head and walked naked into her bathroom.

2

JOSS SLICED THE last crust from Charlie's Vegemite sandwich and wrapped it carefully in cling film until the bread could no longer be seen through the swathes of plastic. It occurred to him that his little girl might never be able to get her lunch out of the wrapping. He smiled, warmth spreading in his chest as he imagined her conscientiously trying.

'Someone will help her at preschool,' he told the sandwich, as he tucked it with a mandarin into her yellow lunchbox. He snapped the box closed, and as he'd been privately doing since she started school, asked the smiling sun on the front to keep his little girl safe. He smoothed the tape upon which her name was printed in Isobel's neat writing. *Charlie Rymill.* Her mother's surname. Good.

Joss had always hated his name. Throughout his thirty-four years, his first and last names had jockeyed for the position of most despised. For the first thirteen years of his life, his first name had held a slight degree of street cred, associated in some way with hashish, but he kept his double-barrelled shocker of a last name to himself whenever possible. No one was going to run in fear from *Joss Preston-Jones* for godsakes.

At thirteen, when the voices had told his mother to throw herself in front of a car, Joss's grandparents had put him in a private school. There, 'Preston-Jones' was completely unremarkable, but 'Joss' had earned him more than one bashing. After school, he'd joined the infantry corps. Within a couple of months, his peers had learned not to exploit the many opportunities to ridicule either name. He had a reputation for never knowing when to stop in a fight.

Since the home invasion at Andy Wu's, Joss had never been more thankful that Isobel had retained her own surname when they'd married, and that they'd given it to Charlie. Those psychos had never learned her full name – Isobel tossing her handbag into the boot of the car before heading into Andy's place for dinner had meant that the offenders had no ID for either of them.

Well, nothing formal.

The worry tape in his mind took up where it had left off before he fell asleep the night before.

Then his girls walked into the kitchen.

Shiny was the first word that came to mind. Charlie's golden hair shone, her four-year-old skin was translucent. She had on a yellow dress – favourite colour – and red shoes. A couple of weeks before, she'd begun to insist she could dress herself.

Charlie launched herself into his arms.

'We're late again, Daddy!' She sounded thrilled. She pretty much always sounded that way.

'Well, you're just going to have to drive fast then,' he said to her beaming face. He turned her around in his arms and deposited her in a chair at the table.

'Go and get dressed, babe,' said Isobel, trailing her fingertips carefully over his bruised face as she passed. 'I'll take over here.' She smoothed a dark lock of hair into place. Damn he loved her wearing that suit.

Joss groaned and headed towards the stairs.

It'd been ten years, and he still couldn't get used to wearing a suit. When he'd become a civilian again in ninety-seven, he'd thought he would never find a job. Do your twenty years, everyone told him. Get an army pension and take a while to make your next move. It wasn't a bad suggestion. But then again, no one but Isobel and his former commanding officers knew about his medical discharge on psychiatric grounds. People thought his tour of Rwanda had changed him; they had no idea how much.

Turned out, though, that his skills were in high demand in civvy street. The ability to lead, proven discipline and analytical expertise – he'd had a choice of jobs. He'd taken a role as fraud investigator for an insurance company, because he thought it sounded boring and he wouldn't have to work in a team. He'd kept these motivations out of his comments in the job interview.

He walked quickly past the mirror, avoiding catching a glimpse of his black eye. The intern at the hospital had told him that they could operate on the cheekbone, insert a screw. Nerve damage was a risk, though. Joss figured his cheek had healed okay the last time he'd fractured it, in Rwanda. He shook his head a little to disperse the memory. Forget surgery, he'd told the doctor. Well, you probably should avoid breaking it again, the specialist had returned dryly.

Downstairs, he got Isobel to do his tie. Six years of private-school uniform had made him an expert at tying knots, but each morning saw him feigning helplessness to his wife. Isobel, amused and frustrated, especially when they were late, like today, would expertly tie the knot, kiss him on the mouth. For two minutes, every morning during this ritual, he breathed her in. A couple of times he'd undone the tie, turned back to her with a look of shocked innocence, like, *how did that happen?*

Not today, though. They really were late.

As soon as the car turned the corner, carrying Charlie to preschool and Isobel to her office in North Sydney, Joss was again lost in images of the robbery. Isobel had wanted him to take some time off, get some counselling, let his face heal. But the last thing he needed was to sit around with nothing to do but think. She knew him well enough to let it go.

Preparing for work last night, he'd presented Isobel with some scenarios to explain his black eye to the other insurance assessors: a water-skiing accident, a fistfight with his mother-in-law; caught up in the latest home invasion? He thought he'd go with Isobel's suggestion in the end: *I fell off a ladder, painting the house.*

He joined the queue for the bus into the city. Usually, he liked catching the bus, people-watching, the relaxed pace of it. It made more sense than getting a lift with Isobel on her way to work, and there was plenty to distract him from his memories of the past: Balmain looked nothing like Rwanda.

Since the thing at Andy Wu's, however, his mind had hardly visited Africa at all.

Those eyes. He'd never have believed you could recognise someone you hadn't seen in twenty-three years just from two eyes staring out of a balaclava. But he had.

Henry Nguyen. Cutter.

Until his first tour of duty, until the Kibeho massacre in Rwanda, Joss's nightmares had all been about the last day he'd seen Cutter.

At age thirteen, two days after the last time he had seen Cutter, Joss and his mum were out the front of Fairfield shopping centre, waiting to cross the road. His mum had told him that they had a meeting scheduled with Jesus. His whole life she'd been telling him stuff like that. He was eight before he realised that people didn't really come into their house each night to poison their food; he'd stayed up one night to check. So, when she wanted to take him to talk to Jesus, the only thing he was worried about was that she didn't start the meeting right there on the pavement in front of Franklins. But she'd grabbed his hand and run into the street. He'd pulled away.

How could he have pulled away?

He used to get so embarrassed when she showed up at the school, wasted, falling asleep in the principal's office. Or when she'd accuse him of being Satan's messenger in front of his friends, screaming into his face, froth on her lips.

Is that why he'd let go of her hand?

Thing is, he knew deep down that he couldn't have known she would run into the path of a car. But a little voice inside asked, couldn't you have guessed? Maybe you knew she was going to do it? Why did you let go of her hand?

His mother had survived, but she'd been scheduled to a psych hospital, and Joss's grandparents had stepped in. He'd moved from Cabramatta to Mosman, changed schools, and had never seen Cutter or any of the others since.

Until Andy's house, the previous Saturday night.

Joss knew Cutter would not have been overjoyed to renew their acquaintance. The feeling was mutual. But that was not the problem.

If Cutter figured out that Joss had recognised him, Cutter would come and find him.

He had to.

Andy Wu would never walk again, and Joss could put Cutter away.

3

THE FEELINGS STARTED the day before, and built until he cut. And if something went wrong, if things didn't go like he planned, it hurt. Bad.

When he was a kid, Henry Nguyen would manage the feelings by slicing his forearms; carving crosses and snakes into his skin. Only when he'd cut to screaming point would the sexual tension ease. The kids who could watch him called him Cutter. The kids who couldn't, never spoke to him at all, kept their heads down when he walked past.

Nowadays, there was nothing he could inflict on himself to stop the feelings. He'd long moved on from that. Blood was still an aphrodisiac, but now he only started feeling normal again when others screamed.

Just lately, though, he hadn't been feeling right until the screaming stopped.

Guns had never done it for him. The pissweak and petrified had brought him plenty over the years, but he'd passed
them on again. What do guns get you? Moments of respect,
and then you've got to do something. Shoot, or move on.
Shoot, and it's all over. Move on and well, what the fuck good
was that?

Tonight was different, though. The hit planned for
Capitol Hill was on a gun collector. A suburban Rambo
getting through his midlife crisis with a new Harley and a
shooting-range membership. Word was, he was cashed up,
and had a nine-piece collection. Licensed and locked down,
of course, but Cutter was looking forward to cracking the
safe.

Persuading the owner to open it for him.

His men felt they needed the guns. Tried to tell him only
guns could get them through doors now, only guns could
convince people to open up and shut up. He saw them look
away while he was working. He knew they didn't have his
love for the knife.

He didn't understand this about his crew. In fact, he'd
given up trying to figure people out when he was in kindergarten. He knew there was a deficit in his makeup. Empathy.
He had figured out what it was supposed to be, understood
the concept, he just couldn't find the switch to turn it on. He
figured it was the same as colourblindness. Some people have
it. Some people don't.

Some counsellor clown had tried to teach him empathy
once – *try to put yourself in the other person's shoes, think
how they might be feeling.* Best counselling he'd ever had.
Helped him imagine just what might hurt the most. He'd used
the tip several times to hone his technique over the years.

Tonight, the feeling became maddening while he was putting on his fatigues, packing his bag. Lacing his boots, his groin burned so much he wanted to screech. Last couple of times, when the screaming had stopped, he'd been surprised to catch himself howling. He laughed aloud when he thought of the other guys' faces.

Cutter's laugh came out a shriek.

4

IT TOOK TEN full seconds for Joss to realise that the face was Isobel's, not Fuzzy's; that she was alive, not drowning in her own blood; and that he was screaming, clutching at his throat.

'Babe, it's okay.' She reached to still his hands.

It's fucking not. 'I know. I'm sorry. Another nightmare.' The sheets stuck to his legs. He shuddered involuntarily as his heart decelerated.

'I made an appointment with Dr Sherif yesterday,' said Isobel.

'I'm not going to a counsellor.'

'It's tentative. I thought we could see how we felt in the morning.'

He said nothing, climbed out of bed.

'What time is it?' he asked from the window, checking the perimeter.

'One. And we've got a visitor.'

He spun; Charlie stood in the doorway, the nose of her yellow dinosaur bumping against her bare feet, its tail in her fist. Her lower lip pouted.

'You shouted,' she said.

'Sorry, baby, Daddy had a bad dream.'

He gathered her up, hot and moist with sleep, and tucked her into their bed, curled in the nest her mother had made of her arms and legs in the bed.

He left the room, knowing he'd not sleep again that night.

He patrolled the house. Over the past two nights, he'd spent more time doing that at night than sleeping. He kept to the deepest shadows in Charlie's room, away from the pool of soft blue light that glowed from the nightlight near her bed. The window was secure. His pulse started with a car engine, but he quickly recognised the vehicle. The Wilkinson kid next door. Got work last Christmas as a baker. His mum got up this time every morning to take him to work.

His mind returned to the night at Andy's. The sights, sounds and smells walked with him through his quiet house. *Thwack. Aaarrgh.*

He chewed at the skin around his thumbnail as he descended the stairs to continue his reconnaissance. Guilt gnawed at his gut. He should've told the police everything straight away, but he had frozen at that point when giving his statement. He knew that if he gave them Cutter, the cops would stick a microscope up his arse. Would want to know everything: how he knew him. He couldn't give them that. Telling the police would mean telling Isobel, and she knew nothing of Cutter. Joss had to make sure it stayed that way.

He looked around the newly renovated kitchen. Charlie's

finger-paintings covered the gleaming stainless steel that had added a grand to the cost of the refrigerator. He couldn't lose Charlie, Isobel. He'd made it out of that life; he couldn't go back to that world.

Maybe it wasn't Cutter, he tried to tell himself. It might not have been him at Andy's at all. Shock can do that to you. Cause you to make mistakes. Shit, it had been twenty years since he'd seen him.

He rubbed at his face and winced; a stab of pain from his cheek started a headache that he knew would last all day.

He felt Cutter's eyes follow him as he continued his patrol.

5

FINDING THE RIGHT house was not easy. It's true there were a million McMansions around these days, usually with a BMW or Range Rover in the garage, but most of them were mortgaged to the hilt. Cutter and his crew had learned that most of these owners didn't have a spare dollar to save their lives.

Some of the fibro houses in Cabramatta were another thing altogether. One family had thirty grand under the bed for fucksakes. Cutter couldn't believe that Mouse, one of his crew, had given up his own aunty on that one. But when he'd cut off the aunty's thumbs to help her calm herself down a little, Esterhase had had to take Mouse out the back. See, you could never figure people out. Why did he put his aunty in it in the first place?

Cutter liked the garage entry best. Kept everyone real quiet until they were all inside. You had to know the house a little: look for one with an internal entry from the garage through to the house. Good thing Esterhase did furniture deliveries for his day job – he got to see these things. Then, wait near the garage, slip in with the car when they come home, and stay quiet till the door goes down. Let them get out of the car. Then they're all yours until morning. Do anything you want, go anywhere you need to go.

Nosy neighbours could be a problem. He tried to stay away from townhouses – connecting walls. It was true they had done one townhouse, and no one had come running. But they'd had to use duct tape to keep her quiet. Cutter preferred it when there was a little screaming room. Houses that backed onto a reserve, a school, an industrial estate; those that had a high brick fence, a busy road, a pool in the yard, just a bit of space around were best.

When Esterhase showed him the house with the guns at Capitol Hill, he'd been in heaven. The Capitol Hill estate was all two- to five-acre blocks. Double brick castles. Pool houses, guest wings. Still a new development, there were vacant blocks everywhere, next to half-finished houses, skeletal in the night. He'd be back for this place. Shit. Maybe he'd do another two here.

Almost time. Cutter couldn't wait.

Esterhase waited in the dark near the garage. The target rarely got home before one a.m. Owned some factory where they worked through the night.

Cutter sat in the van. The rest of the crew sat with him in their balaclavas, wishing Cutter would put his mask on too. They looked everywhere but at him.

Cutter stared out the window of the van into the night, grinning, rocking backwards and forwards in his seat. He kept his hands pressed down tightly into his lap.

6

IN HER UNDERWEAR, face sour, Jill surveyed the wreckage of her bedroom. The only clothes she owned that she hadn't tried on were her swimming costumes.

'So much for a couple of days off,' she muttered.

She settled on narrow grey pants, a fitted white shirt. She smoothed her hair into a high ponytail and scowled at the mirror. New people. Blah. She smudged a tiny bit of colour across her cheeks and eyes. She had no tan yet to hide the freckles across her nose.

At her breakfast bar, she sat with an orange juice and toast, bare feet on the bench, a street directory in her lap. She had planned on plotting her route carefully, maybe taking a drive out to her new workplace before starting. Yeah, right.

The call had come at five-thirty a.m. Another home invasion: Capitol Hill, a wealthy estate around fifteen minutes from the copshop in Liverpool. This time the victim didn't make it to hospital. The ambos had brought his body out in two bags.

'We're going to meet at eight, Jill, but I'll understand if you're not able to get here by then.' Superintendent Last spoke in an unhurried tone. 'We'll catch you up when you do arrive. Again, I'm sorry to call you in today.'

'No problem. I'll be there as soon as I can.'

The most direct route seemed to be Beauchamp Road to Foreshore Drive and then along the M5 all the way to Liverpool. There looked to be only a couple of streets to negotiate once she got off the motorway.

By six-forty, she was in the car heading southwest.

She wound the window down and angled her face into a stream of cool air. The morning sky glowed, and there was a promise on the joggers' faces as they bounded by.

She found a parking spot right out the front of the police station. Metered, but they'd settle that stuff later. The clock in the dash showed 7.38. Early. Good. The last thing she wanted was to start this thing behind everyone else.

Her gut twisted. She hated meeting new people. After nearly a year away from school following the kidnapping, she'd returned to find she couldn't speak English anymore. At least it felt that way. She couldn't relate to the things the other kids said, couldn't fill the silences they left for her. Couldn't make the little noises they did – the giggles, uh-huhs, nuhs, whatevers. What was the point? Once you said what you wanted, or needed, or what was immediately obvious, what was left to say? Some lunchtimes she'd sat, incredulous, listening to the roar of language around her. The words smothered her, choked her airways, and sometimes she would run to a silent classroom, wheezing for oxygen, struggling to clear her throat, trying to prevent an anxiety attack.

The ability to banter, which she'd taken for granted as a younger child, had never returned. The comfortable chitchat that knitted relationships was beyond her. Others saw her as aloof, rude, odd. Some instantly disliked her; resented her for the discomfort they felt when she broke the social rules. In the past, if she could've done anything about it, she probably wouldn't have, given that the distance kept her feeling safe. But today, starting a new job, she wished she had the ability to make the right noises, to help dispel some of the stories she knew would've reached here before her arrival.

She slicked tinted gloss over her dry lips, checked her face once in the rear-view mirror, and stepped out of the car into Liverpool.

The first thing she noticed was that there were definitely no joggers. Not a one. In Maroubra, they were everywhere at this time of day. Here, a few early risers hurried to get to work. Down a block and across the road, a man, his face lost in his hair, screamed ceaselessly at the traffic – *motherfucking cunts! You're all cunts!* A skinny young mum waited with a pram at the lights. A man next to her kept his eyes fastened on the brown paper bag clutched in his hand. Already. What time did the bottlos open around here? She figured that there must be a methadone clinic somewhere close by. A man and a woman in tracksuit pants it looked like they'd worn to bed did the junkie shuffle towards the chemist on the corner. She remembered reading a few years ago that the shopkeepers in the area were furious about the crackdown on the heroin

28

trade in nearby Cabramatta. The politicians had claimed hero status in the war on drugs, but the buyers and sellers had moved just five kilometres down the highway to Liverpool.

Mouth dry, Jill decided she needed a juice or something before she entered the building. On the other side of the road she could see an Asian food store open for business. She crossed the street. Tables of fresh fruit and vegetables, still wet from the markets, spilled onto the footpaths. Moon cakes and dim sum sat in the fridge next to cans of Pepsi and bottled water. She took a bottle of green tea to the counter, where a woman was packing a vegetable Jill had never seen before into small bags.

'Okra. More fibre than any other vegetable! You want some this morning?' The shopkeeper continued to pack as she spoke.

'How do you cook it?' Jill wanted to know.

'I don't know. Never had it! You try it and tell me next time.'

'Okay. Why not. How much?' Jill rummaged through the bottom of her bag for her purse.

'Two dollars,' the woman replied, beaming as she filled Jill a fresh bag containing twice as much as the others she had packed.

Jill crossed the road, cramming the bag of vegetables into her handbag. They poked out the top and she wondered what the hell she had been thinking. It was ten to eight and time to get in there.

Jill found Superintendent Lawrence Last striding down a hallway in her direction. A youth in uniform half-jogged to keep up with him. Last's baggy suit shushed with each over-sized step; grey suit, hair and skin seemed all the same tone. He hunched forward, as though the ceiling hovered just beyond his hair. Plate-sized hands swung by his sides. He saw her ahead of him, and his hand and the crags around his mouth lifted in greeting, then dropped again with his shoulders. He turned his grey eyes to his watch, and was with her in one final lurch.

'I'm so glad you're here, Jill. I really appreciate it.' The quiet voice seemed out of place from such a huge man, as though he'd tried to shrink that too. 'It's all a terrible mess, I'm afraid.'

He seemed so bent with worry that Jill's self-consciousness had already been replaced with a desire to try to lessen his burden. She fell in behind him as he opened the door to a meeting room. The man in uniform handed Last a folder and left them.

They entered a room already occupied by two men.

'David. Derek. Thank you for coming.' Although his voice was low in volume, Superintendent Last carried power into the room.

'Not like we had a choice, is it, boss?'

The words were for Last, but the speaker's eyes were on Jill. Leaning against a wall, arms folded over a bulging chest, he stood straight at the last minute, in offhanded respect to his superior officer.

'Quite,' said Last. 'It's a minute to eight. I expect Delahunt will be here shortly. We'll wait. Maybe if we all take a seat?'

Jill walked around the table to take the seat diagonally facing the door. The dragon seat. According to the rules of feng shui, it afforded its occupant power through placement.

Jill didn't know if she believed that stuff, but she did prefer that position, with her back to the wall – and she needed all the help she could get today. She reached the chair at the same time as the fourth occupant of the room. A flicker of a smile, and then he dropped his eyes, held out a hand, his other holding onto the back of the chair. Assuming possession of it.

'Hello. I am David Tran.'

She took his hand, feeling slightly put out until she noticed a walking stick leaning against the table; he was using the chair for balance while he greeted her.

'Hi. Jill Jackson.' She smiled.

They stood there.

'You take the seat,' she offered, at the same moment as he waved her towards it. They laughed, awkward.

'No, please take this seat. I will sit next to you,' said David.

'Thanks.' Jill dropped into the chair, looking up to see Muscles watching the exchange with an open smirk.

She looked around the table. The men all wore suits. What had she been thinking with her outfit? First day – task-force – suit! It seemed obvious now. She adjusted her shirt a little. Muscles still wore the smirk.

Just in time to save her from doing something ridiculous, like initiating a stare-down match with this idiot, another man entered the room. He must be another taskforce member. What had Superintendent Last said his name was? Delahunt?

Cargo pants. Phew. It was the first thing she noticed. Blue tee-shirt. Yee hah. She straightened a little in her seat.

Dark-haired and unshaven, he walked into the room on an angle, kind of like he was trying to sneak up on something. An A4 notepad, rolled like a trumpet, stuck out of the side pocket of his navy cargos. She figured him for around six foot. Making eye contact with no one, he sat down.

With his entry, Superintendent Last looked up from a bulky folder and rummaged through a box on the table. He pulled out four more folders of the same size, and handed them around the room. Jill left hers closed in front of her, focused her attention on the team leader, eager now to begin.

'Gabriel. Glad you're here,' he said to Delahunt. 'This thing's gone from bad to worse.' A pause. 'I'd like to begin with introductions. I've met all of you previously, so I'll begin with . . . '

A forceful sneeze made Jill jump in her seat. Embarrassed by her exaggerated startle-response, she shifted a little to hide her movement. The new guy sneezed again. An explosion. And again. And again. Each sneeze a shout. The others waited, staring at him. Jill forgot her own discomfort in her mortification for the man. The sound must have been echoing through the hallways.

'Haven't you got a tissue?' the sneezer demanded, looking around at the others. She'd expected 'sorry', 'excuse me', even 'oh dear', but he seemed completely unperturbed.

She grabbed her bag, more to give her something to do other than stare, and reached into it to find her tissue pack. Too late, she overturned the bulging bag of vegetables, and they sprayed across the table, two landing in the superintendent's open folder.

'Bumya,' said the new guy, Gabriel.

'Sorry?' She meant it as a question; as an apology for covering the table in okra; and as an apology to herself, for having to come to this bloody place this morning when she'd so badly wanted a few days off.

32

'Bumya,' he repeated.

She wondered what was wrong with him.

'It's um . . . ah . . .' he tried.

Muscles leaned back in his chair, hands behind his head, enjoying the show.

This was like a car crash.

'Okra!' Delahunt shouted, delighted with himself. 'Bumya. Okra. It's the same thing.' He pointed at the scattered vegetables.

Over the next hour, Jill learned that last night not only had the home invasion gang committed murder for the first time, but that they were now in possession of at least nine firearms. Most worryingly, however, it was clear that the motivation for these crimes was not just robbery. At least one member of this gang was a violent sadist. A sociopath. And his need for violence was escalating.

Six acts to date. Eighteen victims. One dead. One still unconscious, with multiple serious injuries. Reports from past victims had all identified one person who seemed to be in charge. There were four offenders they knew about, each armed with a machete; but only one man in each of the robberies had used his knife. The victims' descriptions suggested that it had been the same person each time: the descriptions of his height, his mannerisms, his voice seemed to tally.

Superintendent Last wanted them all to travel over to the Capitol Hill residence later this morning. He'd been there at five this morning, shortly after the daughter of the deceased had managed to free herself from her restraints and telephone for help. Physically uninjured, she remained in hospital, heavily sedated. Her father's legs, head and arms had been severed from his torso. His safe, containing ammunition and nine registered firearms, had been cleared out.

Almost incoherent, the survivor had managed to let the arriving officers know that she'd heard the whole thing.

Jill imagined that the sound of her father's screaming would have been less horrific than the chopping and sawing sounds that had continued when he stopped.

The taskforce members had been silent during the briefing, transfixed by Last's measured, careful account. Jill and David Tran scribbled notes. During the introductions, she had learned that David Tran and Derek Reid were detectives from Sydney's southwest. Gabriel Delahunt was the surprise – an Australian Federal Police officer, he had most recently been stationed at the police headquarters in Surry Hills, but like Jill, had moved around a lot for his previous big cases. She knew that the AFP often worked major crime investigations with community police, but she'd never worked a case involving them.

'Before we get moving on this thing,' said Last, 'there are two other important matters. First, we'll be looking into a couple of additional home invasions committed prior to the six we have been actively assigned. They occurred late last year, and there are some similarities which suggest that one or more of the same perpetrators may be involved.'

He cleared his throat, sat a little straighter in his seat.

'The second matter we need to discuss involves the media.'

Silence for a few beats.

'I am sure you heard the news this morning.'

Jill did a mental head slap. She'd been too busy figuring out how to get there to listen to the radio.

'I don't know whether any of you listen to talkback, but it seems that eighty per cent of callers want to know why we haven't caught these guys yet. They're talking about being too scared to turn the lights off; complaining that they've spent thousands on new security. Last week, one woman said she'd moved all of her family's beds into the loungeroom, where they plan to sleep every night until the offenders are caught. The idea seems to have caught on, and other listeners report doing the same thing.' He stopped to take a sip of water.

'The news this morning was all over the murder in Capitol Hill. Neighbours must have tipped them off. In fact, channels Nine and Seven and a couple of radio stations held special broadcasts this morning, dedicated to the home invasions. It is now the major national issue. Even the premier's been wheeled out to talk about it.' He paused again and scratched at an island of grey stubble on his face, as though surprised to find it there. Hasty shaving had clawed other patches of skin.

'The pissing contest has begun,' he said. It was the first time Jill had heard him swear.

'I don't know whether any of you have worked a headline case before,' he continued. 'I am sorry to tell you that you are caught up in one now.' He seemed genuinely apologetic. 'The pressure is horrendous. You will work ridiculous hours and be criticised constantly for doing nothing. You can expect no support from above me should things go wrong. Expect hysteria, propaganda and even lies in the media. I can't say it more clearly than this: *do not speak to them.* Come to me with everything. I will do my best to watch your backs.' He paused again. 'Please. Don't speak to the media. They will be everywhere.'

The superintendent unfolded like a giant pair of compasses.

'David, Derek. If you could ride with me please. Jill, would you come behind us with Gabriel? Please follow my vehicle. If we become separated, Capitol Hill is off Elizabeth Drive. You've a map in your folder there . . . ah, Appendix C.' He flicked through the folder to show them. 'We'll enter the house together. Expect crime scene, the coroner, and of course the media. Thank you for your attention this morning. I'll set new directives following our meeting in situ.'

Back in a tick, he'd said.

Jill sat in the Commodore out the front of the police station, motor idling. She stared at the backs of the four heads in the car in front of her, its engine also running. A uniformed officer was in the driver's seat, Last in front, Reid and Tran in the back.

She thrummed her fingers against the wheel, felt like she was doing something wrong. Where the hell was Delahunt?

At last he bounded through the front doors of the station, swung into the passenger seat.

About bloody time, she thought, irritated. She ignored him completely and pulled out, indicating to enter the traffic. Delahunt sat silently, hands in his lap.

She stayed with the car in front, watching for the street sign. Elizabeth Drive. There it was. Straight now to Capitol Hill. She relaxed a tiny bit, rubbed at her neck.

She became more aware of her passenger. Was she supposed to say something? She widened her senses, listened to him moving, tried to learn more about her companion in the quiet car. Her perceptive skills had been sharpened through years of fight training blindfolded, and she could tell a lot from others' barely perceptible movements, the way they breathed. His breathing was even, composed. She felt no tension, but he was not especially still. His active attention was directed to the road, outside the car. There seemed to be no awkwardness or tightness in his silence. She chanced a glance sideways. He'd donned a trucker's cap, the brim pulled low. No sunnies. His eyelashes were ridiculously long. Mediterranean skin, strong nose, generous lips.

'Best way to cook it is with lamb,' he said.

Jill over-corrected the steering a little. 'Sorry?'

'You gotta use heaps of garlic, like a whole thing. A big onion. Then brown the lamb with it. You can use lamb mince if you want, but it smells like shit. Better to use chops, or you could cut up a leg of lamb.'

Was this guy for real? After what they'd just heard? What they were going to see? Regardless, he was on a roll. She sat back and listened, finally realising that he was explaining to her how to cook the okra.

'You gotta have boiling water ready, or you can use stock if you want. Salt and pepper and plenty of tomato paste in with the meat. Add some sugar. A big spoonful. Then you throw the bumya in – you know, the okra – and cover it all with the water. And you have to cook it for an hour. You eat it with rice. But don't do that crappy boiled rice. You've gotta cook it absorption method. You can put lemon and chilli in at the end if you want.'

Was he done? Jill waited.

'Some people eat it with yoghurt,' he said.

He sat silently. Seemed satisfied.

'Right.' she said. 'Um, thanks.'

There were trees on both sides of the road now, large houses thrown around the hills surrounding them. The scrub grew more dense as the car ahead indicated right. Within a kilometre they were on a wide road, sealed, but without curbs and gutters. Jill was amazed at the rural outlook – they were so close to built-up suburbs, but around her were bushland, orchards, grazing cattle and sheep. On the horizon, the Blue Mountains shimmered, opalescent; the sky beyond stretched away forever.

Delahunt was taking everything in, head moving from side to side; at one point, hands on the dash and face pressed against the windscreen, he seemed to stare at something directly above the car. He wound the window down, sniffing the air outside. Jill watched him from the corner of her eye.

She braked with the sudden red lights of the car ahead. They were turning right into a gated roadway. A sign ahead indicated their arrival in Capitol Hill, also announcing that there were acre lots still available for sale.

Jill stared when the first house came into view. It looked like it had been dropped there from Vaucluse, or Hollywood or something. Despite one of the worst droughts in the state's history, manicured emerald lawns and verdant foliage surrounded the gated property. There must be two hundred rose bushes lining the drive, she thought. As they rolled though the suburb, she swivelled her head from side to side. Each home competed with the next for opulence, size, lushness of the gardens.

'Can you believe this?' she asked as they passed a walled

two-storey mansion with single-storey wings either side, each annexe as big as a large home in its own right.

Gabriel murmured something, totally absorbed.

'What do you reckon these people do for a living?' she wondered aloud.

'Tradies, a lot of them,' said Gabriel. 'We've passed electrician vans, building trucks . . .'

'Mercedes, Ferraris. We're in the wrong job.'

'So, that neighbour who noticed the white van at the victim's house last night wouldn't have thought it out of place at all,' he said. 'Most of these people would contract out their cleaning and gardening.'

'Looks like most of them would have live-in help.'

They heard the circus before they saw it. As they rounded a wide bend, the Superintendent's vehicle came to a sudden stop, and Jill hit the brakes hard. Cars and media vans lined the road. Clutches of people stood talking and smoking. A television crew filmed a suited woman gesturing gravely behind her as she spoke. A news chopper droned in the sky up ahead.

The lead car began rolling again, gestured forward by a uniformed officer. Jill buzzed down her window to speak to show him her ID, but he waved her through. The film crew turned cameras in their direction and Jill gave them the back of her head as she motored past the uniformed cop.

A hundred metres in front, unmarked and regular police vehicles indicated the victim's home. Jill pulled up in front of the next-door neighbour's house; behind a wide circular driveway, a curtain moved back into place when she glanced in its direction. She stared at the window a moment longer, then followed her colleagues towards the crime scene.

Nobody bothered to speak; a descending chopper thumping overhead drowned all other sound. The morning was heating up already. Record temperatures were predicted for Sydney this spring and summer. Global warming. It made Jill feel guilty; she loved the heat.

An elaborate intercom system stood beside the open motorised gate and around fifty full-sized palms lined the sandstone drive. A circular fountain the size of Jill's bathroom fluted jets of water into the air. When they reached the open doors, twice as wide and tall as doors on any house Jill had ever entered, she noticed that Delahunt was no longer by her side. She looked back and saw him at the gates, squatting by the fence line, rifling through the dirt with his hands. She followed the others into a marble foyer two levels high.

The cacophony from outside was instantly muted. Jill felt her edginess dissipate slightly. What would it be like to actually live here, she wondered idly, looking around at the opulent furnishings. Given the horror that had unfolded here, she wondered how it could feel so serene.

The superintendent herded them into a room off the foyer, a library. They gathered around him, waiting. David Tran leaned on his walking stick, his face pale. He seemed to be in some pain. Derek Reid, in contrast, almost vibrated with fitness. He brushed unnecessarily close to Jill and she thought she caught the sweet steroid smell body builders often emitted. He gave her a smug smile when he caught her looking.

'The murder took place in the media room.' Last spoke in his usual hushed tone. 'Of course, the body is no longer here. Video footage and photos will be available by the time we get back to the House,' he said, referring to the police station back in Liverpool. He glanced at his watch. 'The autopsy is in progress right now. I wanted you to be here, rather than there.'

Last looked around the group, and finally seemed to notice Gabriel's absence. He did not comment.

'I have no set objective for any of you this morning. Forensics are still collecting prints and trace. Just do what you do. Get a feel for what happened. Take notes.'

From a manila folder, the superintendent handed each of them a three-page photocopied floor plan of the home. He pointed out the murder room.

'We'll meet back here at 1200 hours. If anyone questions your presence, please refer them to me. Good luck.'

Last moved away from their group and Jill was left staring at Reid and Tran. David Tran seemed about to say something. Reid grinned at them and left the library before he could speak.

'Jill,' said Tran, 'you may be best off without me this morning.' He seemed to be still out of breath. 'I'm afraid that walk has already taken a lot out of me. I'll be moving at a slower pace.'

'Sure,' said Jill. She wanted to ask if he was okay, but wasn't sure of the words to use, didn't want to offend.

He seemed to sense her unease. 'I'm supposed to still be at home,' he said. 'Sick report. HOD.'

Hmm. Hurt on duty. She wondered what had happened. Well, this would be the time to ask, Jill, she told herself. But the moment passed while she was thinking of something to say. She nodded at Tran and left the room.

Jill figured Reid would go straight to the crime scene, so she made her way to the garage. She didn't want to see the murder room with Derek Reid.

The MO in three of the home invasions had been access through the garage. Donna Moser, the victim's daughter, had been asleep when her father arrived home. She'd awoken to a black balaclava. So far, she hadn't been able to give the police anything about how the offenders had gained entry. Jill figured if the offenders were onto a good thing, they'd probably stick to it.

Orienting herself using the map in her hand, she walked across marble, granite and thick carpet until she reached the internal entry to the garage, in a room next to the kitchen. The room held a plush couch and large television, and Jill glimpsed a bright, gleaming expanse where a door opened out to a backyard entertainment area and pool.

The door ahead of her stood open; beyond was the darkness of the garage. Jill realised that her tongue was stuck to the roof of her mouth. Maybe she should get some water before going in there.

She was halfway back to the brightness of the kitchen when she forced herself to turn around. It's not the basement, stupid, she told herself. This place is crawling with cops. You're okay. Dark rooms always reminded her of the place she'd been held captive as a twelve-year-old, and it was only six months or so ago that she'd been locked in the same basement, this time fighting for her life.

She stepped down from the living area into a black, cavernous room. Despite its size, it was warm and airless. Her shirt stuck to her back – the air-con obviously didn't reach this room. She smelled fuel. A dark four-wheel drive squatted ahead of her, ghostly smudges glowing from its panels in the gloom. She couldn't see beyond the car. Anyone could be there. Memories of waiting in the dark for the pain to begin crawled from her stomach into her mouth, and she closed her lips tight to keep them there. Heart thudding, she walked backwards until she felt the wall behind her; she slid her hand upwards, seeking the light switch, eyes always focused ahead.

Scrabbling at the wall now, her hand brushed the light panel, and she stabbed the switch on. The lustrous smudges on the Porsche Cayenne were just the chalky residue left behind by the fingerprint team. She stood against the wall a moment, blinked away the memories, already scornful of her weakness. Her contempt gave her the impetus to push away from the wall, and she moved towards the car.

If it had gone down like the others, she thought, Eugene Moser had stepped out of this vehicle into his garage and the point of a machete. The masked man would have led him back into the house, threatening to kill him if he did not comply quietly, and from there would have let in the rest of the crew. Jill imagined the man's terror, the impossible choices: Should I scream, stay here and fight? My daughter's inside – I can't let this man in! But if he stabs me now, he will get in anyway. I have to be in there with her. Maybe he'll just take what he wants and leave us alone. The options would have raced through his mind; his captor aggressive, masked, would have left him no time to think. Ultimately, he would do what he had to do to keep the knife from his throat, to try to placate his assailant.

On tiptoes, Jill peered through the tinted windows into the car's interior. Would they get any prints this time? To date, no fingerprints had been found at any of the crime scenes, and the DNA testing of hair and fibres was still jammed up in a queue with other cases. They'd prioritise everything from *this* case, she thought.

She walked through the rest of the triple-car garage. Along one wall, a floor-to-ceiling shelving system held every type of tool she could imagine. Drawers and cupboards were labelled and colour-coded; hooks held spades and small shovels, brushes and trimming shears. Each had been stencilled in paint onto the backboard. Jill appreciated the order, opened some of the drawers. Suddenly, she stopped walking. A tool was missing. A circular stencilled shape the size of a basketball signalled the outline of the tool that should be docked there. Close by, the hand saw's hook was also empty. She took out her camera, her lips a thin line. Along with the horrendous machete wounds found on a few of the previous victims, Eugene Moser had been dismembered with some kind of saw. Or maybe more than one kind, she thought, figuring a power saw would fit the first stencil perfectly.

The mechanised whirring of her camera droned through the stuffy silence as she snapped the rest of the tool shelves. There was no fingerprint dust on the shelving. She wondered whether the others had noticed that the saws were missing. No weapons had been left at the scene. She turned and stepped straight into Gabriel Delahunt's chest.

Her sharp intake of breath muffled a yelp. You scared me, she wanted to bark, but instead she just glared at him, not wanting to give away more than she already had.

'The others were waiting up the road,' he said.

If he had noticed her alarm, he gave no indication.

'Who?' Jill tried not to convey her irritation. Did this man ever speak in full sentences?

Gabriel held up a sealed evidence bag. 'Forensics missed these.' The bag held cigarette butts.

'Why do you assume they belong to the perps?' Jill stared into the bag.

'These hadn't been there more than a day,' he said, also looking into the bag. 'It rained a little out here the day before yesterday. But these haven't been wet. And a vehicle had been parked off the road next to where I found them. There're ten butts in here. Someone waited there a long time, smoking, yesterday at the latest.' He shrugged. 'Might not have been them. But it probably was.'

Jill stared at his profile as he scanned the tool shelves. Maybe Delahunt had just found their best bet for DNA from at least one of the perps.

'Two saws missing.' He pointed his chin at the stencilled patterns.

'Yeah,' she said.

'You wanna check out the murder site?' he asked. Like he'd asked if she wanted to get a pizza.

'Okay,' she said.

Jill could physically feel Eugene Moser's suffering in the room in which he died. His blood shrieked from the walls, ceiling, floor, demanding the witness understand the horror he'd endured. She stood in a vortex with the screaming, turning slowly in the middle of the room, buffeted by each arc of blood, drenched in the pain.

'The safe's through there.'

Gabriel stood at her shoulder, and she started at his voice, pulled from the nightmare. She glanced around again. The room was every bit as grotesque, but at least it had stopped howling.

The floor plans referred to this room as 'the media centre'. Ten reclining leather armchairs sat in two rows in front of a wall. On the ceiling above the wall, Jill could see a recessed opening where the screen must drop down. In the middle of the house, the room had no windows, and the doors sealed completely to shut out all light. The artificial lights rendered the scene somehow more garish. She could see no surface unmarked by blood.

She followed Gabriel through the room towards an opening in the wall – some kind of door – which stood slightly ajar. It was the same colour as the wall and she could see no handle. Were it closed, she doubted she could have found it again.

'It's not on the floor plan,' said Gabriel. He walked inside.

The size of a large walk-in robe, this room had obviously housed the guns. Display racks were empty, their black bolts open. A small safe stood ajar, some papers scattered on the floor in front of it. A monitor at the back of the room depicted four views of the house and grounds, each scene changing after thirty seconds or so to exhibit another part of the property. On the screen, Jill watched Derek Reid walk into one of the quadrants; in another, two uniformed officers stood guard at the front door.

'So this is a panic room,' said Jill, speaking her thoughts aloud. 'First time I've seen one. Except for that movie, of course.' She looked down at a computer under the monitor. Everything had already been chalked. She noticed the time display on the electronic equipment.

'Shit,' she said. 'It's already gone twelve o'clock. We'd better get back to the library.'

Gabriel was on his hands and knees. Was he sniffing the floor? Hearing her words, he stood and followed her out.

Outside the media centre, Jill made straight for a set of French doors at the back of the house. She needed air that did not reek of blood.

In contrast with the starkly modern media centre, this room held a chaise longue and several ornate cabinets full of trinkets. Jill opened the glass doors onto a pretty courtyard, sheltered from the rest of the yard by flowering shrubs. A semi-circular stone love-seat watched over a fishpond; two fat golden carp swam lazily. Jill followed their movements and saw that the pond flowed under a small bridge and out of the courtyard, apparently to a larger pool elsewhere.

'This is pretty good,' said Delahunt.

'Yeah,' she answered flatly.

'At least one of them can't handle what's going on.'

'What are you talking about?' She realised he was not looking at the fish.

'Vomit.'

'Huh?'

'Here,' he said, pointing to a shrub behind the folded-out doors. 'Someone was sick.'

On the ground, in the bushes, someone had thrown up.

'Could have been one of us,' she said.

'Could have been one of them,' he countered. 'Saw what his buddy did and couldn't take it.'

He watched while Jill photographed the area, and moved the bushes aside for her.

'And that would make it all very interesting.'

He sounded delighted.

7

'I'D PREFER THE movies to the counsellor,' said Joss, falling back on the bed against the pillows. He watched the top of the tree moving outside their window.

'You're bloody hopeless!' said Isobel, dropping down next to him. 'What if I want to go?'

'Do you?'

'I don't know,' she answered. 'But you made me take a day off work for nothing.'

'Well, not for nothing,' he said, wiping drops of water from her bare shoulder, missed when she'd towelled off after their shower.

'But Joss,' she said, pulling away a little and looking him in the eye, 'your nightmares have been worse than ever since the robbery.'

'Haven't you been dreaming about it?'

'Yeah. A few times. I dreamed last night that they broke in here, and we were running, and we couldn't find Charlie.' She paused, pain in her eyes. 'And then there was Andy being cut again, except then it was me getting cut, and you were holding the knife.' She shook her head.

'Shit. Sounds like mine,' he lied. 'Maybe we should go to the counsellor.'

'Would you say anything this time?'

'I think you need it more than me. Talking about shit with a stranger has never helped me. I'll wait outside.'

'It was just so horrible, Joss.'

'I know.' *Thwack. Aaarrgh!* The sound was on loop tape. 'Do you think we should use today to go out to the hospital to see Andy?' Please say no, he thought, hating himself for feeling that way. He wasn't sure that he could handle seeing Isobel's boss again just yet.

'I thought I told you. Sorry,' said Isobel. 'I called Lucy last night. The doctors are allowing immediate family only. He's still unconscious.'

'Poor bastard.'

Isobel sighed, ran her fingertips lightly over his blackened cheek; the bruise was still spreading. 'Anything good on at the movies?'

'I don't know. Let's go find out.'

She stayed where she was; watched the ceiling fan cycling slowly.

'Work organised a collection for Andy and Lucy,' she said. 'We're gonna try to get ramps built so he can wheel in and out of his house.'

'Sounds good.' *Thwack, Aaarrgh.* 'Let's get out of here.'

*

49

The movie had been a bad idea. He hadn't been able to get a seat in the last row, and that left his back exposed. Joss rubbed at his neck: his shoulders ached from the tension of straining to hear everything behind him. It had been a while since he'd had to sit with his back to the wall.

And now there's this freaking crowd, he thought, trying to surf to the front of the wave that had spilled out of the theatre when the movie ended. Isobel half-jogged along beside him, aware of his need to get out.

'Joss, we've got to pay for parking before we go to the car.' She squeezed his hand.

'Where?' All he could see were the exit doors.

'Just back in the shopping centre a bit. Near the lifts,' she said. 'You want me to go?'

Yes. 'Nah, I'm coming.'

He followed her through the cinema foyer to an alcove between the shops and another parking station. The area was quiet and bare, brightly lit and airless, discouraging people from loitering. An elevator whisked customers to the glamour of the shops below, minimising the time they were away from spending.

Isobel had her purse out, facing the machine, figuring out how to insert the ticket, when Joss, reading the instructions over her shoulder, felt movement behind him and spun on the spot.

The fact that time had slowed to half-speed left him convinced for a moment that this was just another nightmare. But even his worst nightmares did not inject this much adrenalin into his gut. He nearly evacuated his bowels. He backed hard into Isobel, jamming her against the ticket machine. Safe. Between him and the wall.

In front of him stood Henry Nguyen. Cutter.

'Hey!' said Isobel, at the same time that Cutter said, 'Hey. Don't I know you?'

Joss scanned the ground, searching for a bottle to smash. Nothing. No litter, nothing he could use as a weapon. A Coke machine in the corner. The bottles would be plastic anyway. Fuck. He opened his arms, protecting Isobel, ready to fly forward and tear this guy's face off.

'Joss. Aren't you Joss? We used to go to school together.'

'Joss, what's wrong?' Isobel sounded unsure.

'Henry. Henry Nguyen. Remember me?' He was holding out his hand.

Isobel was trying to get out from behind him.

'I saw you back in the cinema,' Cutter continued. 'I can't believe I recognised you. How long since we've seen each other, man?'

The question hung in the air.

'I think we were thirteen or fourteen. Shit. It's been forever,' Cutter continued.

He'd dropped his hand, but hadn't moved forward. Joss saw Cutter's mouth moving, but the words were faint, muffled by the pulse in his ears.

Ready. I'm ready, motherfucker, he told Cutter with his eyes.

Cutter was laughing. Isobel was really struggling now.

'Joss, let me out!'

'You're squashing your wife, man,' said Cutter. 'I mean, is this your wife?'

'I. Don't. Know. You.' Joss's voice was quiet. His eyes never left the other man's.

Isobel stopped struggling. Went small behind his back. Knew, when she heard his voice: danger.

'Yeah, whatever man,' Cutter laughed again, only with his mouth, his eyes stayed dead. He flicked long black hair off his shoulders, exposing the gaol tats on his neck.

'Good to see you anyway, Joss. Maybe you'll remember me later. And we can catch up. I'm sure you'll be able to find me if you come around the old neighbourhood. Or I can find you. Think about it. It would be good to see you again.'

With a sideways step, Cutter was gone.

A polished circular table had been moved into the library. When Jill and Gabriel arrived, Superintendent Last was seated with his back to the door. Next to him, his uniformed driver stabbed with two fingers at keys on a laptop. David Tran had the dragon seat, facing the door. Derek Reid slouched in a deep armchair that had been pushed against the wall to make room for the table.

'Did ya get lost?' Reid asked, arms folded across his huge chest, a suggestive smile on his face. 'Big house. Lots of rooms.'

Three empty chairs waited at the table. Jill took the seat that showed Reid her back.

'Jill. Gabriel.' Superintendent Last acknowledged them. 'Colin here is noting our impressions before we leave the site.' He pointed his chin at the officer with the laptop. 'David's just begun making his comments,' he continued. 'Help yourself to some coffee.'

Jill took a bottle of water from the centre of the table instead. She sipped as she listened to Tran talking about his impressions of the site.

'I couldn't help but notice,' David Tran spoke respectfully, with a faint Vietnamese accent, 'how many items of value the group left behind. I think that is what struck me the most while here.' He sat straight in his seat, and looked at each of them as he spoke. 'If we assume that the whole gang was here last night, then they had four men to carry away stolen property. I was expecting to find the house more ... disturbed. I did not expect to find a laptop computer. It was in plain sight in the daughter's bedroom. Also in her room was a box containing some gold jewellery. In the master bedroom, I found an expensive watch, and a mobile phone. These are items that could easily have been taken by the group.'

'Very true,' said Superintendent Last. 'When we first got here, we even found a couple of hundred in cash in the breadbox in the kitchen. Previous victims have reported that all such items were cleared out. What do you make of that?'

'Well, obviously in this case they came for the guns,' Reid answered.

'Has the surviving victim made any comment about the number of offenders?' asked Tran. 'Maybe there were fewer on this occasion?'

'She hasn't been able to cover specifics yet, no,' Last said. 'It is possible there were fewer offenders. That might have left them less time to cover the house thoroughly.'

'Maybe they couldn't focus,' Gabriel spoke for the first time. The group turned to him. 'Could be they weren't feeling well.'

Reid snorted. 'What? You think they all got a headache or something, Delahunt?'

Gabriel paused. 'Yes. I think that's a good way to describe it.' He was silent again; his trucker cap pulled low, eyes on the table, eyelashes brushing his cheeks.

They waited, until Last finally suggested, 'Maybe if you think it through aloud, Gabriel? We'd like to hear what you're thinking. It's all just hypotheses at this stage.'

'I think that the killer, their leader, is a headache for the rest of the gang.' He smiled, happy with his analogy. 'One of them was literally sick last night.' He told them about the vomit in the bushes near the murder room, his language indicating that both he and Jill had made the discovery, although she hadn't had anything to do with the find.

In response, Last opened the mobile phone on the table, and instructed somebody to take a specimen sample from the courtyard immediately. He put the phone down and stared at Gabriel, nodding at him to go on.

Gabriel just smiled back at him.

'Ah, could you talk a little more about what you think happened here last night, Gabriel?' said the superintendent.

'Oh. Okay.' He continued. 'Well, three of them waited in a white van in front of the vacant block a couple of houses up. At least one of them was smoking.' He withdrew the evidence bag from his jacket and placed it on the table in front of him, then skidded it across to Tran, who was staring at the package. 'Then same old, same old. One of them crept in behind the Porsche, got the vic out and let the others in. Then the leader took over. The others kept the girl quiet. They were too panicked or revolted by what they saw in the media room and they weren't able to concentrate on clearing the house of valuables. At least one of them besides the leader had to go right past Eugene Moser's body to help carry the guns. And one of them couldn't keep his food down.'

For the first time, he seemed to notice the insulated cups of coffee in the centre of the table, and he reached across to take one. Jill noticed his bicep bulge as his arm moved. His skin was a dark honey colour.

Gabriel opened the lid on the styrofoam cup and looked at the coffee. They all watched him.

'Why are you sure it was one of them that vomited?' asked Tran. 'We should ask the first officers on the scene if any of them became ill.'

'Betcha forensics'll find the spew belongs to a dog,' said Reid.

'They weren't ready for the saws,' said Gabriel. 'I think it's thrown this group over the edge. All of them. The leader's out of control and the others are pissing their pants. The group's on the brink and they're already making mistakes. It's gonna be easier to find them, but more people are going to die first. The killer's on a spree. He can't stop.' After this rush of words, he looked down at his coffee again, pushed his nose past the rim of the cup and took several deep sniffs.

Last said, 'Saws? You said saws.'

'Jill found them.' Gabriel opened a different coffee and sniffed it, then compared the scent to his other cup.

Superintendent Last focused his attention on Jill.

'The tool rack in the garage,' she said. 'Um. They weren't dusted, and there's a power saw and hand saw missing. We figured maybe they could have been used on Moser.'

'Great work,' said Last, looking over the shoulder of the man typing, ensuring he'd captured the comments. He reached for his phone again and instructed someone to pick up the evidence bag and dust the shelves in the garage. He then called the medical examiner's office and left a message about the missing saws.

While Last was on the phone, Jill tried desperately to find something to distract her from Gabriel. He'd turned to David Tran, asking him, 'So what's wrong with your legs?'

She stood and walked to the back of the room. Floor-to-ceiling bookshelves covered the back wall. A wooden A-frame ladder on wheels waited in the corner of the room, offering access to the books near the ceiling. Leatherbound copies of Dickens, Shakespeare, Austen. Books on architecture, modern art, classical music. She wondered if any of them had been read. It seemed like a designer's idea of a library. She turned when she heard someone moving towards her.

Reid. He leaned in close.

'Well spotted out there, Jackson.' A sheen of sweat, or maybe moisturiser, highlighted open pores across his nose and cheeks. She stepped back a little from the sweet smell of his breath.

After a few beats, he said, 'Look, since you're new around here,' – *Oh God, here it comes*, she thought – 'I was thinking maybe I could introduce you to the rest of the Ds out here. We drink at the Crossroads on Wednesday nights.'

'Yeah. I don't think so,' she said.

She knew she was supposed to make an excuse here, say something conciliatory, even come up with a new topic once she'd declined, but when she could not find even one word, she just waited.

'You can bring your boyfriend, Delahunt.'

Things never changed much from the schoolyard. She almost laughed, but instead moved back to the table. Superintendent Last looked as though he was ready to speak again.

'Good work today,' he told them when they were again

seated. 'Now I'd just like to discuss how we're going to use our time over the next few days. First up, I'd like to meet each morning at eight as we did today. That okay with everyone?' He looked around the group. 'Appreciate it,' he said, his eyes meeting Jill's.

'Next, we'll need to re-interview the direct victims of the past robberies.' He removed two stapled groups of paper from his folder. 'Names and current contacts. David and Derek, I've got you interviewing the vics from robberies one, three and five. Jill and Gabriel, you've got two, four and Donna Moser, who's over at Liverpool Hospital at the moment.' He gathered together his belongings. 'I'm heading back to the House. If anyone wants a lift back now, you're welcome. If you want to stay out here a while, there'll be plenty of people heading back later this afternoon. See you in the morning.' He left the room.

Jill checked her watch. Almost one o'clock. She moved over to Gabriel, and indicated the paper containing the names of the victims they were to interview.

'Do you want to see whether we can get one of these interviews in this arvo?' she asked him.

'Yep,' he answered, pulling out his phone. 'Where do you want to start?'

'Somewhere close?'

'Abbotsbury. Down the road.'

She studied the list. The victims from incident number two lived at Abbotsbury. Ryan Temple and Justine Rice. While Gabriel dialled the number, she glanced over their police statements, although she knew the story already from the meeting this morning. Justine was seventeen, Ryan a year older.

On the night of the robbery, Ryan had been staying over at Justine's house while her parents were overseas. The gang had just knocked on the door this time. Ryan opened it, and in they came. Easy as that. They'd taken Justine upstairs and worked Ryan over in the loungeroom. He'd been bound and beaten, the two offenders upstairs telling Justine they'd kill Ryan if she didn't hurry up and get them cash, jewellery, drugs, everything valuable in the house. No one was cut on this occasion, but the offenders were wearing their trademark black and balaclavas, and carrying machetes.

The apparent leader had been upstairs with Justine. Both she and Ryan had indicated that he'd given orders to the other offenders. Their descriptions of his height and role within the group matched those given by other victims.

Jill read Justine's description of him. She'd guessed he was around 5'8", a little shorter than Ryan, her boyfriend. A thin, black ponytail extended beyond his balaclava; his eyes were dark, Asian. Australian accent. No labels she could detect on his clothing, although the others had been wearing black sports clothes bearing well-known brand names. She'd seen tattoos though – a scorpion on his hip, glimpsed, she said, when he had reached for her brother's Game Boy when raiding one of the rooms, and what looked like crudely inked spiders on the side of his neck between his collar and the balaclava.

Jill caught the end of Gabriel's conversation, and looked up from the file.

'Yes. Thank you, Mrs Rice. We'll see you soon.'

Gabriel closed the phone and together they left the house.

On the way to the car, Jill breathed deeply, ridding herself of the scent of death that had permeated every room of the house. Gabriel stood by the driver's door. Apparently he was driving this time. She threw him the keys and took the passenger seat without comment, putting her sunglasses on and winding up the window.

When they'd left Capitol Hill behind, Jill leaned back in her seat. Gabriel drove confidently, seemingly comfortable with their silence, allowing Jill to think about the kids they were on their way to interview. She thought again about Justine's statement. Something was different with this case. For a start, the violence was much less severe than in any of the others. She thought about the statements she'd read from the other victims. She couldn't be certain, as she'd not had a chance to study them properly, but she was pretty sure this was the only time tattoos had been mentioned.

8

CHLOE FARRELL SHIFTED uncomfortably in the early afternoon sun. The crutch of her tights had been heading south since she got out here this morning. She'd thought about finding a toilet somewhere and taking them off altogether, but the blisters from her new shoes would only get worse. She scowled at her boss, Deborah Davies, as she postured for the camera. Davies had shown up at lunchtime after Chloe had called her, letting her know she'd finally persuaded one of the Capitol Hill residents to be interviewed. Deborah had finished the interview, using Chloe's typed list of questions, and the neighbour had gone back inside her palatial home, thrilled to have met the current affairs presenter she watched in her loungeroom every night. Davies was now recording the fill-ins: asking the questions over and over again in an ever more concerned tone. Giving empathic nods and outraged shakes of her head to her favourite thing in the world: the camera. The gestures and comments would be edited into the piece later, by Chloe, ready for the six p.m. broadcast.

Chloe knew she could've done the interview better. Shit, the stuff she'd got before Deborah arrived was gold. At first, the frightened housewife had refused to speak to her at all, but Chloe had managed to persuade her through the intercom that her comments could help people understand how terrible these home invasions had been. Maybe then the police would do something about catching these bastards, she'd said, knowing the woman was standing just there, behind the door, listening.

She'd opened up, just as Chloe had known she would. Although she lived in a mansion, they were still in the western suburbs. And people around here could tell that Chloe was one of them. She made sure of it with every word she spoke. It got her in a lot of doors.

Born and raised in Seven Hills, Chloe had been one of just a handful from her high school to make it to university. She'd excelled in her journalism studies, taking the university prize two years running. At just twenty-three, and a brand new graduate, she knew a hundred others who would claw her eyes out for this cadetship with the premier news service in the country.

But Chloe was impatient.

Her parents had run their local mixed grocery store for thirty years and they were so tired. Chloe saw her mum every morning, grey-faced and miserable, leaving home to open the shop. Now she was working, Chloe saw her dad only on Sundays. He would be at the markets when they opened at five a.m., and asleep before she returned from work each evening.

Growing up, the shop had been her second home. After school, she'd make her way there and could choose anything she liked for afternoon tea. When she got older, she helped serve customers. Soon she knew most of the neighbourhood. By the time she was thirteen, she knew that Mrs Shanoa's husband was a no-good drunk; that Jeremy Peterson was having an affair with his boss behind his boyfriend's back; that Tania Taylor was on the pension, even though she worked fulltime for cash in hand at the bowling club; and that Mr Mason dressed in drag once a month and stayed out all night in Darlinghurst. She knew plenty more besides, and she couldn't get enough. People opened up and told her things, quietly, while she cut their ham, weighed their frankfurts, rang up their smokes on the outdated till.

Her father stopped her working at the store after the second armed robbery. The man, armed with a syringe, had made off with the day's takings half an hour before Chloe got there for the afternoon. Her dad hated his wife being there too, and had tried to sell the shop, but there were no genuine buyers. Everyone knew that Coles and Woollies made all the money in the industry. Everyone except the junkies, that is: they saw the corner store as a cash register. Her parents had been robbed five times since then.

Chloe had to get them out, and she would. She was going to find a way to get an on-screen position and a six-figure salary. She'd pay off their mortgage and get them out of the shop. And there was something about this story that felt like destiny. She peered overhead at the news chopper, one of theirs, returning after a midday break. Sydney wanted to know what was going on out here.

Chloe surreptitiously pulled at her tights again and made some more notes. Hell, the whole country wanted answers. And she was going to get them.

9

GABRIEL SAT OPEN-mouthed, staring at the enormous television in the corner of the room. Narelle Rice had muted the sound when she'd shown Jill and Gabriel into the living room, explaining that Justine and Ryan were expected home from work at two-thirty. Jill tried to catch Delahunt's eye, but he sat absorbed in the silent TV. On the screen, American soap actors made exaggerated facial expressions.

Mrs Rice returned from the kitchen carrying soft drinks in glasses and a plate of biscuits. She put the biscuits on a low coffee table in front of Gabriel and sat next to Jill on the couch. Gabriel reached unseeingly for the plate and munched while he watched the soap.

'You want me to put the sound on?' asked Mrs Rice.

'No. That's fine,' answered Jill, scowling at Gabriel, who'd turned to nod a yes.

'So, Mrs Rice,' began Jill, 'do Ryan and Justine work together?'

'They do everything together now. Could you just call me Narelle?'

Jill smiled.

'We've only just been able to get Justine to go back to work,' Mrs Rice continued. 'They work over at Orange Grove – you know the Krispy Kreme over there? Ryan's a manager,' she said with pride, 'and Justine was well on her way to management too. Before this happened.' She looked at her lap.

'It must have been terrible for you all,' said Jill.

'Oh you've no idea.' Narelle pulled a tissue from her cardigan pocket. 'We'll just never get over it. Justine . . .' She broke off, smothering a sob with her tissue. 'We've had to let Ryan move in. She wouldn't sleep alone. She said she'd move in with him if we didn't let him stay over.'

Jill nodded.

'He's a good boy, really,' Narelle continued, 'but he's been drinking far too much since this happened.' She shook her head. 'And the arguments! You've no idea. They used to be so close, so kind to one another.'

Jill noted that Gabriel's attention now seemed to be split between Narelle and the soap.

'I'll just get some more biscuits.' Narelle stood. 'Everyone loves them.'

Jill looked down at the empty plate in front of her partner. Are you *serious*, she asked him with her eyes.

He smiled at her with delight, his thick eyebrows raised high. Crumbs covered his dark tee-shirt. She stared at him disparagingly.

'What?' he said.

She pointed at his clothes.

'Oh.'

Still smiling, he brushed at his flat stomach, then stood and dumped the crumbs on the floor. He stared at the little pile around his chair, and then scraped at them with his feet, spreading them into the carpet. She watched, transfixed, as he stopped, then began again, his head down, scraping at the ground with his toe, like a cartoon bull about to charge. Laughter caught in her throat; she wiped the smile from her face when Mrs Rice walked back in, the plate refilled. Gabriel settled back into his chair and took another biscuit.

A scrabbling sound at the front door drew their attention.

'Mum, let us in.'

'Excuse me please. They must have lost their keys again. We haven't left a door unlocked anywhere in this house since the robbery.'

Jill heard a whispered conversation at the front entrance, a disgruntled young female voice louder than the others. Footsteps stamped upstairs and then Mrs Rice re-entered the living room, accompanied by an ungainly youth in a work uniform, baseball cap pulled low, a few pimples scattered across his cheeks.

'Detectives, this is Ryan.' Her hand rested protectively across his shoulders. 'I'll just get you a glass, Ryan,' she told him.

'That's okay,' he muttered. 'I'll get a beer.'

'I'll bring you one,' she said tightly. 'You speak to the detectives.' Turning to Jill, she said, 'Justine's just getting changed.'

'You're not the ones we talked to last time.' Ryan dropped into a chair.

'I'm Sergeant Jill Jackson, Ryan. This is Federal Agent Gabriel Delahunt. We wanted to ask you a few more questions.'

'Yeah, I know. Justine said you called. Is it true those arse-holes killed someone this time? We heard it on the news.' His eyes were just visible under the rim of the cap, his voice flat.

'We're not sure if it's the same people at this point, Ryan, but we need to reinterview everyone who's been through a home invasion lately so we can try to find out.'

Ryan took his beer from Mrs Rice with a mumbled thank you, and drained half of it in one go. Justine's mother gave Jill a resigned look and left the room, worry creasing her forehead.

'They'd better not come here again,' Ryan spoke into his bottle. 'I'll be ready for them next time.'

'Ryan,' Jill had his statement in her hand, 'this is the police report you made. Could you have a look at the section I've highlighted, and tell me if there's anything else you can remember about the offenders? Anything at all could be a great help. The way they moved, talked, anything they said. Sometimes after a couple of weeks bits and pieces come back.'

Ryan swallowed the rest of the beer in two long draughts and stood up.

'I'll look at it, but I'm not the one you should be talking to.' He stood rigid, the statement clenched in his fist. 'Half the time I had my face shoved into that chair you're sitting on.' He indicated to Gabriel. 'The rest of the time I was getting the shit kicked out of me. Justine was upstairs with two of them, and it was pretty quiet up there.' He turned at the sound of feet on the stairs. 'Here she is now. I reckon she got a good look at *everything*.' His voice was acid. 'I'm going to get another beer.'

Justine Rice froze in the doorway, staring after her boyfriend as he left the room, her eyes panicked. Jill was surprised to see she'd changed into flannelette pyjamas. It wasn't yet three p.m. Her hair had been scraped into a messy ponytail and her clear skin was free of makeup. If Ryan had not just indicated otherwise, Jill would have been certain that this was Justine's little sister, a much younger teen.

Justine seemed to register Jill's eyes on her clothing, and hugged her arms around her slender body.

'I've got a stomach ache,' she said, 'so can we do this quickly? I'm sick all the time now, since it happened.' She crawled into the chair furthest from Gabriel and tucked her legs under her. She spoke to Jill only, angling her body so that she could not even see Gabriel.

He stood. 'Jill, I'm just going to see if I can help Ryan with his statement.'

She nodded, grateful Gabriel had picked up the girl's obvious discomfort with him.

'Justine, I'm Jill. Thank you so much for talking with us. I know this is the very last thing you wanted to do today.' Jill leaned forward in her seat and smiled; Justine seemed to uncurl herself a little.

'Are you going to catch these guys soon?' she asked, her voice small.

'Yes.' Jill hoped it was true. 'We've got a lot of people looking for them, and we need your help, Justine.'

'Hah. I can't even help myself.'

'Maybe, Justine, but you saw these guys. You got a better look at them than some of the other witnesses, and that could help us a lot.'

Justine said nothing.

'Justine,' Jill began carefully, 'you were taken upstairs by two of these guys, is that right?'

A small nod.

'And you could hear the others hurting Ryan down here?'

'I could hear everything. He was screaming.' Her mouth was now on her knees, her voice muffled in her pyjamas. 'They said they'd kill him.'

'It must have been horrible, honey. I can't even imagine it.' Jill wished that were true. 'You were very brave to get them what they needed so they wouldn't hurt Ryan anymore.'

'I wasn't brave.'

Jill could barely hear her now.

'Justine, you did exactly what you had to do to get them to stop hurting Ryan and get them out of the house.'

Justine was a portrait of misery, her face buried in her knees, her arms wrapped around them. Her small body shook silently.

'Justine, sometimes it's easier if you keep your eyes open,' Jill told her. 'It makes the images not so clear.'

Justine rocked slightly, her sobbing just audible, and Jill wondered whether she'd told them all there was to know about her time upstairs.

'What happened up there, Justine? Tell me what happened when it all went quiet.'

'They said they'd kill him,' she said. 'The spider one said he'd cut my throat –'

Suddenly she gagged and ran from the room. Mrs Rice hurried after her from the kitchen. Jill sighed resignedly and stood. She followed the sounds of Justine dry-retching and found her sitting on the edge of the bath, her face wet with tears. Her mother bent to comfort her.

'It'll be easier if you just tell me, honey,' Jill said.

'Tell you what?' Mrs Rice straightened. 'Really! She's sick. I think it's best we leave this for another time. I can bring her in to see you tomorrow.'

'Narelle, you've been great letting us come over here, and I know this is horrible for everyone. And I am going to have to get Justine and Ryan to come in and make another statement tomorrow. But right now, Justine has something that she needs to tell me.'

Mrs Rice clasped a hand over her mouth.

Jill continued. 'Narelle, I'm going to have to ask you to just leave us both in here for around ten minutes. Maybe you could duck down to the shop and buy Justine a lemonade? It'll help settle her stomach.'

She spoke firmly. If Justine didn't get this off her chest now, it would consume her from the inside out. Narelle Rice seemed suddenly to know this too, and with an imploring glance at Jill, left the room.

Jill took her place on the side of the bath.

'Let's get this done, Justine. You've held this in too long already. These feelings are poisonous when you keep them inside.' Justine looked up at her. 'You've already told me you've been feeling sick since it happened. You can't get well again until you let it out, until you tell the truth.' It'll take more than that, she thought, but it's a start.

'You said the spider one told you he'd cut your throat,' Jill continued. 'That wasn't in your statement. What happened next?'

Justine pulled away a little from her and turned her head to face the wall. I've lost her, Jill thought, but Justine began to speak in a flat, lifeless voice.

'He'd said he'd cut my throat and fuck the hole in my neck.' Her voice echoed in the small bathroom. 'He said he'd kill Ryan first and then come back and fuck me while I was bleeding. He said I could stop him doing it if I gave the other guy head.' Justine began to cough, then spoke again in a tiny voice. 'So I did.'

'I'm so sorry, Justine,' Jill wanted to reach out to the girl, but she'd moved as far as she could from her.

'Did the other one have any tattoos?' Jill didn't want to press her any more, but this was a race for time now. They had to get these animals.

'No. He didn't.' Justine turned, and faced Jill. 'He made me do it while the spider one watched. But halfway through he pulled away from me and walked out.'

'Okay. I'm so sorry that happened to you, Justine. I'm going to leave you alone soon, honey, but we're going to need you to come in tomorrow.' Jill put her hand on the girl's shoulder. 'You did the right thing telling me.'

'Ryan won't think so. He'll leave me.'

'Deep inside, Justine, I think Ryan already knows what they did to you, and he hasn't left you yet,' Jill said. 'And you know what, Justine? If he did leave you because you got sexually assaulted, then he's not worth it anyway.'

Jill held her while she cried a little, and then said, 'Unless you want to, honey, don't feel you have to tell anyone about this until you come in tomorrow. I'll help you tell your parents and Ryan.'

'Thanks.'

'Before we go, Justine, is there anything else you can think of that they said or did that you haven't told us yet?'

Justine looked up at her. Jill saw her eyes widen with

71

horror; she was remembering, reliving the scene. The girl swallowed, and the dead voice came back.

'Yeah,' she said. 'While he was making me do it to the other one, the spider one started cutting himself on his stomach with a knife, and then he . . . came.'

Jill couldn't speak for a moment. 'He . . . what? He did what?' She listened to the girl crying almost inaudibly.

Finally, she asked quietly, 'Justine, was there any blood or semen left in your room afterwards?'

'Yeah,' the girl nodded, and then hung her head, 'on the floor, but I wiped it up.'

'That's okay Justine. That's okay.'

As she left the house, Jill had her mobile out and was already dialling.

10

'JOSS, YOU'VE GOT to talk to me.' Isobel had tucked Charlie into bed, and now sat down next to him on the lounge. 'Who was that?'

'I told you in the car,' Joss's voice was glass. 'I knew him when I was growing up. He's violent. He's been in gaol. You know I don't want anything to do with my past.'

'Yeah, but I've never heard you talk like that. What would be wrong with just acknowledging him and moving on?'

'For fuck's sake, Isobel! Why do you have to question everything I do? I told you, he's fucking dangerous.'

'Do you think you could try any harder to wake Charlie?' Isobel stood. 'Anyway,' she said, turning away, 'the police called. They have to re-interview us about the robbery. They're going to call tomorrow to set up a time.'

She left the room before he could respond.

Great. Just *great*. What did they want? Joss stared at the blank television screen. He felt hunted, trapped. How had Cutter found him? He knew it was no coincidence. Twenty years and he'd never seen anyone from his past life, and now he'd seen Cutter twice in just over a week. How long had he been watching them? Did he know where they lived? He looked around his loungeroom. How had he let this danger into his life? Why was this happening to him?

An image of Fuzzy, scrabbling at his throat, blood everywhere, flashed into his mind. It seemed to answer his question.

Cursing under his breath, he reached for the remote control, desperate to find something to replace the scenes and sounds in his head. On each station, Fuzzy's fourteen-year-old eyes pleaded with Joss to help him, jets of blood pumping from the gash in his neck. Joss's hands, wet with blood, trying to hold his friend's throat together.

He threw the remote onto the cushion next to him and made his way to the kitchen, unconsciously wiping his hands on his jeans. Reaching into the cupboard, he took out the bottle, a glass. He filled it completely, a wave of the amber liquid sloshing over the side onto his hand. Eyes unfocused, he downed half the glass, relishing the burning. He coughed, swallowed the rest, and poured again, then took the glass and the remainder of the bottle of bourbon back into the lounge-room, noting with relief that he'd seen a new bottle at the back of the cupboard. This was going to be a long night.

Fuzzy's face had left the TV screen, but Joss could still smell his blood. He downed another half glass before the blood of the kids in Rwanda took over. The screaming and hacking of the massacre in Kibeho crowded into his brain and he had to stop midway to the couch; he put his glass down on the dining table so he could hold his head in his hands. Leaning forward, praying the memories would leave him alone, that his brain wouldn't burst, he finally felt his medicine taking effect, the heat of the alcohol in his belly. He fell into the cushions of the lounge, pulled the bottle closer, and turned the volume of the television up a little.

ABC news. He moved to flip the channel, not ready for any more reality, when the top story caught his eye. Another home invasion. Last night. He sat forward in the seat, suddenly very sober. This time someone was dead.

It was as if he'd left the door from hell wide open, and a demon had walked on through. He thought of his girls, upstairs. He had to get them out of here.

Then, he had to find Cutter.

Jill sat at the computer in her loungeroom in her singlet and briefs. She googled 'M5 motorway' to find the site to register for an electronic toll payment tag. The department would reimburse her for the monthly fees. She didn't know how long she'd be out at Liverpool, but she wasn't going to wait in the M5 toll queue with the motorists paying cash every day. She was surprised her department vehicle hadn't been fitted with a tag already. The car was brand new; maybe that explained it.

She sighed and stretched. The trip there and back was a bitch. It took two hours of her day: time she could be training. She looked down at her belly and grimaced. For years, her stomach had been unyielding, creaseless. She poked at a small fold above her knickers and walked into her gym.

Truth is, I kind of like looking like this, Jill thought, looking at her mirrored reflection. She'd had to change out of her push-up bra this morning because her décolletage had rendered her fitted shirt obscene. She smiled at the curve of her usually hard buttocks. The extra five kilos had even changed her face a little – fewer hard angles.

But soft is dead, she told herself.

She scowled at the mirror and increased the angle on her incline bench to forty-five degrees. As she started on six sets of fifty sit-ups, she realised she missed the pain. Her mind drifted back to work.

Following her phone call from the Rice residence, Super-intendent Last had arranged for a tech truck to travel to the house. He'd called her at home at eight with the results. Not only had luminol fluoresced all over the floorboards and the rug in Justine's bedroom, revealing the presence of organic matter, but Justine had also presented the techies with a plastic shopping bag.

'What was in it?' Jill had asked her new boss. What else did this girl have to tell them?

'A bath towel,' he'd said evenly. 'She kept it after wiping up the blood and semen. Can you believe it?'

'She wanted to tell us what happened. She just couldn't put it into words the first time, and then the lie got too big,' said Jill.

'Great work, Jill.' His voice was exhausted. He sounded old. 'We should get results from the sample tomorrow after-noon. What they get from the other trace you found out at Capitol Hill with Gabriel should follow.'

Jill lost count at one hundred crunches, caught up in her thoughts. Before leaving Justine, she'd helped the girl to tell

Ryan and her mother what had happened upstairs. Ryan had taken off, hate and tears in his eyes. She wondered whether he'd returned yet, and what would happen between the young couple.

She'd seen it all before. Sometimes the male ego couldn't take the blow when his partner had been sexually assaulted. All of her tears following a rape were, in some men's eyes, accusations of weakness, reproaches because he hadn't been able to protect her. When the victim also held a corresponding unspoken belief that her partner should have been there, stopped it, the couple rarely made it. When they did, sometimes Jill felt they shouldn't have: the anger would eat them alive.

Jill had ensured that Narelle Rice had all the phone numbers for the community services that could help. She'd follow up and urge Justine and Ryan to have counselling. It had taken a few years and a couple of different therapists for Jill to gain some relief following her own ordeal. Still, killing her rapist years later was what had given her the most release. Now that was something you never got told in therapy. The memory of his death was still a strong, clear image. She tried to tell herself that the healing came from the knowledge that he could never hurt her again. She forced herself not to relive the satisfaction of kicking him to death.

She unhooked her ankles and rolled off the incline bench onto the floor. Nine-thirty. She longed for the shower and her bed. Instead, she walked the well-trodden path to her hand weights and took them back to the bench. Three sets of dumbbell flies first.

11

'I'M NOT GOING.'

'Isobel. I told you. He'll come here. I can identify him.'

Joss stood in the kitchen facing his wife, her arms folded in determination; his, to keep from throwing up. Fortunately, Isobel became very quiet when angry. His hangover was a living entity this morning.

He'd decided last night that he had to tell his wife the truth – that he had recognised one of the men from the home invasion, the most violent of all of them, the man who had almost cut her boss's legs off. He had told Isobel the man's name, Henry Nguyen, Cutter, and that he had known him from his childhood in Cabramatta.

'I understand that we've got to do something about it,' Isobel said. 'But I'm not leaving you. Charlie and I are staying right here. We've got to tell the police. We'll tell them now.'

The most reasonable statement in the world, thought Joss, except that telling the police would change their lives forever, maybe even send him to gaol. He'd left all that behind him. The old Joss was dead. He had to do everything he could to hang on to the new world he'd built for himself.

'I've only told you half the story,' he said.

'You're kidding.'

His eyes showed he was not.

For the first time in his life, Joss told someone what had happened to Fuzzy.

In her kitchen, Jill prepared herself some lunch to take to work, emptied her dishwasher. After stacking her breakfast dishes inside it, she looked around for her handbag. She spotted it near the front door. When she bent to pick it up, she groaned with the pain from her stomach muscles. After a couple of attempts she managed to grab the bag using just one handle. Its contents tipped out onto the floor. For the second time, the vegetables from the Asian food store spilled everywhere, and she remembered the scene from yesterday.

Laughing aloud, Jill squatted to retrieve them, and was still smiling when she left her apartment.

Joss heard the empathy in his boss's voice when he told him he'd be taking a second day away from work. His dangerous 'accident' would be the topic of the lunchroom again today. His colleagues had clucked with alarm when he'd told them he'd fallen from a ladder, leaving him relieved he'd not told them the real reason for his bruised face. It reminded the assessors of the other freak-accidents-around-the-home they'd processed over the years. Apparently, more people died in their bathrooms than in motor vehicle collisions, he'd heard at lunch on Monday.

Isobel had insisted that she would go to work.

'I might be able to find Cutter,' she'd reasoned. When he'd told her about Fuzzy, and explained to her why he couldn't tell the police about his connection to Cutter, she hadn't flinched. Instead, she was in problem-solving mode, and he wished he'd trusted her earlier.

Isobel worked for one of the three largest law firms in Australia. Her role included investigating the paper trail of anyone who wasn't on their side, and sometimes those who were. She had access to almost every piece of electronic information the police did. Privacy meant little if you had the technology and resources to get around the flimsy obstacles set up to protect it.

For his part, Joss was going to see his mother. Back to where it all began.

Tiptoeing up from the loungeroom last night, with most of the second bottle of bourbon rendering the staircase a roiling escalator, Joss had wheeled a chair from the study out to the hallway in front of the linen closet. He'd positioned the swivel chair under the manhole cover and held onto it until the floor stopped moving. Managing to climb onto the seat of the chair, he stood with his feet slightly apart and his hand on the wall to stop the spinning.

As quietly as possible he'd popped the manhole cover, sliding it back into the roof. Ordinarily, he would easily have been able to pull himself from the chair up into the dark cavity overhead. Last night, however, when he'd gripped the edge of the manhole and tried to launch himself up, his feet had propelled the wheeled chair into the closed doors of the master bedroom. With Isobel standing over him holding a tearful Charlie, he'd summoned as much dignity as he could muster and made his way to his side of the bed, where he found himself this morning.

Problem was, now he couldn't keep his mind off the toolbox in the ceiling.

The knife had gone into the box when he'd returned from Rwanda. He'd moved the box from the ceiling in their former home to this house when they moved in five years ago, and as far as he knew, no one else knew what was inside.

Isobel had some idea of the horrors of the genocide in Africa. He knew that when he'd come home, she'd read everything she could find about the Australian peacekeepers' role there. She knew that Joss was one of the thirty or so Australian soldiers who'd been on-site during the Kibeho massacre, when four thousand Hutus had been slaughtered over the course of four days in a displaced person's camp of one hundred thousand people. Thousands more had been horribly wounded. She knew that the rules of engagement for the Australians had prohibited them firing their weapons unless they were directly fired upon. They were expressly forbidden from using their firearms in defence of the civilians.

Two battalions of Tutsi warriors had surrounded the camp, convinced it was harbouring Hutu fighters. In fact, the majority of the camp consisted of women and children, but that had not stopped the bloodlust. The Tutsis had mostly used machetes in order to save bullets. The carnage would have sent any witness mad, but for a soldier, trained to defend and attack, the horror of the utter helplessness had

been unspeakable. Literally. Although Isobel knew the facts
released to the media, no one knew what Joss had seen and
done in those three days. His brothers and sisters in arms
had their own unspoken memories; he read them in their
eyes on the rare occasions they caught up, but only Joss and
the dead Tutsi soldier knew why he kept the knife locked in
the toolbox.

He turned his eyes away as he washed his sodden, uneaten
Weetbix down the sink, rinsed the breakfast dishes and left
the kitchen.

Then he went back upstairs to get his knife.

Despite the humidity, Joss kept the hood up on his jacket
when he changed buses at Wynyard. The bruising on his face
was at its most livid this morning, and he noticed that people
averted their eyes when he glanced in their direction; today
that suited him fine.

As always, he felt guilty on the way to his mother's place.

His maternal grandparents had moved Joss and his
mother out of Cabramatta after the car accident. The fight
had left her after that. The much-loved only child of Richard
and Joan Preston-Jones, lost to schizophrenia, and later
heroin, was finally home.

The house in Mosman evoked a confusing mix of nostal-
gia and pleasure for Joss. After six months of half-arsed
rebellion, he'd settled with relief into the quiet habits of his
grandparents, happy to swap the chaos of his childhood for
their structure and normalcy. The house was the first real
home he'd ever had – he and his mother had bounced
between rental units, her friends' loungerooms, squats and

refuges for his first thirteen years. The sedate mansion that had smothered his mother when she was growing up was, for him, the first place he could breathe.

It hadn't been that way in the very beginning, though.

Now, staring through the rain into his childhood, his breath fogging the window on the bus, Joss thought about the only time he had tried to unite his Cabramatta past with his Mosman present. He'd been living with his grandparents for three months or so, and although he'd made a few friends at his new school, Sandhurst College, the other boys had had a great time at his expense, filling every moment outside of class with stories of his ignorance of the social etiquette they took for granted. After fighting three of the loudest on the oval after school, they began to make comments only when they were in groups so that he couldn't distinguish the speaker, and they developed codes that sent them into fits when he walked by, like raucous packs of birds.

He had missed his brothers from Cabra. Their escapades became heroic adventures in his mind, adventures that he knew the pissants at his new school would never have survived. He remembered his face pushed into the gravel one night, squashed with Fuzzy against a railway wall while a train passed above them, deafened, aware that he would be decapitated if he raised his head just a fraction. Just when he'd thought that the screaming monster above them would suck him up, the last carriage had passed, and he and Fuzzy had risen, their legs trembling in the dark, to finish their graffiti piece on the side of the wall. They'd been legends for a year for that piece, sprayed onto a virgin wall that everyone else had assumed was untouchable.

He remembered running from the transit cops with Cutter, Hendo and Tatts, jumping fences, dropping level to level in carparks, turning back to laugh at the fat fucks running behind them. He remembered, after trashing a school, the searchlights of a police chopper turning night into day. His friends had scattered in all directions, but he'd chosen the worst route – across the school quadrangle. Two cops behind him, guns drawn, shouted at him to stop or they'd shoot. He'd imagined the bullets entering his back, but he didn't stop. He still wondered at his indifference to death that night.

And so he'd invited them over. And, unbelievably, Tatts, Esterhase and Cutter had come to Mosman. Hardly anyone knew Tatts's real name: Guo Qi Xu. Even the teachers couldn't say it properly, so they also called him Tatts. Tatts's uncle, this mad motherfucker who sold smack from his tattoo parlour, had been practising on his nephew since Tatts was six. Tatts loved the body art, and hated his real name, so everyone was happy. Mouse and Cutter wanted Tatts's uncle to do all of their crew with spiders crawling around their necks. Joss and Esterhase had copped some shit from the others when they'd refused.

Joss remembered his grandmother's face when she'd first seen Tatts, but to her credit, she'd welcomed his friends, preparing them sandwiches and juice to eat in the garden by the pool. She'd provided them with tennis racquets and left them alone to spend the day together. Joss had known that inviting them was a mistake from the moment they arrived. Tatts had pulled out a joint as soon as she left. But it was when he'd caught Esterhase with his grandfather's camera in his jacket that Joss told them to leave. He'd never felt so alone. He was no longer one of them, but he didn't want to be a Sandhurst boy.

He got off the bus on Military Road and walked the last couple of blocks to the house. Aged, overhanging trees kept most of the rain off his shoulders, and he breathed in the smell of the wet road, remembering cold, damp afternoons and the welcoming warmth of home. Smiling, he put his hands into his pockets.

His fingers brushed against the knife.

The light left his eyes as he walked up the path of his grandparents' house.

The nurse stepped back and let him in without a smile. He'd seen her here before, but couldn't remember her name. She didn't offer it. She was one of a rotating shift of health-care workers from an agency paid for through his grand-parents' estate.

His mum looked just as she had for the past twenty years. She was sitting by the wide bay window in the main lounge-room, rocking slightly. She looked up when he came in. Her mouth stopped working for just a moment before her tongue continued its rhythmic exploration of her teeth and lips, endlessly pushing in and out of her mouth. Tardive dyskine-sia, caused by three decades of antipsychotic medication – no wonder she hadn't wanted to take the shit, he thought for the thousandth time, bending to catch her head with a kiss as she rocked.

He pulled a heavy armchair over next to hers, and sat down. One of the kinder nurses, Kathy Lin, had told him that his mother liked to be touched, to have her arm stroked, her hair brushed. He watched the rocking slow as he communi-cated with his mother in the only way they had left. He talked to her, the usual one-way conversation, and wondered what she heard, what she took in, just as he always had.

When it was time for her medication, Joss left her with the nurse and the production line of pills and went upstairs to his old bedroom. When he'd left home, his grandmother had not changed his room. There had been no need: there were far more rooms than she could use in the house, and she knew how important stability, the absence of change, were to Joss.

He knew the house now technically belonged to him, but he thought of it as his mother's. He knew he'd never live here again.

He dropped onto his old bed with a pain in his throat; it felt like he'd swallowed an apple, whole. The skin on his mother's arms was almost see-through now, soft like tissue. Her eyes were lifeless; he almost missed the madness that used to shine behind them. At least there'd been energy there.

The rain plashed quietly on the windowsill outside.

At last he rose from the bed and walked over to the cupboard in his room. He'd lived here for more than a year before he'd found the door on the inside wall of the cupboard that opened to a smaller, hidden cavity. Over the years, the space had held liquor, poor report cards, and once or twice a bag of pot. Now his old school backpack filled the space completely. He took the bag back to the bed and opened it. From inside his old pencil case, he unfolded a faded newspaper page. Smiling up at him from the top half of the page was Fuzzy, dressed in school uniform, curly hair completely out of control.

Teenager's Throat Cut! screamed the text below the picture.

12

ISOBEL THOUGHT ABOUT Joss as she scribbled shorthand. Her direct boss was updating the senior partners on their world domination progress since the last monthly meeting. His account was longwinded, as always. When he finally sat, she stretched her cramping fingers and peered through the rain at the bridge.

From the boardroom on the twenty-third floor, Sydney Harbour was typically a gaudy showgirl, but this morning she seemed to have gathered her shawls around her to hide. The mist rendered the wide window a mirror, and Isobel caught her boss, Bob Shields, staring at her in the glass as she watched the rain. She dropped her eyes back to her notepad and held her pen as a pointer, pretending to read over the notes she had taken.

Instead, she worried about her husband. This morning

she'd felt the return of the impenetrable emotional barrier he'd brought home with him from Rwanda. For eighteen months after his return from deployment, Isobel had felt she was living with a different man, a soulless robot who ate and drank – a lot – but had no ability to relate as a human. She'd missed her best friend. But then when the barrier had eventually started to come down, she'd almost wanted it back. Joss had spent months alternating between angry tyrant and melancholy drunk. Isobel had used humour and reason, patience and sex to forge brief moments of connection with the man she'd married. But with Charlie's birth she finally felt him come fully home to her. She'd woken from her first sleep after the eleven-hour labour to find him leaning over her. One look in his eyes had told her.

'I missed you,' she'd said. 'Where've you been?'

'You've only been asleep an hour,' he'd smiled, smoothing her hair from her face, his mouth almost touching hers. 'I've been here the whole time.'

'Yeah? Anyway, welcome back.'

But this morning he was a soldier again: his body in the kitchen, his mind guarding the wire. She wondered whether he was correct about the man at Andy's. She prayed he was just being paranoid. That monster couldn't be the guy he'd grown up with. Could he? She flipped a page in her notebook and stared at the name. Henry Nguyen.

Finally, the meeting was drawing to a close. Isobel forced herself to remain seated until the first of the group left the boardroom before joining the others making their way through the doors. She swallowed her impatience as the two men ahead of her stalled in the doorway to make a final inane joke, the more junior of the two throwing his head back and braying falsely. She'd almost reached the end of the corridor when she felt a hand touch the small of her back.

'You seem a little distracted today, Isobel,' Bob Shields said, close to her ear. 'I'm not giving you too much work to do, am I?'

Isobel kept walking, aiming for the bright hallway flanked by offices outside the boardroom. She worked hard to keep plenty of people around when she talked to her boss.

'Well, yes, as a matter of fact,' she smiled, facing him, her back to the wall. 'I think I'll go to lunch.' It was 10.30 a.m. She strode purposefully in the direction of her office.

Shields's loud laughter followed her. 'I expect the Donatio report on my desk this afternoon,' he called to her back.

She waved her arm in reply. She wasn't sure how much longer she could bear working for that sleaze. She'd known about Shields's reputation for wandering hands before she started working for him – everyone knew – but that didn't make it any easier dealing with the man. She knew she could take it to antidiscrimination, but she wasn't ready to give up working in the legal industry just yet. Though he wasn't her direct line manager, Andy Wu looked out for her, and would assign her duties that kept her away from Shields whenever he could. She shuddered, remembering the last time she'd seen Andy, and wondered how the hell Lucy was bearing up. She and Joss should go out to visit her soon, she thought guiltily, but they had to get on top of this new threat first.

At last she reached her office, shut the door, and began the searches that made her services so highly prized round here. It wasn't the Donatio file she was working on, though. The name she typed into her search engines was Nguyen.

As always, she started wide and worked her way inwards.

The Vietnamese name was one of the most common, and the programs hauled in thousands of hits. She narrowed the fields continually, honing in on his approximate age, geographic location, the nickname 'Cutter', and other small details she'd gathered from Joss. She roughly sifted court reports, quickly discarding mismatches and corralling possibilities to explore more carefully later. She downloaded Freedom of Information applications for credit reports, lease agreements, criminal record history, insurance claims, motor registrations, phone contracts, Medicare and Centrelink records. For the average person, these applications could take months to process, but there were back-entrances for certain groups: finance and insurance institutions, various welfare departments, lawyers acting on behalf of their clients. For her job, Isobel had carefully cultivated contacts with some of the most powerful people in the country – the clerks who held the records to personal information.

She started to dial.

13

JILL FELT LOST in the sterile corridors of the Liverpool police complex. Constructed perhaps twenty years ago, it sat next to the busy courthouse and the mostly deserted public library. An attempt had been made at a contemporary construction, but the bright modern art, glass and stainless steel were at once too slick for the Liverpool streets and too tacky for good taste. A twenty-year coating of grime didn't help. Her boots squeaked over shiny floors as she made her way to the foyer, where she'd agreed to meet her new partner.

Gabriel leaned on the customer service counter. His face appeared serious, but the dark-haired girl behind the barrier inclined towards him, laughing, her fingers twisting a lock of her glossy hair. The girl turned a flushed face and narrowed eyes towards Jill as she approached. Jill felt those eyes on her until they left the building.

A small crowd waited for their turn in front of the court building to their left. Cigarette smoke hung in a pall above them. A couple of ill-looking trees, hopelessly under-equipped to transform the toxins back into oxygen, drooped over the footpath. Two or three man-boys pulled irritably at bright-coloured ties, standing next to resigned parents. Several men in cheap, shiny suits bared tennis socks and skinny ankles. Some of them clustered together, comparing gaol cred, making deals. Others stood too close to their woman, who would today reverse the Apprehended Violence Order protecting her from him; would insist that she would not press charges over the assault that had left her hospitalised and her kids in the care of the state.

Jill and Gabriel passed the courthouse, closely observed by most of those waiting outside, studiously ignoring the news crew on the footpath opposite. She imagined they would do anything to be able to sit in while she and Gabriel interviewed the daughter of the man murdered yesterday. Jill took a deep breath when a breeze momentarily freshened the air. The sun was out on their side of the street; it was another hot day.

Gabriel half-turned to her. 'So, nice place out here,' he said.

She smiled wryly.

'I don't think we'll have much luck with Donna Moser today,' he said next. 'It sounds like the hospital kept her sedated all day yesterday.'

'Worth a shot,' said Jill.

They walked in silence for a while, nearing the sprawling Westfield shopping centre, which had recently undergone major renovations. Its shiny commercial happiness contrasted with the customers and staff who waited at the lights to enter it.

Jill's thoughts turned back to the interview yesterday with Justine Rice. 'I wonder whether Donna was sexually assaulted as well. She's not a great deal older than Justine.'

'It's possible,' Gabriel said. 'But I doubt it. The scenarios are too different. At the Moser house the perp got all his sexual gratification from the torture and the kill.'

'Freak,' she said. They turned off the main street and the huge hospital complex came into sight. 'The violence has escalated so dramatically. It's a wonder we haven't come across this guy before. It's possible he's done a lot of time inside. We should probably look into violent sexual assaults in prison.'

'Good idea. There is some kind of sexual sadism going on, even if we've only seen it expressed in an overt sexual act with the Rice girl.' He stood aside to let a woman with a stroller pass them on the narrow footpath.

When he caught up, he continued.

'Traditional sexual assault doesn't have to take place for these people to get off. Think about it. In a sick way, stabbing flesh simulates the sex act.'

'Yeah, I've heard of that. What do they call it?' Jill felt sweat at her hairline.

'Piquerism. It's a paraphilia common to sexual sadists. Jack the Ripper was a piquerist. And you know what's typical with these guys?' He didn't wait for an answer. 'They also often stab themselves in some way. When they caught the serial killer Albert Fish, an X-ray showed he had more than two dozen needles inserted into his groin. They're sick mothers, I tell you. When I was training, I got called to transport a stiff from this small hospital in the sticks. Bloke had been brought in about ten times previously with self-inflicted stab wounds to the stomach. Would never tell the surgeons

93

what he did it for. When he realised he wasn't going to make it this last time, he told them why he did it.'

Jill looked up at him as she walked.

'He told them,' he continued, 'that he believed he had vaginal tissue in his stomach. When he whacked off, he'd stab his gut to reach the tissue, effectively fucking himself.'

Oh, for God's sake. Jill stared into the gutter, waiting to cross at the lights. Of course she knew they were dealing with a monster in this case, but it was hard to fathom the depravity of a human who could not only deliberately inflict pain upon himself and another, but also become sexually aroused by the suffering. Inevitably, with such thoughts, her own traumatic memories shuddered into view, haltingly illuminated, as though by a fluorescent light stuttering to life. Screaming in the basement for the sexual pleasure of two men. Why did any aberrance surprise her?

Jill lifted her eyes from the ground. Gabriel stood slightly ahead of her. Unshaven again, with his hands in the pockets of his dark cargos, today he wore a light blue tee-shirt. The trucker cap sat low on his forehead. A marked police car passed them, and Gabriel lifted his chin towards the driver in acknowledgement. She saw the gesture returned.

He spoke again, eyes on the hospital across the road. 'The violence is highly addictive,' he said. 'And it has to escalate to satiate their desires. The other thing. . .' He paused, blinking in the sun. 'They never stop until they're caught or dead.'

The nursing unit manager walked Jill and Gabriel towards Donna Moser's room, but warned them that they probably wouldn't be able to get her to speak clearly. The only time the

94

girl had awoken during the night, the nurse told them, she'd become hysterical, waking the whole floor with her screams. They'd sedated her again, and when the psych registrar had visited this morning, he'd authorised another intravenous dose of Valium. A general medical unit was the wrong place for her, in the nurse's opinion.

'Some family friends have arranged to have her moved out of here as soon as possible,' she said softly as she ushered them into the victim's room.

Jill looked down at the young woman sleeping in the bed. She would have guessed her age at maybe sixteen or seventeen, rather than the twenty years Jill knew to be correct. Other than her very white face and some pale shadows under her eyes, Donna appeared unharmed. They waited while the nurse tried gently to rouse her, calling her name, smoothing her hair back from her face. The young woman's eyelids fluttered, but the drugs pulled her back under.

Jill gestured to the nurse to let it go. I wouldn't want to face the world either, Jill thought. She moved one of the heavy bouquets of flowers on the nightstand to leave a card by the girl's bed, and she and Gabriel made their way out of the hospital.

Back on the street, Jill moved towards the pedestrian crossing, but Gabriel pointed in the other direction. She shrugged and followed.

'We'll have to find out where she's moved to when they discharge her,' said Jill, falling into step next to him. 'I'll follow it up.'

He nodded.

Their new direction led them past a large park. Specialists' buildings occupied the other side of the road.

95

'I didn't expect her to look so young,' she said.

When Gabriel again didn't answer, she stared up at him, slightly annoyed, but then noticed that he seemed focused on something ahead. She followed his line of vision. Action exploded immediately ahead of them. A youth wrenched at the handbag of a middle-aged woman as she stood at the side of a vehicle a few metres away. The woman screamed, and Jill tensed to move, but Gabriel held her arm and signalled her to follow him. He stepped off the footpath and into the park. Within seconds, the offender had ripped the bag from the woman's grasp and run straight into the park. Jill stood back slightly, aware she could give chase if she needed to, but that was Delahunt's call. *Let's see what he's got*, she thought.

Gabriel didn't identify himself as the youth ran towards them; in fact, he seemed to make barely any preparatory move at all. At the last moment, as the offender bolted towards them, he turned side-on and swung his arm out into the runner's path at throat-height.

The kid hit the ground hard.

'Get your hands flat on the ground,' Jill yelled, moving quickly towards the youth, now sprawled on his back. 'Face down,' she instructed him.

She followed procedure, but there was really little need. The kid was sucking air, eyes closed in pain. Kicking the bag away, she rolled him over and cuffed his hands behind his back. He was still breathing hard, but managed a couple of hoarse 'motherfuckers'. She kept her hands on the cuffs and looked around at the crowd that was gathering. Gabriel's eyes danced as he watched.

'Up,' Jill ordered, hauling on the handcuffs, and the kid

got quickly to his feet, pulled upwards by the pressure. Gabriel had his radio out, but she could already see a uniformed foot patrol running towards them, and a marked car, sirens on, arriving at the scene. Jill had heard that there were several snatch and grabs a day in Liverpool, and units typically responded quickly.

On their way over to the car, Gabriel spoke.

'Door job,' he said, looking at the perp. His smile was huge.

She couldn't help smiling back. Door job: cyclists collected when a motorist opens the car door without looking. Same principle, I suppose, she thought, and shook her head.

Standing out the front of the Liverpool police complex with the two other lackey journalists, Chloe Farrell had held her breath when she'd seen the man and woman come out of the building. She'd seen these two yesterday out at Capitol Hill, arriving in an unmarked car behind the taskforce commander, Lawrence Last. Slinging a camera around her neck, she'd taken coffee orders from the others and headed off to follow the cops. She did not want passengers.

She kept a reasonable distance behind them. They were easy to tail. Headed to the hospital, she guessed, as they made their way down George Street. She knew the victim's daughter was in there.

Chloe had waited outside the main doors of Liverpool Hospital, wondering whether she should go in and try to find them. They could be in there for ages. Well, one thing's for sure, she promised herself, I am not standing out here any longer than five minutes. Although she was outdoors, she thought she might as well have been in a pub – so many patients and their visitors had come out here to smoke that her eyes were watering.

When the tracksuited drug dealer who'd been staring at her finally walked over to chat, Chloe decided to leave. As she turned to go, she spotted the detectives coming back out of the front doors.

'Hey, princess,' the man in the tracksuit stood in her path, his voice a nasal drawl. 'Do you want to go for a drink or something?'

'Actually,' she said, 'I've just got to catch up with my colleagues over there.' She saw the man clock the detectives. His eyes widened and he began to slink away. 'Maybe later,' she called after him. 'Could I get your name?'

Her would-be suitor broke into a jog, heading back down towards Speed Street.

Chloe smiled to herself and hurried to catch the cops ahead of her. She made a sudden decision that she'd approach them, identify herself and try to get some intel on the case. The worst they can do is brush me off, she thought. I've got to take risks if I'm going to get anywhere in this job.

She'd almost closed the distance between them when she noticed the male stop. The hairs rose on the back of her neck and she took the lens cap off her camera.

It all happened so quickly. Chloe had taken a dozen shots before she even knew what was happening. She got everything. The lot. This would run with the lead story tonight – she knew it. When she tied the two detectives to the taskforce and the murder in Capitol Hill, they'd link it all into one sensational story, with pictures.

98

I'm gonna get a lead reporter's job out of this home invasion story, thought Chloe, trying to run back to the news truck in her stupid new shoes. Hang in there, Mum and Dad.

14

ISOBEL FIGURED THAT if she could give Cutter to the police on a plate, Joss might be able to avoid having to tell his story to them. He'd always shied away from telling her much about his childhood, but she had known that he'd run with a gang until his grandparents had intervened. His account this morning of a robbery in which a boy called Fuzzy had been killed had been vaguely familiar to Isobel. However, the story she remembered hearing as a kid did not match what Joss had told her.

She remembered her parents talking about it after the evening news bulletin. It'd been a big story, back then. Late one night in 1984, fourteen-year-old Carl Waterman – affectionately known to all his classmates as 'Fuzzy' because of his blond afro – had investigated a noise in his father's bike shop. The shop sat underneath the two-bedroom apartment in

North Parramatta that Carl shared with his father. Mr Waterman, waking to a crash, had found his son speared through the throat by a shard of glass from his shattered front window. He'd been unable to save his son. The man's desolate face on the news, pleading for the offenders to come forward, had brought Isobel's mother to tears. Her father had sworn that they should hang the bloody mongrels.

Actually, Joss had told her, what had really happened was that Fuzzy had let him, Cutter and Esterhase into the shop to steal the bikes. They figured insurance would pay for the robbery, and Mr Waterman would be no worse off. The plan was that they'd wheel a bike out each, and hide one for Fuzzy in the flats around the corner. It had gone perfectly until they shattered the window of the shop to make it look like a smash and grab. They knew Fuzzy's dad would sleep till the cops got there – he went to bed with Jack Daniels and nothing could wake him.

They were right. Mr Waterman didn't wake when the huge front window broke inwards and impaled his son. He didn't even wake when Cutter and Esterhase bolted from the shop, knocking over a rack of bike wheels.

Only Joss's screams had woken Fuzzy's dad from his drunken sleep. Joss had done his best to hold Fuzzy's throat together, but his best friend had drowned in his own blood right there in Joss's lap.

By the time he got downstairs carrying a baseball bat, Mr Waterman's son was dead, and Joss was gone.

15

THE CONDENSATION CAUSED by the spring rain combined with the steam of rice and soup cooking in the kitchen. Sweating, Cutter could imagine himself in the Vietnam of his grandfather's era. He rolled onto his side and reached for another tissue, coughed. The routines and rituals of the room comforted him back to his pillow. His aunt fed his cousin's baby on the floor next to him. His grandma sat in her favourite chair rolling sticky rice balls, just as she had every day of his life. He coughed again and groaned quietly, and his grandma glanced up, giving a cluck of alarm. His ma poked her head out from the doorway of the small kitchen and instructed him to drink more of the fish soup that was sitting in a bowl next to his mattress on the floor.

Cutter always came home when he was sick. He'd grown up in this humble house in Cabramatta, as had nine of his cousins and most of their children since. At times, there were up to twenty people sleeping in the house, and it had always been full of delicious smells, laughter and babies.

Because his father and grandfather had purchased the house together, young Henry was the only child to have a bedroom of his own. He would have preferred to sleep in this room with everyone else, on the mattresses that were rolled out each evening; but his grandfather had insisted that Henry occupy his own bed, telling him that he would one day inherit the home and should be aware of his place in the family.

Cutter had had great respect for his grandfather, who'd died when he was only eight, less than twelve months after Cutter's father had been hit by a car and killed instantly.

Cutter's grandfather had been a hero of the war in Vietnam, a general in the South Vietnamese army, fighting for the allies. At night, he had sat with Henry by the hour and verbally recreated epic battles, his role in fighting for the South. He'd prevented the deaths of hundreds of Australian and American troops, teaching them how to recognise and survive the perils of the steaming jungle. There were the panji pits: sticks and branches concealing a ditch studded with protruding spikes that had been poisoned with rotting meat. There were mines suspended from trees, created from discarded Western supplies, set at heights designed to pulverise half the face. He taught them to recognise signs in the bush that the enemy had passed or were waiting – bent leaves, a broken branch. He told Henry of the elaborate Cu Chi Tunnels, designed to house whole families as well as munitions, with deadly snakes kept ready to be released upon enemies brave enough to venture inside. The landmines in the hills of Long Hai; the perils of R&R in the streets of Saigon.

Young Cutter, wide-eyed, sat on his bed with his chin on his knees, rapt, as his grandfather conjured up the tastes, smells and sounds of a country he had never visited.

Of course, the history lessons were not without pain. Henry understood that. One terrible night, betrayed by some of his own villagers, his grandfather had been captured by the Vietcong. Before he was rescued a week later when the Australians overran the camp, he had been tortured almost to death. Grandfather had watched each of his loyal troops beheaded one by one, their heads used as footballs by the enemy. When he'd closed his eyes, unable to watch, his eyelids were cut from his face. Grandpa told Henry that he knew his time would soon come when he had watched his lieutenant's manhood being cut from his loins and forced into his mouth, his lips then sewn crudely shut. He had watched his best friend's eyes pleading with him, the blood from his balls running from his mouth, before he too had been decapitated.

Grandpa told Henry that the experience had made him more than a man; he felt immortal. Death had no power over him. Pain held no fear. But the most powerful lesson, he told the boy almost every night, he had learned from the needles. It was his responsibility, he explained to his grandson, to teach him, to impart to him the same power.

Grandfather told him that the needles were inserted by his captors under the foreskin of his penis. Any sound made caused another needle to be inserted. This continued until the man made no murmur, no sound. The lesson would then be over until the next day.

Cutter learned the lesson in one night when he was four years of age. He'd had the flu and his grandfather had stayed home with him while his family was out celebrating Tet. Most nights thereafter, until his grandfather's death, Henry was instructed in his heritage by the war hero.

As a boy, Henry had loved Saturdays. Once a week on this day, he had the honour of accompanying his grandfather to the local market. There, neighbours and stallholders would pay their respects to Grandpa. Small children would stare at Henry in awe or curiosity as he led the war hero through the bakeries and vegetable stands. Grandpa's eyesight was very poor and he wore his usual huge dark glasses to protect his scarred eyes. He walked slowly; Henry knew his grandfather had terrible arthritis in multiple old injury sites on his arms and legs. Yet his bearing was regal – stallholders would crow to their neighbours with pride when he had purchased from their store.

And then the accident had happened.

It was a wet day, much like this one, Cutter thought now, as he patted at his nose, already sore from blowing it too much. It was a well-worn memory, and he leaned back against his pillow to think it through. His grandma had required medication for one of the babies, he recalled, Chinese medicine from Thanh Kha's store above Dutton Lane. Henry had led his grandfather through the marketplace and into the narrow side street. Slowly, they climbed the stairs to the apothecary's small shop – the living room of an apartment above the market.

At times, at night, the musty smells of the medicinal powders and roots still came to Cutter before he dropped into dreamless sleep.

That morning, Dr Kha's family was eating a late breakfast in the room behind the shop. Cutter remembered that on that day he had been walking as carefully as his grandfather, his groin aching deeply from an extended lesson the night before. As they were leaving, Mrs Pham came out of the gloom of the narrow stairway and greeted them with a bow.

'Please be careful,' she had warned, looking down at young Henry. 'The stairs are wet with the rain this morning.'

Cutter's grandfather had been wrong about being immortal.

You had to give it to him though – he had made no sound as Henry had shoved him hard in the back as he was shuffling down the steep stairway. In fact, the only sound Cutter heard before the stallholders came running was the dull splat when Grandpa's head had split open like a melon on the concrete below.

Cutter thought he could hear the sound now; it caused his penis to harden under the thin bedsheet and set him to coughing again. His grandma stood slowly and came to his side, bending down to feel his forehead with her soft, papery hands.

Cutter always came home when he was sick. He loved the memories.

16

Joss carried his old schoolbag with him when he left his mother's house. He sat directly behind the driver on the bus, shifting from time to time to adjust the position of the knife in his pocket. It seemed to prod for his attention; he couldn't stop thinking about it. He'd have to fashion some kind of holster; it wasn't as though he could just wear it in his belt as he had overseas.

He looked down at his schoolbag – just like any sports backpack, really. It seemed hot in his lap, and he wondered whether any of the other passengers could tell that it had travelled from the past, from another world.

Inside the bag, the boy from the streets waited to get out.

Joss changed buses again at Wynyard, but this time he crossed the road to catch a train to Cabramatta. He swung

his backpack over his shoulder and jogged to the platform.
The knife thumped against his thigh as he ran.

How does one go about making an anonymous call to the
police, Isobel wondered. Can't send a fax or email, of course.
Traceable. Her mobile? She always used a prepaid mobile
phone because she knew how easy it was to find out someone's identity when they subscribed to a plan. Still, she'd heard
that even though a prepaid number wasn't registered, the
phone still acted as a satellite tracking system when it was
switched on. If police had a number that was of interest, they
could find the phone, even if they didn't know whose it was.

How ridiculous, she thought, and snorted as she sipped
her coffee. She felt like she was in a spy movie or something.
The woman from the next table looked up from her novel
and stared.

Isobel got the file out of her shoulder bag and read it
through again briefly. She'd found Henry Nguyen and had
done a work-up on the Donatio file for Shields as well, and
all before two o'clock. I am pretty good at this stuff, she
reminded herself.

Nguyen had no Centrelink file that she could find, but
she'd been able to find his Medicare record. There was also
no hiding his criminal past. From age eighteen – it would take
a bit longer to get any juvenile files – it seemed he had spent
more time in than out of gaol. Violent crime and robbery. She
chewed at her lip, worried Joss could be right – that this man
could have been the one who'd attacked them at Andy Wu's.
Still, she figured, maybe Joss would have a record, too, if he'd
not been rescued from that life.

But that was crazy. It *can't* be him, she told herself. Joss was just shaken up by the robbery. God knows, she still was. And Joss also had his memories of Africa, of the massacre, to contend with. She could easily see how Andy Wu's blood could've triggered memories of his friend Fuzzy's death. Fuzzy made him think about Cutter, and he had just projected Nguyen underneath the mask of the devil at the home invasion.

There was no way Joss could recognise someone underneath that balaclava – there just wasn't any face to see.

The memory of Joss's panic at the movies yesterday surfaced briefly. It did seem a coincidence that they had run into this guy just after the home invasion, but it must just have been spooky chance. She pushed her doubts aside with the remainder of her coffee, not allowing them to fully register. She could not let herself believe that Joss was right about this guy. She'd collected this information just to placate her husband – to give Nguyen's details to the police and let them rule him in or out of this thing.

Isobel left the last bite of her toasted sandwich and stood up. She waited at the lights outside the café with a couple of dozen other people and crossed the street when they got the 'walk' signal. Then she stepped into one of the payphones opposite her work for the first time ever.

'Honey, I really don't think all this is necessary,' Isobel said to her husband in their bedroom that evening. She used her reasoning voice, trying to speak calmly, holding at her side the baseball bat Joss had given her. 'The police have his details now, and if he's implicated in any way, they'll pick him up.' She sighed, looking at his face. Nothing she said made any difference, she thought. He was just waiting for her to finish.

She was right.

'Show me again,' he said.

She gripped the very end of the bat with one hand as he had demonstrated, her other hand in the middle, as though she were holding a javelin. She lunged forward at an imaginary attacker, holding the bat at face-height.

'Remember,' he said, 'You can go for the face, throat, or the balls. Don't go for the chest. Winding him is no good. An eye socket will do.'

He looked her straight in the face, but she felt he wasn't really seeing her.

'Don't forget,' he continued, 'you don't want to hesitate. You don't want to listen to anything anyone's got to say. You'll have one chance only and you've gotta put every bit of strength you have behind it. And don't miss.' He paused, then held his fingers up to emphasise each point. 'One, use all your force; two, don't hesitate; and three, don't miss. Now, show me again.'

Five minutes later, Isobel finally threw the bat on the bed. 'Where are you going to be while I'm hitting this home run?' she asked.

'Don't worry about me. Hopefully, it won't come to this. If they come, with any luck, you, me and Charlie will be on the roof.'

As soon as she'd arrived home from work, Joss had again tried to persuade her to take Charlie to her mother's home in Cairns. She'd turned him down without waiting to listen to his argument. As though he'd known that would be her response, he'd insisted she come up to their bedroom and practise climbing out of the window and onto their roof.

'Can we at least wait till it's dark?' she'd wanted to know. 'And I'm *not* teaching Charlie to climb out a window onto the roof!'

'Fine,' he'd capitulated. 'We take her only if necessary.'

So, when evening had fallen, Isobel had climbed out of the low bedroom window onto their tiled roof. Joss had followed her out.

'Move around to the side a bit.'

He'd spoken softly, thank God. Isobel couldn't imagine trying to explain this to Mrs Wilkinson next door.

Isobel had inched her way around on the tiles; the slope here was gentle, and it was not difficult to move along. Fortunately, the rain had cleared up just after lunch, and the tiles had been dry and still quite warm.

'What the hell's this?' she whispered when she'd come across a dark shape wedged into a corner on the roof.

'The ladder, of course. How did you think we were going to get Charlie down?'

On her haunches on the roof, Isobel had found herself worried far less about a potential home invasion than about her husband's grip on reality. Was she right to humour him in this way? Should she just insist he see the counsellor, refuse to go along with his paranoid plans? Was all this making him worse? What was she doing squatting out here? She'd studied Joss from behind as he negotiated the roof, moving assuredly across the tiles, considering every angle. She determined to try to talk to him again tomorrow.

Back in the bedroom, Isobel put her hand on Joss's shoulder.

'Come on, babe, I'm tired. Let's have a shower and go to bed early.'

Joss picked the bat up from the bed and handed it to her.

'Remember, we're in a confined space,' he said. 'You don't want to have to try and swing it. And you don't want him to get closer to you than a metre. Show me again.'

17

'DO YOU WANT to get out of here today?' Jill asked Gabriel as they sat at their desks in the communal detectives' office in Liverpool. The taskforce meeting had just concluded and Jill was not looking forward to chatting with her colleagues this morning. As Gabriel's smiling eyes met hers over the rim of his coffee mug, she continued, 'It's that bloody current affairs show from last night. I don't want to hear what Derek Reid and his mates have to say about it.'

'You looked pretty tough handcuffing the dangerous assailant in the suburbs,' said Gabriel.

'Don't start, Mr Door Job.'

'Yeah, well,' he said, 'maybe we should go out and do some more interviews.'

'Who's up next?' Jill flicked through the folder in front of her.

'Um, that couple in Balmain,' Gabriel answered. He spoke without looking up, absorbed in the statements in front of him.

'Yeah, that's right,' she said. 'Isobel Rymill and Joss Preston-Jones. That was the Wu case, right?' She didn't really expect an answer and got none. 'Poor bastard, they couldn't save one of his legs, you know. Surgery didn't take.'

'Are you gonna eat that?'

Jill looked down at the banana on her desk. Morning tea. What the hell. She slid it over. He grinned, more at the fruit than at her. He peeled it with his thick fingers and ate it in three huge bites.

'So are you ready to head over there?' He arced the banana skin through the air, and it dropped into a garbage bin on the other side of the room. Reid's bin.

'Yeah, I guess.' Jill thought about the long drive to Balmain, the trip back here to Liverpool afterwards, and then at five or six tonight, the trip back to her unit on the beach. She took a deep breath and stood. God I miss working at Maroubra, she thought.

When they got down to the carpark, Gabriel walked straight to the passenger side and got in, still reading from one of the files he held in his hand.

'So, I guess I'm driving again,' she said to the roof of the car before she climbed behind the wheel.

'You know, these first interviews on the home invasions aren't that great.' Gabriel hadn't heard her. He spoke with his head down, still reading from the case files.

She didn't respond, trying to picture the best route from Liverpool to Balmain. 'Do you know a better way to get to Balmain than the M5?' she asked, tired already.

'Huh? Nuh.'

'So, we'll just take the M5 back into the city, and double back to Balmain?' I could use a little help here, she thought. New girl, remember?

'Okay,' he said.

'Off we go then,' Jill said dryly, making her way back into the traffic she'd sat through not an hour before to get there.

It wasn't until they were at tollbooths that he spoke again. Jill had already worked her way through half a litre of water from a bottle by her side.

'Reid and Tran did most of these victims' interviews,' he said.

Jill waited for his point. Finally, she said, 'Yeah, so?'

'There just seems to be a lot of information lacking. Like Rice and Temple. It didn't take us long to get more information, extra evidence from them. Some of the most important evidence in the case so far.'

Jill thought about the two kids, Justine and Ryan, and wondered how they were doing today. She wondered how Narelle Rice was coping with having her home trashed again by crime scene. In the group meeting this morning, Superintendent Last had told them that the analysis of the towel Justine had kept would be back tomorrow at the latest. She frowned; it *was* pretty sloppy that Reid and Tran had not discovered the sexual assault. Still . . .

'Maybe Justine just couldn't tell two men about the sexual violence,' she said. 'Maybe they interviewed her while Ryan or her mum was there with her. It's not easy to talk about that stuff you know.' God, she knew.

'Exactly.'

115

'What, exactly?'

'Well, that's Interview 101, isn't it? There just seem to be a lot of holes in all of the statements. Maybe we should tell Last that we'll reinterview all of them?'

Jill choked on a sip of water. 'Are you serious?' She could just imagine what the rest of the detectives would say: Yeah, she's been here less than a week, and already she thinks she can do it all better than us. 'It would take forever for just you and me to interview all the witnesses. There's other stuff to be done on this case, Gabriel.'

'Yeah, but the single most important determinant in successfully resolving a case is the quality of information gathered from the interviews with victims and witnesses.'

She looked over at him. His trucker cap hid most of his eyes.

'Anyway,' she said, changing the subject, hoping that he wouldn't try to insist on this, 'what do you think of that anonymous call that came though yesterday afternoon?'

Lawrence Last had mentioned the call in the morning meeting. It was from a woman, identifying a male who might be involved. It had been just one of many calls from the public since their work on the case had started. None of them to date had thrown up anything useful.

'What do I think?' he said. 'I think someone's feeling guilty.'

'Why do you say that? It's not like she was confessing to anything.'

Gabriel kept reading. Jill was getting used to these one-sided conversations. At the moment, she just felt bored and sleepy. The sun beamed in through the windscreen and her cheeks felt hot. She cracked the window a little. The exhaust fumes from the motorway blew in with the breeze. She had found it difficult to sleep last night, waking from a blood-soaked dream in which huge, biting spiders chased her. She'd lain in her bed for an hour afterwards thinking about Eugene Moser's final moments and Justine Rice's horrific confession. Who was this lunatic? It was horrible to imagine him out there somewhere, planning another attack. What could he be capable of next time?

'What was the guy's name?' Jill asked. 'The guy from the phone call? Henry someone? Asian name.'

'Nguyen, Henry. AKA Cutter.'

'That's it. Cutter.' Jill made a scoffing noise. 'Must've been real hard for her to come up with a name like that, given the stories all over the media,' she said sarcastically. 'The call's probably bullshit. Just someone who wants attention, knows nothing about the case at all.' She didn't know whether she believed that, exactly, but she was curious to know more of Gabriel's thoughts about it.

He grunted and kept reading.

Jill high-beamed a car doing eighty in the right-hand lane. It was a hundred zone, and she didn't feel like sitting on this motorway any longer than she had to. The Ford Laser stayed right where it was.

'What's in the file that's so fascinating, anyway?' she said, starting to seriously tailgate the guy in front of her. 'You've read the interview before.'

'It's not what's in here,' said Gabriel. 'It's what's not. You wouldn't believe the questions they forgot to ask this couple from Balmain.'

The truck in the lane next to her was too close to consider overtaking from the left, but the Laser could easily have moved over by now. Jill was considering putting the siren up on the dash and ruining this guy's day.

'So what did they miss out on?' She tried to curb her impatience. Scotty had hated driving with her when she was in this mood. Gabriel seemed not to notice at all.

'Well, a detailed narration of events, for one.'

'Yeah,' she said. 'I read through the interviews yesterday. They did seem a bit sketchy.'

'A bit? Reid did the Preston-Jones interview. He didn't get a description of any of the voices. He didn't ask about incidental sounds from the other room. For God's sake, there wasn't even a word-for-word account of the exact words the witness heard from each offender.'

'Mmm. Pretty sloppy, especially given they had few physical features to go on because of the balaclavas.'

'Don't start me,' he said. 'There's plenty bloody more they could have asked about physical characteristics.'

The Laser finally moved over. A young bloke in dark sunnies. He flipped her the finger before he took the River-wood exit. Dickhead. He probably thought she and Gabriel were a married couple out for a drive. She'd known how to spot an unmarked cop car from age thirteen. This fool had no idea how close he'd come to a five-hundred-dollar headache. He was lucky that Gabriel had finally started to talk and distract her.

'What questions would you have asked to get more from the witnesses about the physical details?' Jill was genuinely interested. All detectives had a different interview technique, and most tended to stick to the questions they had learned from their first supervisor. She'd always been open to learning more sophisticated methods of getting at facts.

'I always teach the witness to use their memory like a video-recording,' he said, suddenly animated. 'I tell them they can fast-forward scenes, or slow the action down. They can take it frame by frame, or just view still-shots. On any given shot they can zoom the camera in, or widen the lens to take in details at the corners of their vision.'

He closed the file but kept his finger inside, marking his place. 'Some witnesses aren't so good at processing visual information, but around a third are brilliant. You can get some people to change the camera angle to get almost any perspective, like a bird's-eye view, looking down from the ceiling, or shoe-view, the camera looking up at the action from the floor.'

'Wow. And that works?'

'Yeah. Like I said, not with everyone, but the least you'd do would be to say, "Stop the picture now. In your mind's eye, stop him right there in front of you. Okay, now tell me what he looks like from the top of his head all the way down."'

'That's good,' said Jill. 'I mean, I do try to get the most vivid descriptions possible, but I'll have to try some of those questions.'

'This,' Gabriel waved the file, 'is shit. He hasn't even asked the witness if he has any thoughts about the perps' motivations. You can get a lot of incidentals when you ask them to just let go and guess why the offenders might have behaved the way they did.'

'You want to know why the *witness* thinks the offender committed the crime?'

'Sure. You know that witnesses are always worried about saying something wrong, or making a mistake. They censor themselves. In a case like this, we can worry about errors in accuracy later; what we want from the witness in an interview is every little thing they can remember, even when they're not completely certain. They're our only eyes in there. They're the detective on the scene.'

'Interesting way of putting it. Do you ever say that to them?'

'All the time. You tell them you want them to guess the thoughts and emotions of the offenders. It widens their viewpoint. Opens them up. You can ask, "Why do you think he did that?", or "Do you think they planned it to go that way?" or even something like "Do you think any of them were angry with, or closer to, any of the others?"'

'Mmm.'

Jill drove silently for a while, her thoughts turning back to the anonymous phone call.

'Why'd you say the anonymous caller was feeling guilty?' she asked again.

'Well, she obviously wants us to investigate someone. You're right, it could be a bullshit call, but I thought her sentence structure was interesting when I listened to the tape this morning. She was really eager to put this guy in. And I don't think she just made up a name. If she did, it wouldn't take us long find out he doesn't exist. Pretty pointless if it's a joke.' He pulled his finger from the file and placed the folder into the door pocket, turning towards her. 'Besides,' he said, 'I think this Henry Nguyen is real, and the feeling I got is that this caller can't live with herself without saying something to someone. She wants us to find him. But she definitely knows more about him than she's told us.'

'It could just be someone she's pissed off with,' returned

Jill. 'Revenge – she might just want us to give some guy a hard time.'

Jill had listened to the call too, and she had to admit that she'd also thought there was something about it that demanded close attention. The caller's voice had been muffled; she really didn't want them to know who she was. At the moment though, Jill was more interested in the way her new partner thought than in discussing her own impressions.

'Could be,' he said. 'We'll have to wait and see. The details she gave don't sound right for that though – not just his address, but his Medicare number, where he's done time? And what she didn't say is just as important. Like, this is how I know what I know; this is why you need to get this guy; and more importantly, my name is . . .'

'Come on, we get heaps of anonymous tips. People don't want to get involved.'

'Yeah, but descriptive information like that is coming from someone who's just a little bit more than a helpful citizen. I think that call's for real and we're looking for a guilty woman. Guilt by association with something. And if she's got anything to do with this case, I'll know her when I talk to her.'

For some reason Jill believed him. That speech should've sounded arrogant, but instead Gabriel just sounded open, matter-of-fact.

She finished the last of her water as the traffic on the motorway slowed to a stop. There was obviously some hold-up ahead. At that precise moment, she realised she was desperate for the toilet. Great. She sighed and tried to distract herself. She just wasn't used to these mammoth drives – maybe it was a conditioned response. It seemed like every time she got on this bloody road she had to go. Could be because there were no service stations: when she knew she couldn't go, she suddenly had to. Thank God, they were nearly at Moore Park.

At the end of the freeway, Jill swung the Commodore into the first service station and bolted to the bathroom. When she got back, Gabriel was standing at the bonnet, food and drink spread out on the hot car like it was a picnic rug.

'So how're we going to handle the interview?' he said, indicating that a plastic-looking salad sandwich was for her.

'What do you have in mind?'

'I want to use audiovisuals to record everything. What do you think?'

'I think,' she answered, 'that you'll completely freak out the victims. They're not going to understand why they would be taped. We haven't even caught a suspect, so it's not like a tape could be used in court.'

'These people are the only experts we have on this gang,' he said, struggling to open his sandwich wrapper. 'They know much more than they think they know. We need as many verbal and non-verbal cues as possible for a full behavioural analysis.'

'It seems like a lot of trouble for a witness interview, but I guess we've got to do everything we can think of at this point,' she said. 'You got the equipment, or are we gonna get them to come in again later?'

'Got everything we need.' He nodded at the duffle bag on the back seat, his still-wrapped sandwich in his mouth, fingers and teeth tearing at the plastic. Jill thought about offering to help, but finally, the plastic gave way. 'We can get it all done today.'

*

As Gabriel pulled his bag from the back of the car, Jill silently repeated the victims' names – Isobel Rymill, Joss Preston-Jones. 'What were they like when you set up the interview this morning?'

'Ah, they said no.' He walked across the street. She stared after him.

'What?' She hurried to catch up. 'Said no to what?'

'The interview.'

They were already at the front door of the freestanding two-storey terrace. Jill glared at Gabriel as he knocked. She heard sounds behind the door, and a deadbolt sliding back. She couldn't see through the crack, as Gabriel's back filled the space.

'Mr Preston-Jones? We spoke this morning,' Gabriel sounded assertive, turned slightly to make space for Jill next to him. 'I'm Gabriel Delahunt and this is my partner, Sergeant Jillian Jackson.'

The man who opened the door looked as though he'd ordinarily be of a more cheerful disposition. An open face, light grey eyes, sandy hair that was buzz-cut close to his scalp. He stood in his doorway in a faded red tee-shirt, tight across his upper chest, loose navy pants, no shoes. He stood a smidge taller than Gabe. He didn't smile. A black-green bruise marred the lightly freckled skin under his left eye.

'I thought we agreed we'd have to do this another time?' He folded tanned arms across his chest.

Gabriel held out his hand. Big smile. Seeing it, Jill couldn't help but smile as well.

Joss Preston-Jones sighed, shook Gabriel's hand, and reached for Jill's. Then he stepped aside and motioned for them to come in.

123

The hallway was narrow. 'Sorry about this,' she felt she had to say over her shoulder. The man smiled tightly.

Jill followed Gabriel to a bright kitchen washed in the midday sun streaming in from the small backyard. Gabriel took a seat on a stool at the breakfast bar. She waited for him to explain what they were doing there, but he seemed content to look around the room, still smiling.

'Ah, Mr Preston-Jones,' she started. Someone had to say something.

'Call me Joss.'

'Great, thanks. Please, call me Jill.' Let Delahunt fend for himself.

'I understand that you would have preferred to do this some other time.'

'My wife's at work.'

Jill stared hard at Gabriel, then turned back to Joss. 'You're probably aware of how urgent it is for us to investigate this case. You might have heard about the latest home invasion?'

'I don't watch the news,' said Joss.

'Well, we believe that the gang that attacked you at Andy Wu's house have now killed a man.' Jill noticed Joss rub his hand across his mouth. 'We need to get as much information as we can about these people so that we can get them off the streets.'

She watched his shoulders relax a little, and his arms, folded across his chest, dropped to his sides.

'I haven't really been back to work since it happened,' said Joss. 'But Isobel had to go. She's bringing our daughter, Charlie, home at about four.'

'Is that Charlie?' Jill pointed to a photo on the fridge. It showed a blonde toddler nursing a fluffy cat almost bigger than herself.

Joss laughed a little. 'Yep.' The love in his eyes looked like pain.

Jill became aware that Gabriel was unpacking his bag.

'The light's probably best in here,' he said, unfolding a telescoped tripod.

'For what?' Joss's arms folded again.

'From now on we'll be videotaping all of our interviews regarding the case.' Gabriel spoke to the small camera he was screwing to the top of the tripod.

Jill glowered at him. This guy could turn the charm on and then drop it in an instant. She guessed that they were about to be kicked out, but instead Joss offered them something to drink. She and Gabriel accepted an orange juice. Joss poured himself a tall glass of water from a filter jug next to the sink.

'Might as well get on with it then,' he said, walking back towards them.

Gabriel set up the recording equipment with more speed than she could have imagined. By the time Joss had taken a seat at the breakfast bar, the contents of Gabriel's modest-sized duffle bag had transformed the small dining area off the kitchen into a studio. He had angled two dining chairs to face one another, and a collapsible reflective screen was positioned behind one of the chairs. He ushered their host towards this chair, motioning Jill towards the other, and took up his place behind the camera.

Jill took her seat feeling nervous and annoyed. For heaven's sake, she thought, we're interviewing a witness, not interrogating a suspect. She opened her notebook and smiled reassuringly at Joss.

'Hang on a sec,' said Gabriel. Incredulous, she watched him drop to his knees and, using a retractable tape measure, calculate the distance between the two chairs. Walking back on his knees, he signalled with his hand for her to rise. She stood and he pushed her chair backwards a hand's breadth.

'Sorry,' he looked up at her.

'Um, yes, maybe we should just get on with it.'

'They were only ninety-two centimetres apart.'

Jill stared. It seemed he was apologising for not getting the measurements right the first time, rather than for the ridiculous fact that he was bothering with such details in the first place.

'Should've been ninety-seven,' Gabriel said to Joss, hands out, as if that explained everything.

I gotta talk to this guy, Jill thought.

'Joss,' she took over. His legs *and* arms were crossed now, and he leaned towards the back door as though he wanted to be anywhere but in there with them. 'We're here to get your full description of what you remember happening at Andy Wu's last Saturday night. Can you tell us everything that happened after you arrived? Please don't leave anything out, everything you've got to say is very important to us. You are our eyes and ears in there.'

Gabriel caught her eye, raised his eyebrows at her.

They listened quietly to Joss's account, occasionally interrupting to clarify a point.

While speaking, Joss stared at a point just beyond Jill's shoulder. She watched him reliving the horror of the night, saw his eyeballs tracking actively as the scene replayed before him. His face was grey and his voice hoarse when he finished. An electronic chime indicated that Gabriel had turned the camera off. Jill looked down at her watch. Three-thirty. The wife would be home soon, but this guy had had enough. His hand shook slightly as he rubbed the bristle on top of his head. When he stood, he steadied himself using the back of the chair, his eyes glazed and unfocused. She and Gabriel gave him their thanks and left, arranging to return to take his wife's statement the following day.

'I hope he's going to be okay,' said Jill, opening the back door of the car so Gabriel could dump his equipment. 'He looked pretty shaken up.'

The steering wheel felt warm when she started the ignition.

'He certainly did,' said Gabriel, absentmindedly struggling to fasten his seatbelt. The plug had caught in his khaki shirt, and she had to stifle an unexpected impulse to untangle the mess for him. She turned on the air-conditioner instead.

'So it's back to Liverpool, then,' she said, mentally calculating the time it would take to get there and back again.

'No. Let's just go to your house.'

'My house.'

'Yeah. I want to watch this tape back. We've got some problems here.'

'I live in Maroubra.'

'Have you got a good TV?'

'Well, yes. But . . . Oh, whatever. We can watch the tape there I suppose.'

She pulled the car out from the curb and headed into the city, finding herself smiling at the thought of the early mark. They travelled against the traffic for most of the trip, Gabriel staring out the window, from time to time jotting in his notebook. As they passed the shops in Randwick, she suddenly wondered what the hell she was doing. Scotty was the only partner she'd ever had in her house, and she trusted him. She'd known her new partner for under a week.

Last night on the phone, her mum had asked her what he was like, and she'd been unable to find the words. After a few moments, she'd laughed, and told her mum that she'd have to get back to her. She hadn't figured him out yet.

Jill drove towards the ocean ahead.

After seeing the detectives out, Joss found himself back in front of the cupboard in the kitchen. Describing the night at Andy's in such detail had unshackled the demons in his brain. Memories howled in his head now, each clamouring for processing, hurling up image after horrifying image. He gave in to the kaleidoscope, knowing from experience that he was incapable of stemming the flood once it had progressed unchecked to this point. He reached unseeingly for the bottle of bourbon. The interview had prevented him utilising his routine avoidance strategies – hard exercise; forcing himself to remember he was home, safe, in the present. He had only this recourse left. He swigged directly from the bottle and then reached for a glass.

Back on the sofa, he steeled himself for the show; he drank quickly to put as much distance between himself and the images as possible.

Kibeho, 1995. The definition of human depravity. From every angle someone died in agony, or, much worse, survived, a machete wound through the middle of their face; a limb or genitals missing; intestines exposed for the birds that dived sorties in screaming, black-eyed packs. He moved through the blood and body pieces, pulling a dead woman away from her wailing infant before the child suffocated under her weight, dragging a breathing body from a pile of corpses and handing him to the medics. A small team from Médecins Sans Frontières and the medical section of the Australian peace-keeping force patched up those they could, medivaced a fortunate few, and provided morphine to many others, who would at least die oblivious to their own screams. For many years, he envied them that.

Another glass. The bourbon burned.

The boy and his family. The memory kicked in at the worst part, of course. The father lay dead, feeble spits of blood still exiting the mess of his throat. A girl, maybe ten, waited, mute, for the next act of horror life would bring her. Her mother, a baby on her hip, keened quietly, a steady, emotionless moan that conveyed more pain than a scream. And the new man of the house – the boy, younger than his sister – shaped up with a stick to the Tutsi warrior with the machete.

The devil with the knife turned to smile at Joss; to tell him with his eyes that he could cut this family to pieces, and that Joss could do nothing but salvage anyone left when he'd had his fill.

Not this time.

Joss watched himself moving forward to meet the enemy.

On the couch, feeling as though his head had played host to a wasp's nest, Joss's hand reached between the cushions, and pulled out that for which it had been searching. He wiped the knife against his thigh, and put it back in its resting place. Close.

He let his head fall back against the lounge.

18

'YOU SEE, HE'S doing it again,' said Gabriel, cross-legged on her floor. The glow of the TV screen lit up his face. They otherwise sat in shadow, the gathering gloom of dusk waited on the balcony.

'So that would be another cluster?'

'Yup.' He kept his eyes on the screen, but she saw him make a mark in the notepad perched on his knee.

There hadn't been time to be awkward. Gabriel had walked straight to the TV upon entering Jill's apartment and had wheeled it around to expose the leads at the back. Before she'd even offered coffee, the Balmain room and Joss Preston-Jones had filled the screen. Gabriel had been animated from the start.

'I don't get it,' he'd said to her. 'I've got to see it again. This guy was throwing up deception cues all over the place. Come in here and watch this.'

She'd taken a seat on her chocolate leather sofa and leaned backwards, her arms across her chest, an eyebrow raised.

'You're sceptical,' he said.

'You think he's lying?'

'He's not telling us the whole truth. He's being deceptive again and again and again.'

'How do you know?'

'Same way I can tell that you think I'm full of shit right now. Incriminating and discriminating stress cues; verbal and non-verbal signs.' He turned back to the TV. 'You gotta watch this.'

Jill had always been interested in the principles of interrogation, and had thought she had a good sense of when a subject was lying. She knew well that most of the time what a suspect actually said during an interrogation was only half the story. The way they said it, their body posture and movements told the rest. What she learned in her loungeroom over the next two hours, though, surpassed all of the behaviour analysis training she'd had to date, and gave words to a lot of her instinctual knowledge and hunches.

'Okay, so we know that no single behaviour can tell us whether someone is being truthful or deceptive, right?' He continued without expecting a response. 'But when we repeatedly observe some kind of stress reaction, or even better, a *cluster* of stress reactions when a particular issue is being discussed, then we can assume it's not a random behaviour.'

From Jill's point of view, anyone speaking about a brutal home invasion would radiate stress signals. Preston-Jones was wrecked after the interview, as was almost every victim she'd ever talked to. Gabriel's eyes and voice were compelling, however. She leaned forward in her seat.

'Of course, even innocent subjects will be nervous, and we'll detect that every time. But Joss exhibits markers suggestive of poor credibility at several key points through the interview, signals that I wouldn't expect in subjects who are telling the whole truth. What we've got to figure out now is what he's omitting from his statement. What he's not telling us. But more importantly,' Gabriel turned his eyes from Jill back to the screen, 'why he's omitting it.'

Jill finally found herself on the rug next to Gabriel, propped cross-legged with her back against the lounge to better see the screen. He paused the tape at key moments and time and again showed her movements made by Joss that stood out from his typical signs of tension.

'I'm picking up more evasion than deception,' he said.

She estimated that they were around halfway through the tape.

'It could also be embarrassment,' he continued, 'but it's more likely to be guilty knowledge: withholding information.'

The discriminating stress cues, once Gabriel had pointed them out, began to appear obvious.

'Negation!' Jill pointed at Joss on screen, once again rubbing his palm up and down his nose, briefly covering his mouth. Negation behaviour, Gabriel had reminded her, was a subconscious effort to hide leaks of emotion from the face. In the video, Joss repeatedly put his hands up to the facial touch zone – the area from mid-nose to mid-chin – hiding his mouth when he spoke about the ringleader of the gang.

'Right. And what's that?' he asked her, tape paused on

Joss making a sweeping gesture in response to a question asked by Gabriel.

'Aversion behaviour? He's blocking you, isn't he?'

'Figuratively, he's sweeping the question away. Remember I asked him to expand on what happened when the leader was questioning him on the ground. He used a bridging phrase: what did he say?' Gabriel looked down at the pad on his knee. '"The next thing I knew they were gone." *The next thing I knew* . . . It's a typical phrase used to cover gaps and omissions. He doesn't want to talk about what happened just before the offenders left.'

Gabriel paused the tape again and performed a yoga stretch on the loungeroom floor. His khaki shirt stretched tight over the muscles in his chest and back. Her shoulders felt stiff and she considered copying his pose, but instead she contented herself with stretching her neck from side to side.

'What else do we know about this guy?' he asked.

'Just the basic demographics, I think,' she answered. 'Age, address, family, his job. Probably we should look deeper.'

'Definitely. Look at the screen now.' Gabriel again sat up, cross-legged. 'See. That's another control behaviour. He's sitting on his hands. I think that he knows about stress cues and he's trying to suppress his nervous behaviours. Problem for him is that this tells us just as much – he's trying to be deceptive about his true emotions. When he freezes, or grips the chair, or sits on his hands within three to five seconds of a hot topic, he might as well have just let his hands do what they wanted to.

'But what I really want to know,' he said, standing and clicking off the TV, 'is where he learned that he should be monitoring his signals. I don't think he's always been a civilian, Jill.'

Jill also stood. She walked into the kitchen, and for no reason felt suddenly self-conscious. She wiped her hand across the four switches in the panel on the wall and flooded the apartment with light. What was it, six o'clock? She glanced at the clock on her wall.

'It's almost seven,' he said. 'What do you want to eat?'

'Ah . . .'

'We could just go grab some laksa?' He seemed to notice the startled expression on her face. 'Or maybe you're too tired. That's okay. I'll head off.'

'Where do you live?'

Was she supposed to offer to drive him home? This sucked. She didn't even know this guy, and now she felt responsible for getting him home. What do you do in these situations? The awkwardness of such personal exchanges was almost physically painful for her.

'Bus to Central. Central to Ryde,' he answered. 'I live in Ryde. It's an hour from here. I come out here all the time. I love the Thai restaurant up the strip.'

'Hang on a sec,' Jill surprised herself by saying. She suddenly realised she was starving. 'I'd love some laksa.'

She walked into her bathroom, splashed her face and fixed her hair in the mirror. Just before leaving, she turned back and slicked on some lip-gloss. *What are you doing?* she asked herself in the mirror. She left the room quickly and grabbed her handbag, not looking at Gabriel.

'Let's go,' she said, walking out of her flat.

19

'YOU LOOK LIKE you know your way around a gym,' he said.

It was only 7.45 a.m., and Jill had made the mistake of entering the taskforce meeting room without considering that she might be alone in there with Derek Reid. He'd moved on from his first-day suit to more casual clothes, and the three buttons undone at the top of his thin beige shirt showed too much tan and too little hair. She couldn't help but look twice. Yep, he waxed his chest. His sleeves barely contained his biceps. His eyes took her in, whole.

'You look like you could stay away from it for a couple of weeks,' she said. Stupid! Where did that come from? Oh my God, he thinks I'm flirting, she thought, horrified.

Reid's mouth turned up. The sheen on his copper skin caught the light as he actually flexed one bicep, pushing the fabric of his shirt almost beyond its limits.

'Maybe we could work out together this afternoon, what do you say?'

Maybe I could throw up now, she thought, but answered, 'I don't think so. I'm booked in for a spray tan.'

The corners of his smile dropped a little as he thought that through, and Jill turned to see David Tran entering the meeting room, leaning on his cane. She smiled, more than pleased to see him.

'Superintendent Last asked that I apologise for his being late this morning,' Tran spoke to them both. 'Apparently there's been a step forward in the case.'

'Do you know what it is, David?' asked Jill.

He shook his head, and they fell silent for several moments.

'So I wonder what Delahunt's excuse is for being late,' Reid said. 'I guess the Feds can show up whenever they're ready, huh?'

Jill ignored him. The service was full of people like Reid – always looking to put someone or something down. She found the constant negativity boring. She wondered what Tran was like. He certainly didn't seem to fit the usual mould. She decided to try to find out more about his experiences when he interviewed some of the past victims.

'So what did you think of Justine Rice?' she began. She directed the question to David Tran, but Reid answered.

'She gave us nothing,' he said. 'Not surprising, really, now it turns out that she was sexually assaulted by these freaks. She's not going to speak to a couple of blokes, is she?' He sounded defensive.

'There was more to it, I think, Jill,' said Tran. 'She and Ryan Temple took an instant dislike to me in particular.

While it's often an advantage being an Asian cop around these suburbs, I'm afraid that it's alienated some of the vics in this case.'

Jill nodded. She could see his point. Even people who'd denounced racism all their lives could find themselves fearful or hostile towards people of a particular nationality when they'd been attacked by a member of that community. She knew from experience that when violent crime was paired with a certain ethnicity, many victims forever after avoided all members of that race.

'I have already made the observation to Superintendent Last. It is probably a good thing that some of these interviews are repeated,' said Tran. 'Because of my presence, there could be other things people are holding back.'

Reid turned away, but not before Jill caught him giving his partner a foul look.

Lawrence Last walked in, looking as haggard as ever, but this morning there was a light behind his eyes. Gabriel Delahunt followed him into the room.

'We've had the biggest breakthrough so far,' he told them as soon as everyone had taken a seat. 'Forensics came through late last night on the evidence collected at two of the crime scenes. Both names are in the system. The organic matter collected at Capitol Hill belonged to the stomach contents of a Dang Huynh, AKA Mouse. He last did time at Junee for an aggravated rob. Time before that at Parramatta for vehicle theft. He's got a bit of a juvie record. He's thirty-four now.'

'We don't know for sure that this bloke's got anything to do with the murder, do we?' Reid wanted to know.

'No, Derek, we know nothing about why Huynh was at

the property. Jill and Gabriel haven't yet been able to speak to Donna Moser, the victim's daughter. He could have been there for some other reason, but we know that there was an eight- to twenty-four-hour window during which this man vomited at the residence. Beyond that, we don't know any more about the suspect than what I've just told you.

'The second piece of remarkable news, folks,' he continued, fixing each of them with an intent look, 'comes from the Rice crime scene. The lab has analysed the semen and blood sample collected on the towel by Justine Rice. It belongs to Mr Henry Nguyen.'

Jill gasped and turned to Gabriel. He raised his eyebrows at her, his face otherwise impassive.

'Yes, the name should be familiar to each of you,' Superintendent Last continued. 'On Wednesday afternoon we received an anonymous call from a woman claiming that Henry Nguyen, AKA Cutter, was the leader of this gang. I believe some of you have listened to the tape. I have arranged for a copy of the sound file to be emailed to each of you this morning. It appears that this caller does know what she is talking about, and we need very much to speak to her again. We issued a media release first thing today, indicating that we want the caller to contact us again.'

'What do we know about this man so far, sir?' Tran asked, as Last took a sip from his coffee.

'Nguyen's last known address was John Street, Cabramatta,' said Last, 'excluding, of course, his time spent in prison: Parklea, Parramatta and Long Bay. Ah, hold on a moment.' He looked down at his notes, and then read, 'Maliciously destroying property; break, enter and steal; take and drive conveyance; assault occasioning actual bodily harm.

'As a child,' he continued, 'Nguyen also appears to have been locked up for more time than he was at school, including in Minda, Mount Penang and Dharruk. Let's see . . .' – again he bowed his large head to his notes – 'charges whilst an inmate include fighting; threatening language; assault; and damaging property.

'And people,' Lawrence Last paused to ensure they were all listening. 'Apparently Mr Nguyen likes a knife – hence the nickname, Cutter. He's had multiple self-harm attempts in every lock-up, and most of the time he did not report them. In fact,' he cleared his throat, and then continued in the same measured tone, 'he was transferred to the hospital at Long Bay when his cell-mate went to the guards for help. Apparently Mr Nguyen had opened a wound in his stomach, and under his covers had been manipulating the area for over a week. The cell-mate informed the guards when he could no longer bear the smell.'

Jill unconsciously smoothed her hair when Joss Preston-Jones's wife, Isobel Rymill, opened her front door. A dark, glossy ponytail snaked around one side of the tall woman's neck, contrasting with her simple white shift dress. She welcomed them into her home with a smile, but hugged her arms around her slim body as they walked together towards the kitchen. Her face was shiny and clear, but her eyes were red-rimmed, her lips slightly swollen.

Superintendent Last had insisted that the taskforce continue with the witness interviews today, despite the developments. He had four officers collecting further intelligence on their two suspects, and would not hear of any definitive action being taken until they had done more surveillance to better determine their whereabouts. He was adamant that no one went anywhere near the suspects' families, or their last known addresses, until they knew exactly where the two men were. It was important not to tip them off in any way.

So Jill and Gabriel sat sipping orange juice at the breakfast bar of the terrace house in Balmain for the second time in as many days.

'How was Joss after yesterday's interview?' Jill asked Isobel Rymill. Despite the evidence on the tape that he was holding something back, Jill had instinctively warmed to this woman's husband, and she couldn't help but wish that this family had not come into their investigation in such a brutal way. She felt guilty that she and Gabriel would this afternoon be finding out everything they could about Joss Preston-Jones. This was not the way she was used to working with victims.

As Isobel told them that her husband was bearing up relatively well, Jill couldn't help but notice the aversion behaviours she displayed – the 'liar's lean', Gabriel had called it – her body angled sharply away from Jill, almost toppling her off the back of her stool. Her eyes darted around the room like a small bird, and she twisted her fingers together in her lap.

Isobel's account of the home invasion was just as harrowing as her husband's. Jill liked to think she had a sense for detecting offenders, and Joss and Isobel did not fit the pattern. She noted the carefully maintained furniture, the mementoes, the photographs on the walls. It was a family home, an ordinary home. She had to agree with Gabriel, though. Joss and Isobel definitely seemed to be keeping something back from them. This did not necessarily mean that they were hiding something related to this case; Jill had seen this kind of behaviour before. Sometimes police involvement in the life of a victim of a particular crime unearthed their involvement in a completely unrelated matter.

Are you up to something? Jill mentally questioned Isobel, as she was tearily finishing her account for the camera.

By the time the interview was over at two o'clock, Jill was already regretting that she'd agreed to analyse the tape at Gabriel's apartment in Ryde. His suggestion that they use her flat yesterday had caught her by surprise, but in bed last night she had mentally kicked herself for not suggesting they use the police station in Balmain, or even in the city, rather than her unit. And when Gabriel had suggested his house today, she'd agreed immediately. What was going on with her? Breaking her own rules, backtracking on decisions. She was lowering her guard too fast. The thought bunched her shoulders. Still, she told herself, they were achieving a lot together in this case. Just let it go at that.

20

CHLOE HAD BEEN extra careful with her makeup this morning. With her first pay cheque as a journalist, she'd been able to buy some serious-looking suits. The dress she chose this morning, however, she had purchased for eveningwear. Perhaps for a date with some fascinating scientist or a doctor she'd have interviewed, she'd thought at the time. Although it wasn't at all low-cut, and dropped to her calves, the caramel jersey clung to her breasts and hips, and she felt more sexy in it than in her skimpiest sundress. It had not even been on sale. This morning, she'd twirled, delighted, around and around in front of the mirror, just as she had in the change rooms of the boutique in which she'd bought it. The snooty salesgirl had actually smiled at her. A woman from the next stall had come out of her cubicle just after her, wearing the same dress. Chloe, four inches taller than her in her bare feet, had given her a big smile, but the other woman had stared briefly at both of them in the communal mirror and ducked back behind her door. Chloe had bought the dress and a pair of knee-high, chocolate brown boots. The boots were the same shade as her eyes and hair.

She stood now in George Street, Liverpool, regretting her decision this morning. A group of four workmen in the Spotlight carpark behind her had been making comments since nine a.m. and it was now after twelve. She'd seen the same man in a suit walk past her and the cameramen three times. She knew he was working up the courage to come over to her. His smile lingered longer with each trip. Keep walking, she tried to tell him with her eyes.

Thing is, the guy behind the counter in the copshop had been the reason for this dress this morning. Constable Andrew Montgomery. He'd asked her if she'd be back today, and yep, here she was, but she hadn't yet been in to say hi.

Yesterday, she'd entered the station full of confidence, given her name and implied that she was an important investigative journalist working on the home invasion cases. The female police liaison officer had tried to blow her off with the standard spiel for the media, but Chloe, undeterred, had said that she'd wait to speak to someone for as long as it took. The dark-eyed girl behind the counter had just smiled sardonically as Chloe settled in for the wait, somewhat dispirited.

She had spotted him first, sat a little straighter on the rigid plastic bench seat. He was looking for something behind the counter, flustered, in a hurry. Two high spots of colour stood out on the smooth skin of his face. Along with Chloe, the dark-eyed girl tracked every move he made. He seemed to spot what he was searching for and moved to pick it up from under a counter. Chloe caught her breath when his shoulders flexed in the short-sleeved police uniform. She'd never realised until that point how much she liked uniforms. At that moment, when Chloe was midway through a slow, secret smile, he seemed to realise that there was someone else in the room and his eyes cut to hers.

She dropped her notepad.

'Here, let me get that for you.'

He was out from behind the counter and by her side in a heartbeat. He passed her the writing pad and she felt compelled to stand: he was so tall from her vantage point on the bench. Chloe was as good as six foot without the kitten heels she was wearing. He stood a head taller. His dark hair was closely cropped.

'Thanks,' she said. Then cleared her throat.

'Is someone looking after you?' he asked.

'It's okay, Andrew,' the liaison officer called from behind the counter. 'She's with the press. I already told her there are no updates this morning.'

'Ah, a journalist,' he said to Chloe. 'Here to keep us on our toes?'

Chloe figured that she should use this opportunity to try to get some kind of quote from one of the officers working here. Any comment could be useful when her bosses were demanding fresh input for three news programs and eight updates a day.

'Actually,' she said with a smile, 'have you got a minute?'

'Is that all you need?'

Chloe laughed. She couldn't help it.

'What I need is some information about the progress

being made on the home invasion gang. Have you guys interviewed any suspects?'

He looked uncomfortable.

'What's your name?' he asked finally.

Chloe withdrew a card from the top pocket of her shirt
and handed it to him. He read it, and then held out his hand.
She shook it, briefly. He smiled into her eyes.

'Well, Chloe Farrell, my name's Constable Andrew Montgomery, and all I can tell you is that we are unable to provide
the media with any new information at the present time. We
will release further statements as facts become available.' He
used a mock-formal tone to deliver the standard line.

'Thanks a lot. Very helpful,' she said with a pout, gathering up her bag.

'Hey,' he said. 'Things change every day. You never know
what's gonna come up. Are you coming back tomorrow?'

'You never know, Constable Montgomery,' she said,
turning to leave. 'Things change every day.'

Now, on the pavement opposite the station, Chloe had
half made up her mind to cross the road and enter the
building again when she spotted an unmarked vehicle leaving
the parking area under the police complex. She nudged her
colleague with the camera.

'Another one,' she said. 'Could be one of the taskforce.'

She was correct. It was Sergeant Jillian Jackson, the
woman she'd photographed on Wednesday, driving with the
dark-haired man in the trucker's cap that she'd been unable
to identify. Even Deborah Davies hadn't been able to get the
guy's name. I wonder who he is, Chloe thought.

When the car was out of shot, Chloe guessed that these
detectives leaving the building would be the most exciting

thing that would happen in the next couple of hours. She thought it might be time to try to get something from someone behind the desk. She combed her fingers through her hair and strode across George Street.

Chloe smiled deliberately at the one-way mirror directly behind the liaison officer before stating her request. Constable Andrew Montgomery skidded out from behind the panel before she'd even finished her sentence.

'Chloe Farrell,' he said. 'It's lunchtime. Hungry?'

'Starving,' she said.

21

'EVA!' KAREN MICEH dropped the platter she was drying, and it smashed into pieces on the tiled kitchen floor. Her two-year-old daughter, Eva, began to cry at the noise and the shock of Mummy yelling at her.

Within three lurching strides, Karen had reached the child sitting cross-legged under the dining room table and removed the pointed filleting knife from her lap. Eva howled more loudly.

'Oh my God, Eva! How many times have I told you, you mustn't play . . . *owww*!'

Karen banged her head on the table as she bundled wet-faced Eva up from the floor. She held her close, stroking her back, automatically jiggling her little body up and down. Manoeuvring one hand out from under her daughter's chubby legs, she glanced at her watch. Oh for heaven's sake,

147

she thought. How am I going to get everything done on time?

For the third time already this morning, she cursed her ratbag husband, Eddie. *Ex*-husband, she reminded herself, and good riddance. She didn't miss his lazy, bludging friends calling at all hours of the night; she didn't miss his subtle put-downs and the way he leered at other women. She certainly didn't miss the bong under his side of the bed. When she'd found her daughters, Maryana and Eva, giggling and grimacing over its stink one morning, she knew her fool husband would never grow up, and that her marriage was over.

Actually, in some ways life had never been so peaceful for Karen as it was now – just her and the girls, homework and shopping, and her part-time work as a sandwich hand at Castle Towers. The one thing she couldn't do without, though, was Eddie's pay cheque.

She walked the sniffling Eva back to the sink and settled her into the highchair she'd set up so her little girl could 'help' with the dishes. This time, though, she pushed the chair further from the sink. How had she missed Eva grabbing the knife?

She sighed tiredly and looked into the loungeroom of her Baulkham Hills home. This place is perfect, she told herself again. I can't move the girls now, they're just settling down after the separation. She bent to pick up the shards of the ceramic platter. One of her favourites; her brother, Ken, had bought it for her in Spain. She turned to frown at Eva, but her daughter's self-occupied chortling over her tea-set left her smiling instead.

It was her brother who'd given her the rental idea.

'This is really a great room,' Ken had said to her the previous month, when he'd come to install the above-ground pool he'd bought for his nieces – getting it ready for Christmas, he'd said. He always spoiled them.

'Yeah, the girls love to play in there,' she'd said around a peg, as she hung out the washing on the hoist next to the lemon tree.

'You could rent that out to another family,' he'd laughed.

Karen didn't know anyone who'd ever taken in a boarder, but actually it was the perfect solution for her. With the extra income, there'd be no need for her and the girls to find a cheaper place to rent. Of course, the self-contained space under the large balcony couldn't actually house a family, but a single person would have plenty of room.

The problem, the real-estate people had warned her, was that her house was some distance from public transport, and the sort of people wishing to rent a single room typically didn't have their own car. This would reduce the number of applicants, they told her. Karen was not daunted. She knew she might be idealising it, but she had an image of herself selecting from a few young people first moving away from home, preferably a girl – Karen would be her mentor, a friend; she'd really enjoy the company. Maybe her tenant would be from the country – here for her first year at university. She could imagine how the girl's family would appreciate the family home away from home that Karen would provide. Macquarie Uni was not too far from here, she reasoned.

Six months had passed with just a single application submitted. The couple had been young, but that's where her fantasy tenants ended. They'd pulled up to Karen's house in a car she was certain was their home at the time. Even had there not been boxes and clothes piled high, the driver would have been hard pressed to see through the grime that covered the windows. The occupants didn't alight for a good five minutes, and from behind the curtain in her loungeroom Karen watched them screaming at one another. At least their windscreen was relatively clear. From this vantage, she could also see the drapes moving surreptitiously at number nineteen. Mrs Robotham. What would she have made of Jackie and Troy as new neighbours? Jackie picked at sores on her arms while Troy did the talking. Neither of them really made eye contact with Karen. As soon as they crossed the threshold, she was planning their exit. Troy smelled like Eddie's bong water and Jackie couldn't negotiate around the furniture. Karen couldn't be certain, but it seemed Troy's interest lay more in her electrical goods than the room for rent. His eyes lingered on the microwave, the DVD, the clunky laptop she used to play Solitaire.

Karen had resignedly begun searching for less expensive properties for herself when someone else had answered her ad.

Now, she threw the last of the scatter cushions onto the couch and kicked one of Maryana's rollerskates back under a chair. Maryana, her six-year-old, was at school. Karen bustled back to the kitchen to grab Eva – couldn't leave her near the knives again – and hurried over to respond to the doorbell.

I hope he likes the room, she thought, opening the door with a smile.

If it hadn't been for the old woman, Karen's first reaction would have been to shut the door again immediately. As it was, however, the tiny, bent lady looked as though she could not stand up for much longer, despite the fact that the man was holding her arm so solicitously.

She showed them in and asked the old woman if she'd like a drink.

'Just some water, please,' he answered for her.

'My grandmother has lived through war and famine,' he said when Karen returned with the water. 'She has arthritis and she turned ninety last year, but she still insisted that she come and inspect the room before I take it.' He smiled fondly at his grandmother as he helped her accept the glass.

Karen smiled uncertainly. She did not like his long hair, but he seemed a much nicer person than her first glimpse of him had indicated. Anyone who was this close to his grandmother must be a good person. She had a sense about these things. Just goes to show, she reminded herself, you can't judge a book by its cover – her own grandmother had taught her that.

'I'm afraid there are a few stairs,' she said, shifting a shy Eva to the other hip. 'But when you're both ready, I'll take you down to see the room, Henry.'

'That'd be great. Thanks.'

Karen smiled more brightly and led Cutter and his grandmother from the room.

In one of the Department of Community Service's many attempts to 'help' him, at thirteen Cutter had been sent to a small group home for troubled children. The house was in leafy Baulkham Hills, and he was pretty sure that most of the neighbours didn't know the purpose of the home. A couple, Debbie and Ian, chosen and paid by the Department for their extraordinary progress with even the most difficult kids, ran the home.

Cutter had loved Baulkham Hills. Sure, everyone was racist there, but that was the case pretty much everywhere when he was a kid. The Australian families fascinated him, and after twilight, he would sit in the bushes for hours watching the mums preparing dinner, the kids doing their homework, their dads arriving home from work. He'd laugh quietly at the funny way they ate, the way the kids were disciplined and ran crying to their rooms. Better than any TV show he'd ever seen, however, were the backhanders he saw some of the perfect dads give the perfect mums. He'd found at least four of these households, and he would sit in their azalea bushes, the camellia shrubs, and stuff his hand in his mouth to stop his laughter being heard. The suburb was so quiet in the evenings that he'd even taken to bringing a towel to muffle the chortles while he watched his special TV screens – their well-lit loungeroom windows.

Debbie, his group home 'mum', had told him he should be coming home earlier. She would sit with him at night and quietly ask him where he went, why he never ate with them. He couldn't tell Debbie that he skipped school and went home most days to eat rice balls and fish soup. Debbie would be furious that the school had not told her he was seldom there. Things were going just fine for him at that school – he didn't want to be there, and they couldn't have been more delighted with his decision.

Debbie just wouldn't give up on him. She'd bring Ian into his room at night and they'd play good cop/bad cop; she'd read the Bible with him; she learned about Vietnam, and even tried learning some of the words to encourage him to speak to her. One night, when he'd broken into a face-splitting smile, she'd thought it was working. She was winning him over.

Cutter couldn't bear that her efforts would now redouble and he'd have to sit here for hours more, listening to her shit. Instead, he spoke his first full sentence ever to Debbie.

'You know why I smiled, Debbie?' He looked up at her through straight, black eyelashes, shadowing bottomless black eyes.

He really is a striking boy, she thought, reaching out with her foot to touch just the tip of his shoe, the first time she had ever touched him. Finally, she was getting through. All they need is a little love, she told herself.

'Why Henry? Why were you smiling?' She leaned in close.

'Because I can smell your cunt, you slut. You fucked Ian just before you came in here, didn't you?' He spoke quietly, concentrating on every feature as the horror flared her nostrils and dilated her pupils. Before she could physically recoil, he grabbed at her crotch under her pretty, yellow skirt, and managed to push his finger through her panties and hard into her hole.

'Or maybe,' he continued, holding her arm now as she screamed, 'you were waiting for me, with your finger going round and round in there. I've seen the way you look at me.'

He could no longer hold her and she fell off the bed, screaming and screaming, scuttling backwards on the floor. He jumped out the window before Ian could grab him, but not before slowly sucking his finger on the window ledge.

Debbie could tell Ian all about what that gesture meant later, when she was feeling better.

Cutter checked out the basement underneath Karen's huge back patio. He showed his grandmother carefully to a chair by a desk. She'd been wonderful. He knew he would never have got this place in Baulkham Hills if he'd come alone. And he knew his grandmother would always do whatever her number-one grandson asked.

He smiled at the two women, walked to the small window looking out onto the backyard and breathed in the lemony air.

'Perfect,' he said.

22

'YOU WANT SOMETHING to drink?'

Jill looked at Gabriel standing in his kitchen. Yeah, white wine, she thought. Where did that urge come from, she wondered. She hadn't had a drink in ten years. 'Um, some water would be great,' she said.

'Help yourself.' He pointed his chin at the fridge, his hands expertly paring the skin from two fat, brilliant-orange salmon steaks.

She opened the refrigerator and looked around, almost disappointed to find there was no wine in there anyway. A tall bottle of water stood in the door. She pulled it out and put it on the bench, then stuck her head back in the fridge.

'You want me to make a salad or something?' she asked, spying bags of lettuce and carrots.

'If you want,' he said. 'And pass me those beans.'

She grabbed the vegetables and set them next to the water on the bench, then stood for a moment, figuring he'd tell her where things were. When he didn't, she went looking for the glasses, a knife, a salad bowl and chopping board. She also found some warm, ripe tomatoes, a lemon and a Spanish onion in the fruit bowl, and set to tearing lettuce leaves. She stole glances at him as he worked. Without his cap, dark curls fell into his eyes. He kept wiping them away with his wrist, careful not to touch his hair with his fishy hands. She realised she had never seen him clean-shaven. He always had a dark stubble; she noticed for the first time that it was flecked with just one or two greys. His full lips moved unconsciously as he concentrated completely on the food.

She looked away and checked out his apartment instead, stamping firmly down upon the stupid thought that this felt more like a lunch date than a day at work. We gotta eat, she told herself. Might as well be here as anywhere else.

Actually, this is quite nice, if kind of weird, she thought, looking around the apartment. It felt more like a treehouse than a two-bedroom, third-floor unit in Sydney's northwest. A giant eucalyptus tree that danced literally at the edge of the balcony established the effect. Midway up the tree trunk, the view from the unit was of spinning lime-green leaves and gnarled branches, with just a few glimpses of the sky beyond. This apartment building felt as if it had been surgically inserted into one of the rare pockets of original Sydney bushland.

She drizzled olive oil onto the salad, and walked over towards the balcony to take a better look. Sliding open the glass door, she stepped into a greenhouse, took sips of the green, oxygen-soaked air. Had she dared, she could easily have climbed onto the balustrade and down the knobbly trunk of the huge tree. She could see no sign of other humans living anywhere nearby. She imagined strolling as far as she could see along the bush-gully floor, through fallen leaves and stands of stringybark and gum trees. Half-tempted to do just that, she suddenly noticed a smoke-like shape break away from the base of the tree and hurtle up towards her. She almost stepped back in fear until she recognised the lithe movements. She waited to see where the small cat would go. Within half a second, it sat staring at her from the branch closest to the balcony. Entranced, she froze, and they stared at one another until she had to blink.

The cat sprang silently from the branch to the balcony floor and rubbed its chubby grey cheeks around her ankles. She blinked down at it for a few moments more, hoping it would not run away, and then bent carefully to pat it. There was a rumble of purring, and then the little cat lifted high its tail and sauntered into Gabriel's apartment.

Jill followed it in, leaving the doors open. Inside, from this angle, the room was less remarkable. A couple of squashy lounge chairs and a coffee table, a TV, no dining table. The light in the apartment was a cool, flickering green – the effect of the tree outside, breathing through the room.

'Ten,' said Gabriel, matter-of-factly, from the kitchen.

'Pardon?' she said.

'That's Ten,' he pointed at the floor.

She looked down, lost.

'Oh, the cat!' She finally got it. 'Why do you call it Ten?'

'Her. She's a her,' he said, and then, 'Lunch is ready.'

They ate on the lounge chairs with their plates on their laps. Gabriel had coated thick fingers of the salmon in the most translucent tempura Jill had ever eaten. The fish had barely been cooked through, and when her fork caused the soft pieces to flake apart, she copied Gabriel and ate it with her hands. It was deep-fried, and the delicious sin of this made her lick her salty fingers with each bite.

'You ready to look at the tape?' he asked eventually, the first words either of them had spoken since they'd sat down.

'Huh? Oh, yeah.' She stood. 'That was just . . . great. Thanks.' She took the dishes to the sink, and tried to rise out of the strange mood that had enveloped her since she'd walked in here. She dropped her fork when she identified the feeling.

She was relaxed.

The knowledge made her hands shake.

23

'AW FUCK, MOUSE, now look what you've done!' Simon Ester-hase threw his snooker cue into the rack in disgust. 'I sank the black, man. Why don't you stop bitching for a while? It's getting old.'

'Are you fucking serious?' Dang Huynh, known to most people as Mouse, chewed at his thumbnail. The skin around all of his fingernails was red-raw. 'I'm telling you I can't take anymore of this shit. He's a fucking psycho! What's to stop him from chopping one of us into pieces?'

Esterhase rubbed at his neck. He'd had diarrhoea every day since the Capitol Hill thing, and he just couldn't sleep right. But what was he going to do? Mouse and Tatts were losing it, and it was true that this could get them all killed. They'd all known Cutter was mental since they were kids, but he'd never done anything like this before. Now, though,

Esterhase agreed with Mouse that it wouldn't take much for Cutter to turn his radar on them. He winced as images, sounds, flashed into his mind.

Esterhase sat down at his coffee table, chopped up some more pot. The ritual soothed him. He'd smoked twenty cones a day for the past fifteen years. Truth was, now when he had to be straight for some reason, he felt stoned.

Fuck, Mouse had paced the same circle fifty times.

'Man, can you sit down, Mouse? You're making my dick itch.'

'Why did he have to start with the killing? He's not going to stop,' said Mouse. 'How are we going to get out of this? He's going to get caught and we're all going up for fucking murder, man.'

Esterhase knew it. He packed a cone tightly and lit it, his lungs burning as he pulled the hit of marijuana, clean. They had always been scared of Cutter, but you just kind of ignored his sick shit back in the day. They'd all done so much time since then that none of them really knew how bad he'd become. Maybe Cutter didn't even know. The fucker was mad, that was for sure. Esterhase packed another cone.

'Here, Mouse, have this. You'll feel better,' he said, holding the bong out to his friend.

'I don't want it. I'm paranoid enough already!' Mouse wrung his hands. He had dark circles under his eyes and Esterhase noticed grey shot through his greasy dark hair. 'I keep thinking he's gonna break in my house and cut me up.' His voice cracked.

'Well, what do you want to do, Mouse? We go to the cops, we'll go down with him. They won't stop until they get the rest of us.' He lit the bong and had half the cone himself.

160

He stared at Mouse through the smoke, red-eyed. 'We can kill him.'

Esterhase expected Mouse to freak at the suggestion. He, Tatts and Mouse had never done more than give a bloke a good flogging. The machetes were all for show. At least they had been.

Mouse said nothing.

'You wouldn't want to fuck a thing like that up though, now would ya, Mouse?'

'How would we do it?' Mouse's voice was tiny.

'You're fucking kidding me!' Esterhase gave a dead laugh. 'You've thought about it then?'

'What else are we gonna do?' Mouse pleaded. 'We've got to get out of this shit somehow.'

Esterhase looked around his rumpus room. He saw a luxurious, relaxing room to chill out in. In reality, the room was like the rest of the house, crammed with mismatched stolen property, half of it broken, all of it coated in a thin layer of grime. The walls were yellow with cigarette and marijuana smoke.

Esterhase was the pride of his family. The only child to have a job for more than six months straight, and to make it out of the housos. Shit, even his dad had only had a job once for about a year, back when Esterhase was a kid. Removalist too, just like him. But while his father had fucked his back up early, Esterhase had been smart. He'd always got others on the job to do the heavy lifting. The Maoris would work all day for smoko or some speed at knock-off time. And the job was perfect for finding places to do over.

Everything was pretty good in his life, he thought, finishing the rest of the cone.

Except for Cutter.

*

Lunch had been perfect, really, in every way. Well, except for the food.

Fortunately, Chloe Farrell and Andrew Montgomery had not been interested in the food. A newly retired couple sharing a muffin at the next table in the small café had wriggled closer on their bench seat while watching them. The man even moved his foot to touch his wife's shoe under the table. They'd been that way, once.

Andrew knew he was going to be late back, but he ordered a coffee anyway. Chloe had sparkling mineral water.

'Off the record,' Andrew said, watching her sip her drink through a straw.

'What is?' asked Chloe, ready for another joke, or flirtatious comment.

'A call came in late yesterday about the case.'

Chloe tucked her hair behind her ears. Sat forward.

'It could be nothing. Jane took it at the front desk. I was getting ready to knock off.'

'What was it?'

'Some woman. Anonymous. Gave the name of someone we should be looking at for these home invasions.'

'What was the name?' she asked, palms flat on the table, eyes serious, face angled up to his.

Andrew gave a laugh. 'You're a real little newshound, aren't you?'

'Come on, Andrew. It's my job.'

'Yeah, well, it'd be my job if anyone knew I even told you that much.'

'But you said it could be nothing. If I knew the name, I could dig around. Maybe I could help.'

'You digging around would not help, Chloe. If the tip was straight up, you would not want to go poking a stick into this guy's nest.'

'Is there anything I could say that would get you to give me the name?'

'Baby, I could think of a million things you could say to me that would make me give you anything. But that's not playing fair.'

'Okay,' she said, standing. 'Well, we'd better get back then.'

Andrew's expression was surprised, then hurt.

'I'll pay for lunch if you'll get dinner.' She smiled over her shoulder, as she walked to the cashier.

24

JILL STOOD IN the doorway after lunch, silently taking in the bank of audiovisual and computing equipment in Gabriel's second bedroom. It wrapped around three walls: PC monitors and TV screens, cameras and tripods, speakers and hard drives. Electrical cords and cables snaked across the floor, climbed walls, and trailed sinuously across most surfaces. A curtain was drawn across the single window, and the room was shadowy. Green and red LED lights blinked rhythmically in the gloom.

Gabriel cleared his throat behind her; she stepped aside. Smiling broadly, he wheeled a second chair into the room, bumping it four-wheel-drive-style over double-adaptors and a couple of magazines. Jill, flattening herself against the bookshelf next to the door, turned and read some of the titles. *Crime Scene Investigation*; *Criminal Profiling*;

Forensic Interviewing and Interrogation; *Serial Killer Typology*.

'So what sort of cases were you on before this one?' she asked, pulling down a thick tome. She flicked through it before closing it on a page of corpses, a black and white photograph of a child's dead eyes the last image in her mind. She blinked it away.

'Oh, this and that. Same as you I suppose,' he answered, smashing the second chair into a space at one of the terminals. He couldn't quite get it to fit, so she walked over, and with her foot, nudged aside a book caught between the wheel and the desk. The chair bumped hard against the table with Gabriel's final shove, and some of the equipment atop it lurched. 'There!' he grinned delightedly and threw himself onto the seat.

Jill took the other chair as Gabriel pressed buttons and moved a mouse to wake some of the slumbering machines. She looked at the screen in front of Gabriel too late to identify the official-looking logo that preceded the program he had opened.

'Could you just access my email, Jill?' he said, pointing to the monitor in front of her. 'I sent myself the voice recording of the anonymous phone call. It should be in there somewhere.'

She opened his email program, surprised at his lack of concern for his privacy. Probably this isn't his only email account, she thought. She found the MPEG file near the top of his unopened mail and double-clicked. Under it were a couple of the pharmaceutical and penis-enlargement spam emails that also choked her mailbox every morning. It seemed not even all this technology could stop them getting through.

'So.' He pushed his chair back a little from his screen and looked at her. 'What did you think of Isobel Rymill?'

'She seemed even more nervous than her husband,' she said.

Gabriel pulled a USB flash device from his pocket and plugged it into his terminal, where it began downloading a large document. 'Anything else?' he asked, eyes back on his screen.

'Well, I noticed clusters of deception signals.' The words she'd learned from him yesterday seemed cumbersome.

'And they could mean . . .'

'She's hiding something. It could be guilty knowledge, something shameful, or the truth. She might be lying to us, or just holding something of importance back.' Jill felt half-curious and half-annoyed by this oral examination.

'Exactly.' He nodded and smiled slightly.

She waited for him to add something. He seemed delighted by their exchange, but as she had come to learn, he didn't always conclude his train of thoughts aloud.

She waited while he clicked on some icons on his screen, and a computerised drone started up from the terminal as it obeyed his commands. Suddenly he reached straight across her and used the mouse for her computer. His back touched her chest and her mouth was almost on his neck. She pushed her chair backwards, startled by his abrupt invasion of her space, but he continued what he was doing without heeding her movement.

'Just saved the audio MPEG to my machine,' he said, straightening up and turning to face her. 'Remember I told you that if I heard the anonymous caller again I was sure I would know her?'

Jill stared at him, the realisation raising the hairs on her arms. 'Isobel Rymill – she was the one who called and told us to investigate Henry Nguyen?'

He didn't answer, and she watched as he used the program he'd opened to compartmentalise parts of the recording they'd made of Rymill earlier that morning. He created a series of digitised sound bites and lined seven or eight of them up next to the file that held the recording of the anonymous tip-off. He then opened another program and opened two of the files with it. When he pressed 'Enter' the drone of the computer kicked up a notch. Almost immediately a coloured graph and readout appeared on the screen.

'Ninety per cent match,' he said, white teeth flashing. 'Not bad, considering the distortion from the phone call caused by her covering the receiver.'

'Wow,' said Jill, leaning close over Gabriel's shoulder. 'Where'd you get this voice recognition software? I don't think we've got anything that good at work.'

'I know. It's amateur hour in there. What are you gonna do?'

'So, we've got a clear new line of inquiry,' he continued, opening another program. 'We need to know everything about Joss Preston-Jones *and* Isobel Rymill, and we need to know why they so desperately want us to investigate Henry Nguyen.'

Joss had thought his day at work would never end, but he was surprised at how quickly he'd slipped into robot-mode and completed his chores for the day. He'd brushed aside the concerned comments about the fading bruises on his face, and left the office at 4.30 p.m. exactly. He called the house phone, knowing Isobel would not yet be there with Charlie – tonight Charlie had dancing lessons – and left a message indicating that he would not be home for dinner. Then he turned his mobile phone off and caught the lift down to the employees-only gym. He changed out of his work clothes and shoved them into his backpack. Imagining Isobel's face when she saw the clothes, he took the trousers out again and folded them neatly.

He went to the weight rack wearing a singlet and shorts and loaded fifteen kilos onto the hand weights. He moved rapidly through six sets of fifty bicep curls, dissociating through the pain, then hit the showers. He held his face under the water, eyes open, breathing in the steam.

He could see only Cutter.

He changed into jeans, a dark tee-shirt and runners. And for the second time in two days, Joss went back to his old world. He caught the train from Central to Cabramatta.

Isobel had grudgingly told Joss the things she'd learned about Henry Nguyen.

'I don't see why you need to know this stuff,' she'd protested. 'The police have it now.'

In Cabramatta two days before, he'd visited a medical centre. Isobel had found Cutter's medical records and they showed monthly visits to the centre, mostly on Thursday afternoons. The timing was about right, but Joss, waiting at a bus stop directly across from the front door, had seen no sign of Nguyen. He'd had no firm plan as to what he would do if he did. All he knew was that his life had changed completely since the home invasion, and he was not going to let it fall apart without doing everything he could to stop it.

He considered staking out Cutter's grandmother's house. When they were kids, he, Fuzzy and Esterhase had dropped Cutter there at around five one morning using a car they'd stolen the night before. Half asleep, they'd driven the car over a couple of streets and dumped it at a soccer field before walking home. Joss remembered that he'd helped his drunken mum from the lounge up to her bed before he'd gone to bed for the rest of the day. He shook his head. What a way to grow up.

He decided against the trip to Cutter's old home. He could think of no obvious information he could get from the family at this point. It was unlikely Cutter still lived there anyway. Joss needed to know more about his associates – who he hung out with now. Maybe he could find out the name of the arsehole that'd stood on his head at Andy Wu's house.

He got off the train at Cabramatta station and the smells of his past slapped him in the face. The area had been predominantly Italian when he was a kid, but since then Asian, and particularly Vietnamese, communities had been steadily migrating to the suburb. Now, most shop signs were in both English and Vietnamese. The rest were in Vietnamese only.

He made his way to the pub closest to the station. Back then, he and his friends had sold stolen watches and cameras, typewriters and aftershave to the patrons of this pub. It could be that some of the old crew still came here.

The ground felt gummy out the front of the hotel. Because of too many broken heads from the bashings and paralytic falls, the council had replaced the pavement with the rubber material used in children's playgrounds.

169

Joss left the last of the warm twilight behind him and stepped inside the pub. Like most hotels, it was always the same time once you entered those doors. Ten a.m. or midnight, it all felt the same, with the aim of aiding the punters to forget the troubles of the outside world, kick back for a while, lose some more money.

Cigarette smoke already impregnating his tee-shirt and whispering its way down his lungs, he took a seat at the end of the main bar, facing the door. Determined to ask for a light beer and sit back to sip it slowly, he found himself instead ordering a schooner of full-strength VB. Ten minutes later he asked for the same again and for two packets of chips. He hoped the grease would counteract some of the alcohol.

Tragedy performed a series of vignettes around the hotel. A woman sat with two men, her features sliding off her face with her lipstick, gazing with naked desperation from one man to the other as they spoke the inscrutable language of the drunk. Her expression altered to one of begging appeasement when she had their attention. He twice watched her flinch when one of the men moved his arm suddenly to sneeze, to make a point.

A bloke in the fluorescent shirt that was the uniform of unskilled labourers kicked his workboot in disgust against the base of the poker machine he was feeding. When he stood up from his stool, Joss was surprised to see he looked no older than twenty or so. He made his way to the front of the room, but instead of leaving, he withdrew two fifties from the ATM near the door. He returned to his stool, slid in a note, his jaw slack, his eyes on fire, as though he was watching pornography.

A wizened man laughed into his glass on a stool next to Joss. A section of greasy hair that had long abandoned its comb-over position slipped in and out of his beer as he drank. The bald spot on his head was beaded with sweat, despite the refrigerated air. A dark area at his groin signalled that he'd found the trip to the toilet a waste of good drinking time. He's probably a digger, thought Joss, draining the last of his beer. The thought made him want to order another, but he figured he'd use the toilet instead. He swayed a little when he got off the stool.

He splashed his face with cold water before leaving the bathroom.

Eyes always on the door, he saw a face from his past walk into the pub.

Fuck, what was his name?

The man walked towards the bar, not looking in Joss's direction. Joss ordered another beer and took it back to a small table; he angled his chair towards the bar. The man looked around the room after he'd ordered his drink. His eyes moved past Joss, then whipped back again, his obvious movement almost comical to someone trained in surveillance.

Joss sipped.

'Hey, man,' the bloke had his drink and was making his way over. What was his frigging name? 'Aren't you Joss?'

'Yeah. Rodney Harris?' said Joss, remembering at the very last moment.

'Yeah, man! How the fuck have you been? What are you doing back in Cabra, dog?'

Rodney Harris was a wannabe back in the day. He would try to hang around whenever he saw Joss and his friends, and sometimes they'd let him. Other times they'd tell him to piss off, or make him steal them some food before he could stay.

Today, his features were blurred, his once-blond hair thin, translucent. He spoke in the nasal gaol-whine of the streets. The heels of his shoes were rounded with wear.

'Oh, you know, nothin,' Joss tried to dumb down. 'Thought I'd come see if there's any action around here, you know.'

Harris looked at him sidelong, and took a sip of his dark-coloured drink.

Joss pushed out the chair opposite with his foot. 'You're not still drinking Jackies are ya?' he said.

Harris laughed. 'Yeah, man, always.' He took the seat.

'So what have you been doing?' Joss asked before the other man could. 'I haven't seen you for years.'

'Since we were kids, dog. Not since Fuzzy died. How fucked up was that, man?'

'Yeah.'

'I've been doing shit. You know, this and that. I got a coupla kids.' He put his hand-rolled cigarette on the edge of an ashtray on the table, pulled out a flat, shredding wallet and showed Joss a green-tinged laminated photo of a young girl and boy. 'Course they'd be older than this now,' he said, looking at the photo. 'Their slut mum took off with them to Queensland when I was inside.'

'Yeah?' said Joss. 'Bitch. They're all the fuckin' same.'

'Too right, dog.' They drank together. 'So what about you? Where'd you piss off to? We heard your mum killed herself. Sorry, man.'

'Nah. Crazy bitch. She just threw herself in front of a car, but she survived. Probably dead now though, for all I know. Who cares? I got locked up for being uncontrollable.'

'No waaay.' Harris laughed. 'Unlucky. So what brings you back to the 'hood?'

Joss inwardly cringed at the American gangster-speak. Didn't these idiots ever grow up? Harris drained his drink, crunched the ice.

'Let me get you another one, man.' Joss stood and made his way over to the bar. He shouldn't have another, but this was a critical point. He had to ask about Cutter. He ordered another beer, and, overly careful, carried the drinks back to the table. The rigid walk of the almost drunk.

'It's a spinout to see you, Rod,' he said when he got back to the table. 'Do any of the old boys still hang around here?'

'Yeah, man.' Harris listed off a few names, all of them familiar, none of them the right one.

'So where do you go to score now?' Joss lowered his voice.

Big smile. 'What are you into?'

'I just want some pot, maybe some pills.'

'You know who's selling some great shit right now? Simon Esterhase. Remember him?'

Yeah, you could say that. 'Bullshit. Esterhase? I haven't seen him for ages. Does he still hang around with, ah, what was his name . . . Cutter?'

Harris's mouth turned down at the name. 'Yeah, man.' He looked around the room. 'Crazy motherfucker.'

'Does he come around here much?'

'Who? Cutter? Nah. I see him around the station sometimes. I think he still goes over to his olds' house a lot. That's when he's not inside.'

Joss laughed hollowly.

'Yeah?' he gathered himself together, spoke calmly, a pulse ticking in his temple. 'You know I wouldn't mind catching up with them again, now I'm doing the whole memory lane thing. You wouldn't know how I could reach them, would ya?'

'I got Esterhase's number right here. I go see him whenever I can afford it. You wanna go out there tonight?'

'Maybe. What about Cutter's number, have you got that?'

'What do you want his number for, man? Don't you remember him? Well, he's a lot worse than that now.' He pulled from his wallet a worn, folded sheet of paper, torn from an exercise book. 'Got a pen? Don't tell Cutter I gave you this, man.'

Joss copied the numbers, both mobiles, onto a coaster and dropped it into his backpack. He'd had half of his latest beer and needed the toilet again. The woman sitting with the two men began crying loudly, but there were no tears in her eyes. She stopped when one of the men raised a fist.

Joss stood, suddenly exhausted. His head buzzed and his hands felt filthy. He looked down at them and they seemed hazy, indistinct. He went to the toilet. When he returned Harris was crunching ice again, looking up at him expectantly, eager to continue the party.

'I'm gonna go, Rod,' he said, leaving his beer.

'Nah, dog, where are you going?'

Joss was already halfway to the door.

He salivated with the scent of coriander, rice and fried garlic as he hit the night air. Isobel would've left him some dinner, of course, but he had to eat now. He remembered there used to be a good noodle house around here somewhere. He wondered if it would still be there.

The streets were quiet. A few late travellers made their way home from work, but it seemed that most people were indoors now, cooking up the smells that were driving him crazy. He turned a corner that seemed familiar and pulled his wallet from his pocket, hoping he had some cash left. He had to walk over to a street light to see the inside of his wallet.

Friends since kindergarten, Frankie Danang and Tua Lataafa had always played together well. Whispered, when it was certain they were nowhere listening, their classmates called them Quick and Thick. On the footy field, Frankie ran faster than anyone, and when it came to defence, no one could get past Tua, who was bigger than all of the teachers by Year Six. Today, at eighteen, and already done with school for five years, most people in Cabramatta ducked into a shop, crossed a street or hailed a cab when they spotted Tua and Frankie in the distance. If you got off at the station and saw them sitting there, most people knew it was best to hop back on the train, catch the bus back from the next stop. Better half an hour late for dinner, than the next three days in Fairfield Hospital.

Frankie and Tua had rolling down pat. They averaged five hundred bucks a day, but three grand was their record. Frankie used a knife and Tua his fists. Sometimes a boot was required, but most people were quite obliging within a minute or two. They'd never gone much for excessive violence; had never seen the need, really.

The strategy was simple: approach and ask for a smoke; Frankie – twenty centimetre switchblade punched into the thigh; Tua – king-hit to the face: nose, jaw, depended on the angle as they dropped, really. They used to relive the action highlights over a beer afterwards, but the novelty had mostly worn off by now, and they tended to talk more about football and girls.

Tua spotted this one. He touched Frankie on the arm, nodded his head in the man's direction. The day had been slow. They'd met up pretty late this arvo, and there'd been no one in the quiet spots around Cabra this evening. Frankie had recommended a trip to the Quay, and they had been heading to the station.

Frankie scanned their environment. Perfect. He'd lost count of their hits in this alley. And the guy had a slight lean on. He wouldn't even know his leg had a hole in it until the ambos told him in half an hour or so. No one around, should be sweet.

Still, he didn't give Tua the signal straight away. There was something. Could this guy be a cop? Something about the way he held himself? He didn't seem to have any idea they were there, but . . .

Tua was staring at Frankie. What? His eyebrows asked.

Frankie shrugged. The blade snicked out by his thigh, a scissor snip in the night.

The signal.

Joss checked his wallet under the streetlight, but its contents didn't register. Nothing in his face or posture had altered, but he was now completely sober. He put a seemingly steadying hand upon the pole and bent awkwardly, pulling at his shoe as though to dislodge a stone. The angle widened his peripheral vision, and he was now certain that one of them was carrying. Gun or knife? The answer was essential in determining his first move. He couldn't tell – the knuckles on the hand holding the weapon were pointed down, but still, it could be either.

Eight metres, seven. *Make a decision.*

Most places in Sydney, chances were this would be a knife. Guns were relatively scarce, but this was Cabramatta after all, and if there was going to be a gun, it would be here.

Six metres.

He was going to guess knife. Something about the hang of the kid's shoulders, the grip on the object, the fist closed hard, pumping it up. No need to do that with a gun.

Five metres.

Okay, come.

'Hey, you got a smoke there, mate?'

The big one spoke (to distract), the little one moved closer (to strike).

Joss drew in a deep, delicious draught of night air. The effect was soporific, but his senses could not have been more acute. A sensation of peace came with a feeling of alignment. Sometimes in life it was much more difficult to play nice than to just be real. Just you and me, boys. The violence was hot behind his eyes.

'I don't smoke,' he said.

The little one knew, now.

Three metres, two.

Wait.

Frankie realised he had missed the feeling of adrenalin pissing into his gut, the flurry of fear constricting his anus.

This guy was going to need care, he thought. In times to come, he and Tua would talk about tonight. He tried to signal to Tua, to let him know to beware, but his best friend was in the zone, pumping up.

Frankie knew he'd have to go in fast.

He felt his heartbeat in his hands.

Tua knew that somehow he should've been calculating a new strategy, but the first thing he felt was admiration for the guy's block and duck from Frankie's knife. Still wondering whether he could use that move playing footy on the weekend, he found himself on his arse. The cunt had kicked him! He stood and lurched forward, enraged, and he was on the ground again. Huh? No one had touched him, 'cause the fucker was busy kicking Frankie. He stood. He fell. What the . . .

Tua looked down at his legs and blinked. He screamed.

His left shinbone had burst through the skin above his ankle and stood like a forty-five degree erection out from his flesh, some of which was clinging pinkly to the bone.

He fainted.

Joss could see that the little one was just conscious; he was nursing his broken arm as he lay in the gutter.

'Don't go to sleep now,' he said calmly to the Asian youth at his feet. 'Your friend needs an ambulance.'

A couple of people stared as he jumped on the train just before it pulled out from Cabramatta station. Joss looked down at his hands, clothes. No blood. What?

He didn't realise that his eyes glittered and his grin had stuck his lips to his teeth.

*

The unit felt empty tonight. In the past, that had been the only way Jill could bear it. She liked it locked down and silent – the only noises those she generated herself, or the familiar hums and purrs of her cleaning appliances. On odd occasions, she'd feel an urge to invite her mum and dad over for dinner. Sometimes her brother and sister-in-law would drop by with Lily and Avery, her four-year-old niece and six-year-old nephew. More often, she'd visit them in their homes. She could probably count the number of times Cassie, her sister, had been by. When she did have visitors, while she wanted to be with them, Jill also found herself watching and waiting for the cues that indicated they would soon leave.

Control. It meant everything to her. And when people were in her house, when she couldn't see where everyone was, or identify each noise in her space, she couldn't relax. She'd do her best, but couldn't resist the urge to maintain her order – surreptitiously re-straightening magazines, re-aligning cushions when she thought people didn't notice. She often caught her mum at such moments, smiling in her direction, cueing her to try to let things go until everyone left.

Tonight felt different. She frowned at her apartment. For the first time ever the gleaming surfaces, blonde beech, stainless steel and cool granite seemed sterile somehow. She wondered whether more colour could help – some jewel-coloured cushions on the chocolate sofas, maybe a big painting on the loungeroom wall. A rug?

Maybe I should move altogether, she thought suddenly. This unit had quadrupled in value since she had taken out the mortgage ten years ago. The outrageous Sydney property boom, coupled with her gorgeous ocean view, had made her rich. Well, on paper. Of course, as soon as she purchased another Sydney property she'd be back in debt.

She'd never thought this way before. She hated change. Anyway, where would she go? It would be pretty hard to give up living at the beach. The noise of the inner city would drive her crazy. And she couldn't see herself in a house in the suburbs, mowing the lawns.

Why was that? Where was that urge for kids and a husband? Holidays to the Gold Coast, school fetes, a four-wheel drive? She paced her kitchen, opened cupboards, closed them again, looking for something.

She walked to the phone. Punched in seven digits and hung up before dialling the eighth. Scotty. What would he be doing now? Probably Emma Gibson. She smiled viciously, thinking of the grey-eyed glamour girl they'd worked with at Maroubra. She's one person glad to see me out of there, she thought.

The next number she dialled unconsciously, listening to the machine's familiar message while she pictured Emma's shiny black hair in Scotty's big hands. Her mum picked up at the end of the recorded spiel. She always let it play whether she was home or not – stopped the telemarketers, she said.

'So, how's the case going, darling?' her mum wanted to know.

'Mmm, okay. Not fast enough though of course. It never is, is it? Especially this case.'

'It's just terrible. I hate to think of you working on these things. The stories on the news today were just awful.'

'Don't watch the news.' Jill modified her tone when she realised how abrupt she sounded. 'Yeah, it's a pretty bad case. We hope to get a breakthrough soon.'

'How's everything else out there, Jill? What are the people like? You didn't manage to tell me anything about Gabriel last time we spoke,' her mum reminded her.

'They're okay. I don't really know anyone yet. Gabriel seems okay, though.'

'How old is he?'

'Mum. I don't know how old he is. Maybe the same age as me.'

'And he's nice?'

Jill paused. Nice? It was probably not the first word she'd use to describe her new partner. What could she say about him him?

'He's a good cook,' she tried.

'He's *cooked* for you? You had dinner at his house? Was his wife there?'

Oh boy. 'He doesn't have a wife.' As far as I know. 'We had to watch some videos from the case. His house was close and he cooked. Lunch.'

'So what did you eat?'

'Fish. Look, Mum, tell me what's happening out your way. How's Dad?'

'Your father – I don't know what's got into him lately. He hasn't been himself.'

'What do you mean? Is he okay?' Jill sat up straight at her breakfast bar.

'Oh, he seems healthy enough. But he's . . . well he's doing a lot of shopping.'

'Shopping. Dad?'

'I know. Stuff for the house. Clothes for him. Yesterday he bought me a swimming costume.'

'He did not.'

'With parrots on it.'

Jill felt her eyebrows rising. Her father could not be dragged into a shopping mall, and had always made her or Cassie buy his presents for their mum. He had no difficulties at the hardware shop – but visiting a store that sold women's clothing? She couldn't imagine it.

'I know what you're thinking,' her mother continued. 'Midlife crisis. I bought a book today.'

Jill smiled. Pop psychology. Her mother had a library.

'Oprah recommended it. He's a little old for it all, according to the book, but I'll finish reading it and let you know.'

'How's everyone else?'

Frances Jackson sighed through the phone.

'Cassie.' Jill guessed.

'I don't know, love. I think she's not eating again.'

Jill's younger sister made a living as a swimsuit model. Like the rest of her colleagues, she perennially flirted with anorexia nervosa. Jill shifted on the barstool. Not a lot she could do about it: she found it harder to talk to Cassie than almost anyone, and when she tried to discuss weight with her sister, Cassie would scoff – Jill's own struggles with food from time to time made her concern seem hypocritical.

'Bob and I called around there on Tuesday,' Frances continued. 'It was after lunch, Jill, and she was still in bed.'

'She'd probably been on a shoot, Ma.'

'That's what she said, but it looked more like she'd had a party over there. It was a mess.'

'Good for her,' said Jill, suddenly almost envying her sister's glamorous lifestyle.

'Mmm.' Jill's mother did not approve. 'Some of her friends had stayed the night.'

'Uh huh.'

'They're all very beautiful, Jill, but none of them seem very . . . diligent.'

'Diligent?'

'Oh, I don't know. I just wish she'd settle down a bit. She's thirty now. And you should have seen the empty bottles everywhere.'

Jill rubbed at a non-existent smudge on her breakfast bar. 'Well, you said it was a party.' None of them spoke overtly about the fact that they rarely saw Cassie without a drink in her hand.

'Yes. Anyway, darling, I don't want to worry you. I'm sure things will be fine. How's Scotty? Have you seen him since you started at Liverpool?'

'No. Oh, Mum, I just got call waiting.' Jill lied. 'I'll give you a ring again tomorrow.'

Jill hung up feeling slightly guilty about lying to her mother. But speaking about Scotty was the last thing she felt like tonight. Right now, she just wished he was here scoffing food in her loungeroom, his huge feet overhanging her lounge.

She walked dispiritedly around her empty unit and finally found herself in her gym. She got to work.

25

SATURDAY MORNING SAW Jill at a computer terminal in the detectives' quarters of the Liverpool police complex. She and Gabriel had decided to split tasks; the pressure from the media upon the investigations team was huge. Jill would've preferred Superintendent Last to get angry, scream at them – anything other than having to watch his stoop deepen. He had chewed through half a packet of antacid tablets in the meeting yesterday morning.

Jill and Gabriel knew they needed to find the connection between Henry Nguyen, Isobel and Joss. At the same time, because they had learned so much from re-interviewing the victims of the home invasions, they'd decided they couldn't afford to abandon that process. The logical choice was for Gabriel to continue the interviews, while Jill investigated Isobel and Joss's backgrounds, looking for links with Nguyen.

She'd expected another warm day, and now Jill sat freezing and miserable in shirtsleeves in the squadroom. The temperature on the air-conditioner, she was convinced, had been set by some demented maintenance guy who hated cops. She knew without checking that her top lip would be blue; she had the kind of headache she usually got when she ate ice-cream too quickly. No good trying to get someone to make the thing warmer. In these buildings the thermostat was always 'centrally controlled' and adjusting it 'a major drama'.

She stuck her hands under her armpits for a moment and then turned her attention to Henry Nguyen, creating a file of what they knew about him already. The anonymous caller – Isobel Rymill, they were almost certain – had rattled off a series of his convictions and sentences. Jill opened another window on the computer and called up his sheet. There was a long list, as Superintendent Last had indicated yesterday, and the caller had missed a few. Juvenile record, Jill noted. Career criminal. She copied the information and tidied it up a little; pasted it into her own file.

One of the juvie cases caught her eye. Nguyen had done nine months at Dharruk for a smash and grab that had left an adolescent dead, his throat cut. She calculated dates and figured young Henry had been thirteen. The charge was break and enter – with the actions leading to accidental death – but she wondered whether there had been more to it. What did they call Nguyen? Cutter. Maybe he'd started early? His record did not include murder or manslaughter, or anything involving serious knife attacks, but she knew that a charge sheet generally only reflected a fraction of what an offender had been up to.

She searched the COPS database for the juvenile case and

scanned it quickly. She copied it, deleted irrelevant notations, and pasted it into her file. The smash and grab had been at a bike shop; the deceased, the owner's son. Henry Nguyen's fingerprints, already on file even at that early age, had been found at the scene, and when they'd gone around to his grandmother's home in Cabramatta to pick him up, they'd found one of the stolen bikes in his bedroom. Jill could remember nothing of the story at the time. She'd have been about eleven when this went down. Eleven. A year before her own world went to hell when she was abducted.

The victim, Carl Waterman, had been around the same age as Nguyen at the time; the cops investigating figured that the boy, who lived with his father above the bike shop, had heard the noise when Cutter broke into the store and come down to investigate. There were ten COPS entries on the same event.

According to the files, Nguyen had told the investigating officers that he'd broken into the store alone by smashing one of the two glass panels at the front of the shop. He'd told the officers he hadn't seen the Waterman boy in the shop and couldn't explain how the kid had come to be impaled by a large section of the glass. He also could not explain how he'd managed to steal five bikes on his own.

Jill skimmed the wrap-up on the case. The officers assumed that Nguyen had committed the robbery in company with at least a couple of older youths, possibly adults – people smart enough not to leave fingerprints. They believed the second panel of glass, destabilised when the first had come down, was what had killed Carl Waterman. The prosecutors had had to ask for a committal, given the child's death, but Jill figured that the relatively light sentence reflected a belief that Nguyen had been led astray by more seasoned criminals.

She wondered whether the smash and grab had really gone down that way. The case could actually establish a very early propensity for this Cutter to make people bleed. They knew he liked blood a hell of a lot nowadays. She thought with horror of young Justine Rice watching this sicko bring himself to orgasm by cutting himself. They had to find him fast.

Jill needed to stand up. Pins and needles throbbed in her fingertips. This cold is ridiculous, she thought. She stared at the ceiling above her terminal. A half-metre air-conditioning vent was positioned directly above her chair. She imagined she could see the frigid air streaming from the vent, drenching her desk. She cupped the tip of her nose in her palm to try to get some feeling back. The back of her throat felt scratchy, and she wished she could be doing this work from home. Or at Gabriel's. She bet his computers would have access to these databases.

She walked to one of the windows of the squadroom, hugging her arms around her body, and stared down into the street below. A camera flashed. She stepped sideways, back against the wall, and angled her head to peek out without showing her face. Two media trucks occupied the parking spots in front of the courthouse below. She saw a third in the Spotlight carpark across the road. A news camera was now angled up at her, two men and a woman sidestepping, heads weaving, trying to see behind the window. Anything at all to do with this case was big news. Not since the 'Bodies in the Barrels' homicides in Adelaide had Australia been as deliciously terrified. People in the

immediate area, however, got no thrill at all from it. Coun-
sellors had been brought into local schools because children
had been producing artwork depicting their fathers and pets
dismembered.

Jill wondered what Gabriel would be able to get out of the
dead man's daughter, Donna Moser. He planned to interview
her sometime today. She was well enough to have been moved
to a private psychiatric hospital in Burwood, so she should be
up to talking, they'd figured.

On her way to the coffee machine, Jill passed another
woman, head down over a computer. Muriel? Marilyn?
Lawrence Last had introduced them a couple of days ago.
Marion? Yep, that's it, she thought. The woman raised her
head briefly and nodded at Jill. She looks comfortable
enough, thought Jill, starting to shiver. The extra twenty kilos
Marion had on her would be helping. She slid a mug under
the expensive espresso maker and added two heaped
teaspoons of sugar. Wrapping her hands around the cup, she
held its warmth to her body as she walked back to her desk.

Next step: known associates of Henry Nguyen. There had
been no mention in the meeting yesterday of any known past
connection between Nguyen and Dang Huynh – the suspect
forensics had identified as having vomited at the Capitol Hill
crime scene. Jill thought about Gabriel's rapid conclusion that
the vomit indicated that at least one member of the gang
didn't have the same bloodlust as the killer. Huynh hadn't
been able to keep his dinner down, so there was little chance
he was the one doing the butchery.

Jill wondered how long Huynh had known Cutter as she
typed and underlined his name in her notes. She entered his
nickname, 'Mouse', and called up his sheet. Car theft, aggra-

vated robbery. She kept digging. Well, well. At age seventeen, Dang Huynh had gone up on an assault charge in company with Henry Nguyen. They'd bashed a boy and a teacher at Bonnyrigg High during school hours. Neither attacker had been a student at the school. Jill remembered the case from Nguyen's criminal records. The school's vice-principal had lost an eye when Nguyen had smashed a bottle into his face; the teacher had been trying to break up the attack. Nguyen had been sent to Mt Penang that time. She read on. Yep, there it was, Mouse had also been remanded at Mt Penang after the assault.

So at least these two members of the home invasion gang went back a long way. The thought gave Jill an idea. She pushed her already cooling coffee aside and bent back over the computer.

Cutter tucked his lucky socks into a drawer inside his wardrobe. Head on an angle, he peered into his black eyes in the mirror stuck inside the wardrobe door. He closed it and lowered himself onto his carefully made single bed. It and the wardrobe were the only furniture he'd moved over from Cabramatta. Same bed he'd had since he was a boy. In fact, his grandfather used to sit just about there, as he taught him the needle lessons. Cutter's orange towelling bedspread was so worn it was transparent in patches. So soft. He smoothed it over and over under his palm.

He felt very pleased with this basement room. The door was heavy, made of metal for some reason, and when he closed it, the small window, and the curtain covering it, he could hear nothing at all from outside. He felt certain that no

189

one outside could hear him in here, either. The walls were double brick, coated in thick white paint, and he sniffed in the dirt-tang of mildew that bubbled underneath. He loved that smell. His grandmother had not. No, she had told him, you cannot live here! The water is stagnant. Your luck cannot flow. Your cold will be worse! Come home with us where you belong, she'd entreated in Vietnamese as he signed the simple, single-page contract that his new landlord, Mrs Miceh, had produced.

Karen Miceh. So sweet. He'd had to almost pull the piece of paper from her grip, as though she'd changed her mind at the last minute. Face to face when he'd handed it back again, he'd quickened his breathing to match her own, his chest rising and falling in rhythm with hers, listening for the sound of her pulse, hypnotised.

The sound of a dog barking blew in with the breeze from his open window. He frowned, rose from the bed and stepped into some slippers. He walked around the clothesline and the wading pool, passing the squat lemon tree, thick with bees sipping at its blossoms.

Just past three p.m. in Baulkham Hills. He loved this hour. On weekdays at this time, mums, dads and nanas would wait at bus stops and pedestrian crossings outside the schools, lined up in Taragos and four-wheel drives. When the weather warmed up, it would be straight to the local pool and then to pick up a barbecued chook on the way home. Today, it would be softball tryouts and piano lessons, maths tutoring or karate class. When living here as a child, he'd seen these routines as a pantomime just for him – a whole cast of humans playing sugar and spice, frantically ignoring the rot and disease that was born within all of them, that was feasting away as they grew older.

He had reached the back of the large suburban garden. Behind the huge, netted fig tree, a low wire fence hid behind feral camellia bushes, marking the boundary between Karen Miceh's home and her neighbour's. The barking stopped with Cutter's last footstep and was replaced by a pleading whine, a snuffling whimper. The dog wanted a pat. Cutter manoeuvred through the scented bushes and a wet, yellow nose pushed through the mesh of the wire barrier.

'Good doggie,' Cutter crooned, hand outstretched. The golden Labrador thumped the lawn behind the fence in delight, strained to get closer for a good scratch.

'That's a good boy,' said Cutter softly, reaching over the fence.

Jill absently wiped the back of her hand across her nose. Ugh. She reached for a tissue, and then picked up the phone on the desk.

'Gabe, where are you?' she said into the handset.

'At the hospital,' he said.

'Have you interviewed her yet?'

'Nope. Three o'clock.'

'I'll meet you out there.'

She printed out a single page and shut down the computer. She'd finished earlier than she'd thought, and was glad to have the opportunity to watch Gabriel interviewing another victim. She gathered up her bag and the case-file, and stood to leave the squadroom. At the last moment, she grabbed the phone again and left a message for Lawrence Last to let him know her movements.

She jogged down four flights of stairs to the basement

carpark and threw her bag in the backseat of her issued Commodore. It wasn't until the M5 on-ramp that she pushed the dashboard vents away from her face and turned the heater down, realising she was now stifling hot. Nudging the bumper of her vehicle into the near-stationary traffic, she waved to pretend that she was grateful to the driver behind for letting her in. She knew she'd be still sitting waiting to merge if that motorist had had anything to do with it. It was dog-eat-dog on this motorway.

Too late, she realised that it would've been far quicker to take the Hume Highway to Burwood. She thumped the steering wheel with the heel of her hand and settled in to wait in the traffic.

Her hot nose throbbed.

'So, guess who used to hang with Henry Nguyen back in the day?' she said to Gabriel in greeting when they met in the foyer of the hospital. There were still twenty minutes before they were due to meet with Donna Moser.

'Joss Preston-Jones,' he said.

'Well, yeah,' she said. 'Good guess. Also, Mr Chew and Spew – Dang Huynh.'

'Hmm.'

Gabriel led her to a tiny cafeteria just off the entrance. 'You want something to drink?' he asked her, gesturing to a half-finished milkshake and hamburger at a table. He'd obviously started before she got there.

She walked to a fridge at the back of the café, selected a glass bottle of orange juice and pressed it, cold, against her cheeks. At the counter, she paid for it and a six-capsule box of

Panadol, and walked back to join Gabriel, popping two of the tablets and draining half the juice before she reached the table.

He watched her, eyebrows lifted, as he ate his hamburger. It smelled pretty good.

'Joss was arrested, age twelve, in company with Nguyen, a couple of other juveniles and a nineteen-year-old,' she told him. 'The North Sydney cops caught them stealing petrol from a caryard. The yard had a single fuel pump for its own use and the kids decided to stock up. They filled their car and a couple of containers in the boot. The North Sydney boys released Joss and Henry and the other kids, but the adult copped a charge.'

Gabriel slurped his shake.

'So all these years later, Henry and Joss meet again,' she said. 'Or had they been hanging out all along? Joss has no adult sheet, but maybe he's been in touch with this gang since he was a kid. What if he knew all about the thing at Andy Wu's? What if that's what he and his wife are hiding?'

Gabriel raised one dark eyebrow.

'I know,' she said. 'Just brainstorming. They're not the type. And if it was the case that Nguyen and Joss are still mates, why would Joss and Isobel tip us off about Nguyen?'

He nodded.

'So, what: they're just at this dinner party and it all goes down just as they said? But then somehow Joss recognises Cutter and tells his wife, and she tells us?'

Gabriel shrugged.

'What, are we playing charades here or something?' Jill rubbed at her eyes in irritation. They felt hot and itchy. She took another sip of juice. She thought *she* didn't have a lot of words to say to others. Gabriel was so odd sometimes. She sighed and continued. 'Why didn't they just tell all this to Tran and Reid when they interviewed them the first time? Why did they keep Nguyen's name from us when we interviewed them?'

'Scared.'

'Yeah, I get that. But they're gonna be better off with him locked up, aren't they? Wouldn't it be better for them to help us catch him?'

Gabriel shrugged again. Jill finished her juice.

'Are you ready?' She looked down at her watch. Already three p.m., and they hadn't even begun the interview with Donna Moser. She wanted to be at home in a bath.

Maryana Miceh held her finger to her lips, motioning Eva to be quiet. Two-year-olds are so dumb, thought Maryana, as Eva giggled and twirled around and around on the balcony above her. At six, Maryana felt she should be the boss of her little sister, but Eva never listened to her. She knelt down in the grass near the wall under the veranda and crawled carefully forward. When she drew close to the spot with the crack, she held her breath. Mummy had told her five times already not to go near the new tenant, but that just made her want to see him more. At recess, Jasmine Hardcastle had said that maybe he was a murderer and he would kill her family in their sleep. Maryana had squealed and laughed with everyone else, but since then, the idea made her feel kind of like she had worms in her tummy. Standing up slowly in the grass near the wall, her tummy felt fluttery, like the worms had hatched into moths. She heard Eva singing 'Jingle Bells' above her.

Ooh! He's got tattoos, was the first thing that Maryana thought. She pressed her eye closer to the crack in the wall. She wasn't sure what he was doing, but it looked like it had to hurt. Maybe he was sick? He was lying on his bed with his hands on his stomach and it was all bloody!

'Maryana!'

At her mother's voice, the squeal slipped out before she could stop it, and Maryana ran as fast as she could. She felt as though a dragon were chasing her, and when she arrived, flushed and panting in the kitchen, her mother asked her what was wrong.

'Nothing,' she said, mouth turned down, shifting from foot to foot.

Karen Miceh looked twice at her little girl, then bent to pick up Eva, still singing. She put her arm on Maryana's shoulder and led them to the front door.

'Girls,' she said, 'Kylie and James are here from next door. They want to know if we've seen Buffy. He's gone missing.'

'I've never done this before,' said Chloe, propped up in the bed, Andrew's white quilt clutched to her chest.

'Well, you seemed to know what you were doing.'

Andrew ducked when she threw a pillow at his head. He had a towel slung low around his flat stomach.

'Not *that*, stupid!' she said. 'I mean I've never gone to bed with someone when I've known them less than a week.'

'Actually,' Andrew looked at his watch, 'we met almost exactly seventy-two hours ago.'

Chloe groaned. 'Don't rub it in,' she said, but she felt

kind of pleased that he'd memorised the time of their first meeting.

'What are you gonna do while I'm at work today?' he asked, opening a cupboard and pulling out an ironed shirt.

The uniform. Chloe smiled widely and leaned back against the bed head to watch.

'You'd better stop looking at me like that,' he said. 'I can't be late to work today.'

'Anything happen with that name that came through on Thursday?' she asked, wondering if he'd tell her anything else about the anonymous call.

'Yep,' he said, buttoning his shirt. 'They think it's one of them.'

'The home invasion gang? You're shitting me! How do you know?'

He grinned at her. She'd leaned forward, all attention, forgetting about the quilt. She clutched it to her chest again, red-faced.

'A few of us got a memo,' he said. 'There's a rotating shift to watch this guy's last known address. We got instructions not to approach; it's just surveillance right now. At least this nutjob's good for something – me and Hendo pulled tonight's watch. Should be some good overtime.'

'What's his name?'

He looked at her sideways.

'Henry,' he said.

'Go on! Henry what?'

'Yeah, good try, beautiful. That, I'm not gonna tell you. Now come over here and give me a hand. I've got a bit of a problem with this towel.'

*

196

At four o'clock, Donna Moser's godparents arrived at the hospital and, seeing her distress, asked Jill and Gabriel to leave. They had arranged for Donna to be moved from Liverpool Hospital to this private psychiatric clinic. They were now the only family that she had – an only child, her mother had died of breast cancer when Donna was in her first year of high school.

Donna had told Jill and Gabriel that her godparents, Eugene Moser's business partner and his wife, had asked her to live with them and their sons in Strathfield. She wasn't yet sure what she was going to do. She and her father had only just moved into the house in Capitol Hill, working together with an architect and designer to incorporate the features they wanted in their home, but right now, she didn't want anything to do with the property.

It's good that she has some choices at least, thought Jill – Donna Moser had just inherited fifty per cent of a multi-million-dollar metal fabrication business.

As they left the room, Jill could see a male nurse gently try to encourage the pale, hollow-eyed girl to take some medication. Donna stared into space, tears coursing unchecked. Jill knew she and Gabe had pressed play on the animation reel of her father's murder. She imagined that the soundtrack was the worst part.

'Do you want to come over to my house?' Gabriel asked Jill as they stood in the carpark.

'What? No. Why?'

'Got some more stuff on Joss Preston-Jones,' he answered, looking at his shoes. 'I thought maybe we could put it all together.' He paused. 'And I'm making penne alla vodka.'

'You're making what?'

'It's pasta in a vodka-cream sauce. Really, you have to try it.'

Jill thought about the contents of her refrigerator. She hadn't been shopping since she'd started working at Liverpool. She had a bag of carrots, some olives and anchovies. Her mum's frozen meals had run out days ago. It would have to be takeaway, or . . .

'I've got garlic bread. And pistachio gelato,' said Gabriel.

'I'll follow you,' she said.

As much as Chloe had wanted Andrew to tell her the name of the suspect in the gang, she was kind of pleased that he hadn't. She respected that he took his job so seriously.

She smiled slowly, thinking about the dinner they'd shared last night. When they couldn't stretch dessert out any longer, they'd had to make a choice. Another venue, or his house. Parting hadn't even been an option. She stretched her neck against the headrest of the driver's seat. Her Mazda 3 was really a little squishy for her long legs, but it had been a good price. Tucked in behind a ute in the Spotlight carpark, Chloe had a good view of the vehicles leaving the Liverpool police complex.

The black Magna was not the Commodore she'd been expecting, but she could never have mistaken Andrew behind the wheel, even though he'd changed out of his uniform into civilian clothing. A red-haired guy in a white tee-shirt laughed in the seat next to him.

She pulled her car into the traffic a few vehicles behind them.

26

How it had happened, Jill couldn't figure. She had been curled in a lounge chair listening to the sounds of Gabriel cooking in the kitchen, the little grey cat named Ten warm on her lap, smiling at her, eyes closed.

She woke to Gabriel speaking her name quietly. Her heart shot to her throat and free-fell back again. She stared around wildly, still saturated with sleep, and when she realised where she was, she wanted to cry. Horrified, she felt hot tears well. She couldn't believe she had let her guard down so quickly with him. She straightened in the chair; a bolt of tension fused one side of her neck; her face felt scorched.

'You look like shit,' said Gabriel.

She stared at him, desolately.

'Probably we should eat something,' he said.

Dull pain pressed at the back of her throat and pulsed behind her eyes. She still felt utterly exhausted, and she allowed Gabriel to grab her hand and drag her from the chair. What am I doing here? she thought. She recognised the aches she felt in her elbows and knees as signs of a cold. The travelling, the new people, the case, the fucking air-conditioner. It had worn her down.

'Come and tell me how much you want.'

She followed him to the kitchen. And this guy. Never before had her nervous system habituated so rapidly to the presence of a man. She couldn't believe she'd fallen asleep in his house. She glared at the back of his head, angry with him somehow for that.

The smell of garlic finally made it past her muffled senses and Jill began to salivate. She hadn't eaten since breakfast. Unself-consciously, Gabriel helped himself first, filling a deep bowl with pasta from the pot on the stove. He handed her the spoon and stood back to watch. While she filled her mismatched plate, he began eating as he stood there, waiting for her. When her plate was full, he opened the oven door and pulled garlic bread off a tray with his fingers, dropped two fragrant wedges onto her plate. She hurried to sit, starving. The creamy sauce had a grainy heat behind it. It was almost gone before she reclined back in the lounge chair. She licked garlicky butter from her fingers.

Ten sat propped against a wall like a polar bear, her legs spread out in front of her, cleaning her stomach. A cool rivulet of breeze from the balcony washed over Jill's flushed cheeks. Gabriel spoke.

'I spent the morning here on the computer,' he said. 'Checking out our boy, Joss.'

Jill tucked her legs up under her and leaned back into the cushion, listening.

'He moved from Canley Vale High School when he was thirteen and finished his schooling at Sandhurst College,' he continued. 'He must've hung out with Cutter while he was living with his mother. She has schizophrenia. Been in and out of Rozelle and Cumberland for the last thirty years. Joss did his Higher School Certificate. Joined the army, Infantry corps. Went with the second contingent of Australian peace-keepers to Rwanda in 1995. The Australians on his tour got caught up in the Kibeho massacre. Do you remember watching the news about the war in Africa in ninety-four, ninety-five?'

'Yep.'

Jill had grown up horrified, along with the rest of Australia, by the famines in Africa. When Australians troops had joined the UN peacekeepers over there in 1994, she'd avoided the news programs for weeks because it seemed every story was about the 'rivers of blood' in Rwanda; images of mounds of corpses and scores of bodies floating down a river had left her feeling helpless, ill. Just as she'd changed the channel and ignored it, the world had also looked the other way.

She thought about the wars in Iraq and Afghanistan. Supposedly the allies were there to liberate the people from the tyranny of their governments. No soldiers had been sent to fight for the tens of thousands of people who were slaugh-tered in Rwanda. Australia's peacekeepers had been impotent. Their rules of engagement had not allowed them to fire a shot in defence of the victims. They were there simply to observe and to assist the wounded when they could.

201

There was no oil in Africa.

'Preston-Jones was medically discharged from the army on psych grounds,' Gabriel continued. 'He married Isobel Rymill in ninety-three. As we know, they have one daughter, Charlie Rymill, aged four. His maternal grandparents are deceased. His father's name was not listed on his birth certificate. He works for a large insurance company in Martin Place.' Gabriel stood and stretched.

'You want a drink?' he asked, on his way to the kitchen.

Jill unfolded her legs on the couch. Ten now slept with a paw over her eyes, blocking out the soft light in the room. Her little body twitched as she dreamed. Jill took a look at her watch. Seven o'clock. I should go home, she thought, and sat up.

Gabriel returned with two cups. She took hers and sniffed it. Held the cup back out to him.

'It's butterscotch schnapps. It'll be good for your cold,' he said.

She lifted an eyebrow, stared flatly. He took a sip from his glass, a china teacup bearing red roses, and licked his lips, grinning at her.

She looked down into her brown earthenware mug; in an inch of amber, viscous liquid, two fat ice cubes circled lazily. It smelled great. She took her first sip of alcohol in ten years. The toffee liquid coated the back of her throat, burning and freezing at the same time. She had another taste, her lips sticky.

The ice cubes clinked softly and Jill leaned back into the couch. Ten breathed heavily as she slept. The peal of a phone suddenly split the silence, and Jill snapped forward, grabbing for her bag.

'Jackson,' she said.

'Yo, J.'

'Scotty! What do you want?'

'What do I want? Nice. I have to want something now to say hi?'

'Sorry, Scotty. I didn't mean to say that. It came out wrong. How're you doing?' Jill stood and walked with the phone, acutely aware of Gabriel staring at her openly, as though she were a live stage show, or a scene from a riveting movie.

'Okay, but I miss you. Well, I miss beating you at things. It's not the same thrashing Robbo on the bike. He doesn't try as hard as you, and he never gets as pissed when I teach him a lesson.'

She smiled wryly.

'Jackson. You still there?

'Yes, Scotty. I'm still here. You don't always win, you know.' She found herself almost whispering.

'What are you doing now? I could whip your arse with a game of squash and then we could have a swim?' He cleared his throat. 'Or, maybe we could get something to eat?'

Jill's stomach lurched a little at the sudden vulnerability in his voice.

'I, ah, I already ate. I just finished working.' Why did she feel guilty?

Right then, Gabriel called from the kitchen.

'Jill, you want some ice-cream?'

'Ice-cream,' said Scotty. 'Working hard?'

'I said I just finished.'

'Uh huh. So who was that?'

'Gabriel Delahunt. New partner.'

'Gabriel,' said Scotty. 'Girl's name.'

Jill sighed. Oh for goodness' sake. 'Look, I was just about to head home. I think I caught a cold today. I just want to get to bed.'

'Yeah, well, don't let me keep you, Jill. I'll catch you later.'

'I'll call you next week.' She closed her phone.

'I think we should go to Balmain first thing Monday morning,' Gabriel said when she joined him in the kitchen. 'Speak to Joss and Isobel before they go to work. What do you reckon?'

'Yep. Good idea,' she answered sleepily. She drained her cup.

'So, you want some dessert?'

'No thanks, Gabriel.' Her voice sounded formal to her ears, and she felt suddenly shy, then annoyed that she should feel this way. 'I'm going to head home.'

'No worries. So, we'll make it six on Monday then?'

She nodded and moved to leave, determined to get out of there, her thoughts churning. Why did she feel like she was cheating on Scotty when she didn't think of him that way? And why should she feel like she was cheating at all when she barely knew Gabriel? They'd only eaten together, for heaven's sake.

She climbed into her car and threw her bag onto the seat next to her. That's why it's easier not to get too close to people, she told herself. These confusing feelings.

She buzzed her window all the way down as she drove, the evening breeze helping to dispel some of the dullness that smudged her senses. She still could not believe she'd fallen asleep in someone else's house.

Not counting her parents' home, that was a first.

*

Chloe returned to the house in Cabramatta at eight-thirty that night. The black Magna had left and she could see a green late-model Falcon sitting in its place. She chewed her lip.

What was the good of knowing about this place if she didn't get some more on this guy? Investigative journalists are like detectives, she reminded herself. They've got to have a cover and they've got to take some risks.

She knew by the end of this year there'd be a hundred new journalism graduates hungry to take her spot. That was not going to happen. Chloe got out of her car and opened the gate out the front of the small fibro house.

Cutter's house.

Mrs Tu Ly Nguyen wasn't sure what she should do. Although her English was limited, she knew enough to know that this lovely young girl wanted to speak to Henry. Henry had always told her never to speak to anyone about him. And her daughter-in-law and children were out visiting this evening.

It would be best to say nothing, to close the door, and she determined to do so. She sighed. The girl was so pretty.

Mrs Nguyen worried so much about her first-born grandson. He should have had a wife, a family by now to take care of him. She had hated leaving him in that room under the stairs. He should have more friends like this one.

She looked up at the girl on the porch. So tall. So beautiful! Something told her she could trust this girl. But she worried that Henry would be angry. She sighed.

Certain now that she was doing the right thing, Cutter's

grandmother turned away from the door and walked back into the house.

She returned thirty seconds later with a piece of paper and an orange.

Mrs Tu Ly Nguyen pressed the fruit and the scrap of cardboard into Chloe's hand. Upon the paper was scribbled an address. A street number in Baulkham Hills.

No one should live under the stairs, Mrs Nguyen thought, shuffling back inside to pray to her ancestors at her shrine.

27

KAREN MICEH WAS torn. Her parents had taught her to share, to treat others with respect, and she wanted to pass the same morals on to her daughters. It was Henry's first weekend living downstairs, and before she'd met him she'd always intended to invite the new tenant to Sunday lunch with her, her brother Ken and the girls. She and Ken had kept the Sunday ritual going after their parents died, although her dropkick husband had often stuffed things up by getting stoned and trying to start an argument with her brother or hitting on whichever girl Ken might have been seeing at the time. The lunches since Eddie had been gone had been lovely. She had thought that inviting the new tenant along would be a pleasant addition to their party. She loved to cook.

But then she'd met Henry. Something about him made her uneasy, although she felt guilty about that. Her grandmother had always told her not to judge people by their appearance alone, and she tried to live by that saying, finding that she'd met many beautiful people who maybe hadn't seemed respectable at first glance. When she'd seen Henry with his hair tied back for the first time, his tattoos visible, she had freaked. But it wasn't just the tattoos – even Ken had tattoos – although the beautiful tiger on Ken's deltoid was hardly the same thing as spiders on one's neck, she thought. She hoped that she wasn't a closet racist. She'd heard you could be such a thing without even knowing. Her good friend, Jamie, who was a lesbian, had told her that, saying that even members of the gay community could be closet homophobes. Ashamed of their own sexuality, even when they were out and sup-posedly proud! Imagine that.

That decided her at last. Karen had always prided herself on denouncing racism, and if it did turn out to be bigotry that was holding her back from giving this man a chance, then she'd face it and fix it.

Besides, she thought, twisting at the hem of her apron, it would give Ken a chance to meet Henry, to see what he thought.

Karen stood at the door a few moments before knocking. She was pretty sure he was in there – her front gate made an awful squeak when it was opened, and she hadn't heard it this morning, so she reasoned that he couldn't have gone out. She raised her hand to knock, and then lowered it again, her stomach flip-flopping.

She looked around her yard, stalling. It was a beautiful day. The sun was warm and she could hear the bees in the lemon tree. She had to get the first load out on the line soon and get on with the day, or no one was going to be eating lunch. She stepped closer to the door and knocked firmly.

'Henry,' she spoke to the door, smiling. 'I wonder, have you got a minute?'

She suddenly worried that he could be asleep, and she could have slapped herself. It hadn't occurred to her that someone could still be asleep at ten o'clock in the morning. She hadn't slept that late since she was a teenager. But it was Sunday morning, she chastised herself – not everyone is up at six o'clock like her.

'I can wait,' she sang through the door. 'I'll wait for a moment. I just wanted to invite you to lunch.'

She heard nothing from behind the thick door and thought about retreating. Maybe he was coming, though; she must've already woken him up. She remembered when she'd been painting the room that sounds from outside were deadened. Maybe he hadn't heard her. She could just walk away.

She stood a moment, studying her nails, and, hearing nothing from inside, turned to go. Maybe he doesn't want much to do with us anyway, she thought. That would be a relief, she decided, if he'd come to that conclusion himself.

Karen's thoughts had turned to her washing, and she had taken a step away when the door scraped open behind her, and she raised a hand to her mouth.

'Oh, Henry,' she said. 'I hope I didn't wake you.'

The man stared at her from those curiously black eyes, and she could read nothing in his expression. He didn't say a thing. He seemed to be wide awake, though, as far as she could tell, and thank goodness, he was fully dressed. She noticed a nasty smell from the room behind him and blushed in embarrassment.

'Henry, it smells like the mould's coming back in there,' she prattled, unnerved by his silence and slow-blinking eyes. 'Ken and I – he's my brother, I think I told you – we did our best to get rid of it all in there, but I think it must be coming through the paint. I'm sorry about that. We'll get onto it again.'

He said nothing, continued to study her.

'Anyway,' she continued, overly bright, 'I thought you might like to come to lunch with me and the girls. Oh, and Ken, that's my brother. Although of course if you don't want to . . . it's only a roast. I don't want to be intrusive; I thought I'd just ask, but . . .'

'Lunch would be lovely. Thank you, Karen.'

He smiled. She wished he hadn't.

'Okay, great then, that's great,' she said, backing away. 'Well, we eat at twelve, usually, although some people might think that's a bit early. It's the girls . . .'

'Twelve's great, Karen. I'm really looking forward to it.'

Karen Miceh managed a weak smile and half ran up her back steps to her laundry.

In the end, the roast was dry, because she wasn't sure whether he'd like it medium, as she and Ken did. The girls always preferred the crunchy edges anyway, but Karen felt miserable carving the juiceless meat. She smiled at her guest, who'd changed into a collared shirt and tied his long hair back into a ponytail. Somehow, his attempt to appear civilised rendered him even more alien.

'So, Henry, were you born in Australia?' she asked. Good one, Karen: go the race card already.

'Yes,' he said, 'and you?'

'Yes, yes. Ken and I were both born here. Our parents were proud Macedonians, but they wanted us to be Australian. They thought the names Karen and Ken were as Aussie as you could get.' She gave him a wry smile as she passed him a plate.

'Thank you,' he said, accepting the sliced roast lamb from her. 'Looks delicious. I'm glad it's well cooked. I can't stand blood.'

Her smile was forced as she fixed Ken with a stare. Great, so she and her brother should eat overcooked meat every Sunday now? Why does it have to be so hard to be neighbourly?

'You have beautiful daughters, Karen. You must be very proud.'

'Yes. Thank you,' she said. 'Maryana, sit up straight in your chair. You know better than that. I've told you twice already.'

Karen frowned. Her oldest daughter usually swamped strangers with questions and chatter, and it was all Karen could do, typically, to stop her little girl climbing all over them. Today, Maryana seemed almost to be trying to hide under the table. Eva prattled away in her highchair, playing with her potatoes.

'So, Henry, what do you do for a quid?' Ken spoke up. 'Are you in a job at the moment?'

'In and out, Ken. I'm in sales. I do a lot of door-to-door work.'

Karen almost snorted. No wonder he didn't get a lot of

211

work. Most people wouldn't want him in their house. Damn Eddie for putting me in this situation, she thought. Still, Henry seemed to be nice enough now that she was getting used to the way he looked.

Karen finished serving and began to eat. She listened to Ken and Henry speaking for a while and tried to encourage Maryana to settle down, but her daughter had eaten none of her lunch.

'What's the matter, little Maryana, don't you feel well?' Henry asked during a break in the conversation with Ken.

Maryana squirmed in her chair, her hair covering her face.

'Did something make you feel sick?' he said.

Maryana started to cry.

'Oh baby, what's wrong?' Karen stood and went to her daughter. 'Henry, I think you're right.' She reached down and scooped Maryana into her arms. 'She's all hot. Are you feeling sick, darling?'

Karen took Maryana from the room, her daughter clinging to her like a baby. She settled her into bed and smoothed her hair a little until she stopped crying.

She returned to the table when Maryana had relaxed under her quilt, tired out by her sobs.

'Is she okay, Karen?' asked Ken.

'I don't know what's wrong with her,' she said. 'I gave her a Panadol. I'll let her sleep now and take her up to the medical centre this afternoon.'

Maryana Miceh felt a lot better.

As soon as she got away from that Henry, she didn't feel so woozy. He was probably a very nice man, she told herself.

It was just that the sore on his tummy made her feel really sweaty and hot. She kept thinking about what she had seen him doing through the crack in the wall. Maybe she should tell her mum?

She decided it would probably be best to ask Jasmine Hardcastle tomorrow before class started. Even though Jasmine thought she was better than everyone else, she did seem to know a lot of stuff. Maryana didn't want to get in trouble for spying on Henry, but maybe her mum should know about his stomach. Maybe she could get him some bandaids or something. And he didn't have a car. Maybe he needed to get a lift to see Dr Kim at the medical centre.

Alerted by a sound out the window, she scrambled up and knelt on her bed.

Wow, she thought. There's a pretty lady on the lawn. She's coming to our house!

Maryana slipped off her bed and padded through the hallway to the front door. She pulled the door open and walked out onto the front steps. She held her hand up to her face to stop the sun hurting her eyes. The lady waved. Maryana could see that the lady couldn't open their gate.

'That gate's stupid,' said Maryana, hopping on one leg down the path that ran from the steps to the fence. 'My dad was supposed to fix it, but Mummy said he's stupid too.'

'I've come to visit Henry,' said Chloe Farrell, smiling. 'Does he live here?'

'No, silly!' Maryana laughed.

'Oh . . . okay.'

'He's *renting*!'

'Uh huh.'

'You know you can just climb over that gate. Uncle Ken

does that. *He* says my dad is stupid too. Do you think that's rude?'

Chloe stepped over the low fence easily.

'My name's Chloe,' she said.

'I wish that was my name,' said Maryana. 'I'm Maryana. Everyone's in there having lunch.' She pointed back inside. 'Come on. I'll show you where Henry is renting.'

Maryana ran around the side of the house.

Chloe followed.

Chloe now felt certain that the police had this all wrong. She'd been told that the first suspect police investigated was most often the wrong one, and it was with this in mind that she'd decided to risk asking after this Henry person at the house in Cabramatta. The fact that he hadn't been brought in for questioning also strengthened her doubts that the police seriously thought this guy was one of the killers. And then she'd met Henry's grandmother, and she was so sweet! But it was little Maryana and this gingerbread house that finally convinced her. Would a bloodthirsty psychopath be eating Sunday lunch with a family in Baulkham Hills? She didn't think so.

So it was all good for her. She could get an interview with a police suspect and show that they were still a long way off the mark as far as solving the case. She wondered if this bloke even knew he was under surveillance. She suspected that the cops didn't even know that he'd moved on from the family house in Cabramatta. She smiled to herself as she followed little Maryana's chubby legs into the backyard of the home. Maybe she'd get to present a piece live to camera. The anchor, Deborah, would burn.

'Maryana!'

Chloe heard a call come from inside the house.

'That's my mum,' the little girl said. 'I gotta go. His room's in there.' Maryana pointed to a door tucked beside the stairs leading to the house above them. 'You wanna come up?'

'No, that's okay, Maryana. I should go back around the front and knock on the door. I should introduce myself to your mum properly.'

'Okay, then,' said the little girl, giving her a quizzical look. She ran off.

Chloe decided to have a quick look around before going back to the front of the house. She was surprised at how easy it had been to find this guy and wanted to think of a few questions to put to him before they met, but she wasn't sure whether the little girl would tell her mum she was down here. Chloe didn't want to meet these people that way. She quickly ducked around the side of the rented room and realised that it was partially dug into the ground. She spotted a window on the back wall and tried to peer through. She could see nothing.

She made her way back around to the front of the room.

'Lunch was great, Karen, Ken.' Henry stood. 'Thank you. I might just use the bathroom before I go.'

Ken stood as well. 'You might have to go downstairs, mate. I'm just on my way to use the toilet up here myself.'

Karen smiled at her brother, grateful. For some ridiculous reason she didn't want this man becoming too familiar with her house.

'I don't know why everyone needs the toilet all of a sudden.' Karen tried to laugh. 'And Maryana feeling sick too. I hope it wasn't my cooking. Where has that child got to?' she said, calling to her daughter again before seeing Henry to the back door.

Karen shocked herself by turning the deadlock when she closed it. Must be that closet racism, she thought, forcing herself to open the door again. Her six-year-old scooted past her into the kitchen.

Cutter could smell her.

He moved from the final step of the house onto the concrete that led to the washing line. Not Karen's sweet, ripe tang. No, no. We've had a visitor, he thought. Musky smell. He turned his nose into the light breeze and sniffed again. Why would anyone be down here?

Cutter didn't believe in coincidence. He didn't believe in chance. If something didn't feel right, it was wrong. There was something wrong in Baulkham Hills.

His head whipped around with the sound. There. There she is. Anyone with her? He could see no one. Still, he kept his options open as he moved forward a little to greet the guest.

'Henry?' she said, doubt in her eyes.

Now that was a surprise. No one knew he was here. She didn't look like a cop. Maybe a friend of his landlord – had Karen told people about him already?

'My name is Chloe Farrell,' she said, extending her hand. 'I'm an investigative journalist working on the southwest Sydney home invasion case. I wondered if we could speak for a few moments?'

He took her hand, breathed with her for a few beats. He had to blink to break the spell.

'To me? What about?' He walked closer to his door.

'I don't know whether you're aware, Henry, but the police think you might know something that could help them with the case.'

'Did you get my address from the police?' he asked, putting his key into the lock on his door.

'No,' she smiled. 'I'm pretty sure they don't know you live here. Don't be angry, now,' she said with a big smile. Her teeth are so white, he thought. 'I got your address from the sweet lady at your old house in Cabramatta. Is she your grandmother?'

Cutter grinned and the girl stepped back a little. He lowered the wattage.

'Yes, that's my grandma. Look, I don't think I can help you with any of this, but I wouldn't mind knowing what's going on. You want to come in for a moment and we can talk for a bit?'

28

JILL SAT UP quickly in bed and wished she hadn't. A ribbon of pain that began in her neck and extended down one shoulder pulled her back down to her pillow. After falling quickly into a deep and dreamless sleep within twenty minutes of arriving home from Gabriel's last night, she'd awoken at three a.m. feeling she was drowning. She'd spent the next fifteen minutes blowing her nose, and the hour after that punching her pillow into some kind of shape conducive to sleeping again. She'd ended with the pillow bunched high under her neck, a position that always left her sore the next morning.

Sunday. She could not believe that just a week had passed since she and Scotty had packed her belongings at Maroubra police station. So much had happened. They'd uncovered a lot of important information about the home invasion gang, but they still had no one in custody, and had yet to interview a suspect.

She wondered what Scotty was doing today, and smiled, certain that he would wonder the same thing about her at some stage today. Usually they went for a run or a long bike ride together on Sundays. She thought about the butterfly pendant in her underwear drawer, the jewellery so unlike her. She smiled again, but the back of her throat suddenly ached with sadness. She hoped that the butterfly did not symbolise her relationship with Scotty: a fragile, beautiful, brief life. She considered all of the relationships she'd had. Her habit had been to flit from one to the next, alighting briefly, fluttering away with any minor disturbance or change in the wind. And she'd been so careful with Scotty, never allowing more than a friendship, to try to preserve what they had together as partners at work.

So. She should do something with her day off. She could go out to Camden and see her family – she'd love to see her niece and nephew right now. Even with a red nose and headache, it would be great to have little Lily sitting with her on the bed, prattling on about the most important things in the world to her – frogs, her best friend Tracey Timmons, her Bratz dolls. But Jill could not imagine getting in the car and driving that far.

She could call Scotty. He'd love to see her, and she realised that she missed him a lot. Most weeks for the past couple of years they'd seen each other six or even seven days a week. She convinced herself that she wouldn't call because he'd want to do a bike ride, or a swim, and she didn't feel well enough today. She quickly pushed aside the real reason she wouldn't call: she couldn't bear it if the awkwardness that had ended every past relationship suddenly materialised between them.

She pulled her knees up to her chin, unwilling yet to get out of bed and face the day. She should be able to call a girl-friend, catch up for lunch, she thought. That's what other people did with their weekends. The fact that she didn't have close friends had never bothered her until the last six months or so. In the past, there'd only been time for training and work, but even with her obsessive dedication, they had been mere hobbies compared to her fulltime occupation: keeping herself safe. Safety entailed distance from others. The fewer people you let into your heart, the less likely that one of them would rip and shred and tear it to pieces.

She sighed. Although she'd killed Alejandro Sebastian – the man who'd kidnapped and raped her as a child – his legacy lived on. She'd hoped that his death would burst the bubble that had simultaneously protected and alienated her from the world. Over the past few months she'd thought the bubble was becoming a little more permeable, but she could still feel its barricades at the periphery of her psyche.

The thought of the schnapps at Gabriel's last night suddenly rose like a spectre in front of her. Changing routines meant losing control. She thought about a story the therapist, Mercy Merris, had told her when she had been forced to have counselling several years ago. Mercy had spoken of a Vietnam veteran who'd been an inpatient at the hospital where she worked. The man had seemed to be fitting in well, participating in group sessions and joining in the 'veranda therapy' with the other vets, who swapped jokes and ciga-rettes, life lessons and sometimes their meds.

One day Mercy had seen the man sitting alone by the

rose garden with his head in his hands. She'd approached and asked him what was wrong. The look in his eyes had been wretched.

'What are you people fucking doing to me?' the man had demanded. 'Don't you know I've killed people?'

Mercy had told Jill that the question had surprised her. She'd been working with this man so he knew very well that she was aware he had killed people.

He'd continued, 'I've been fucking *laughing* over there!', pointing to the veranda behind them. 'If I let my guard down like that, who knows what the fuck I'll do next? I've killed people – if you try to get me to start feeling again, what if I can't control that part of me?'

Although Jill had understood the man's dilemma when Mercy had first related the story, its meaning was deeper for her now. Her life had so long been lived in absolutes that she was not sure she could tolerate the shades of grey that other people seemed to accept. The one glass of liquor last night would be just that to anyone else, but for Jill it could mean that she'd just taken her first step into the alcoholic spiral she had lived through for a year in her adolescence. It had always been all or nothing for her.

She got out of bed, the cramp in her neck finally demanding a stretch. She picked her tissue box up from the nightstand and walked with it to her loungeroom, slipping between the blinds and sliding the balcony door open a crack. She couldn't smell the surf through her blocked nose, but the sea breeze slapped her in the face. She took a few deep gulps of the cool morning air.

It wasn't just the alcohol. Other rituals were blurring, too. The exercise, for one. It was now every second day. Was that enough? Could she still fight for her life? Did she still need to? And then there was Gabriel. A *week*, she'd known him, and last night she had been drinking at his house. If someone had told her a week ago the way she would spend last night, she'd have laughed in their face.

She made up her mind. Despite this head cold, she couldn't spend the whole day inside feeling miserable. She needed some groceries and she wasn't going to let the day go by without some form of exercise. She quickly showered and dressed in leggings and a long-sleeved tee-shirt.

The Maroubra shopping centre was an easy three-kilometre walk. Jill wasn't going to do easy. No way she'd allow herself to get weak, she decided. She'd go to Eastgardens at Pagewood, and she'd take the long route, via Matraville.

When her feet hit the pavement outside her unit block, she started to run. Habit. At first, her lungs burned with the effort, and her feet felt heavy, but by the time she got to Beauchamp Road, she had found her rhythm and zoned out the pain.

Her thoughts turned again to the case. She considered the answers she wanted to get out of Joss Preston-Jones and Isobel Rymill tomorrow. The time had come for them to stop screwing around. In full flight at the Anzac Parade intersection at South Maroubra, she didn't bother to stop at the lights. Dodging through the traffic, it suddenly occurred to her that Joss and his wife could be in danger. She hit the pavement on the other side of the intersection. If Joss had recognised Cutter wearing a balaclava, surely it was possible, even probable, that Cutter had recognised him.

She thought about what she told most victims who were worried about offenders coming back to find them after they'd been robbed or attacked. The adrenalin rush the criminal experienced during the act of crime typically diminished their memory for incidental details of the crime scene. These incidental details included the features of their victims. She'd seen survivors sell their homes within weeks, quit their jobs, leave the state, even their families, afraid that the offenders would return and attack again, certain they were still on a hit list. When she spoke to the perps, however, Jill noticed that most of them wouldn't have a clue that their targets were still petrified that they'd be back. Most of the time, Jill's words didn't comfort the victims. Hell, her behaviour over the last twenty years indicated that she didn't believe them herself.

And the stakes were higher in this case. Cutter and his crew had committed murder. There were witnesses. If they believed that those witnesses could send them to gaol, they might try to return and take them out.

Heading downhill now, Jill ramped up the pace and felt her drug of choice – endorphins – kick in. She considered whether telling the couple about this risk might convince them to open up to her. She had no real evidence of a threat to their safety – in fact, she decided, the events so far would indicate otherwise. The offenders had done nothing to harm Joss at the time of the home invasion. Surely if he'd recognised Joss, Henry Nguyen would have taken him out that night? Jill knew that during robberies, mass murder would sometimes take place when the armed robber had gone too far and accidentally killed someone at the scene. Realising that the consequences of being caught were now far worse, sometimes the perps went postal and took out all of the witnesses.

After the five-kilometre run, she automatically took her pulse out the front of the sprawling Eastgardens shopping complex. A little higher than usual. She waited outside the huge glass doors for a moment, letting her heartbeat slow. She detested crowds, and she knew that she didn't need any extra stimulation when she entered the centre.

It seemed as though the spring weather had created a nesting frenzy. It looked like people had come from all over Sydney today to purchase their summer fashions, new cushions or a barbecue. She knew from her mother that around this time of year people started to think about a new lounge suite or plasma TV to impress their Christmas visitors. Hell, Jill thought, as she looked around her, some of these people would probably have their Christmas present lists on them. In October! Jill usually bought her presents on the twenty-third of December. She had promised herself she would use the internet to do her Christmas shopping this year, but she guessed she probably wouldn't get around to it.

Breathing normally again, she followed a twenty-something couple in through the doors. They held hands, but the woman was a step ahead of her man, her face shining, entering her Sunday house of worship.

Jill just needed some fresh vegies. She'd get fish, milk and coffee locally, but the vegetables were better in the larger centres. Music poured out of a huge boutique to her left and she paused. She really liked this song. The mannequins in the window angled bony hips and arrogant eyes down at her. Summer dresses. Full, floaty fabrics held onto bare shoulders by impossibly thin shoestring straps. Jill couldn't imagine herself wearing something that offered so little protection from the outside world. The jewelled colours conjured images of cocktails by the pool, tropical birds, sunsets and balmy evening Christmas parties. A world Jill wasn't part of. She knew there were others in the community also barred entry to this world, who malevolently resented its inhabitants. Isolated, violent males, who took this rejection personally, plotted revenge against girls who wore dresses like these. 'Paint it Black', the Rolling Stones song, came to her mind – for some people the bright summer clothes brought forward their darkest fantasies.

The opening notes of another track that Jill liked came from the boutique's sound system. She stepped inside and immediately regretted it. She usually purchased her clothing from Myer or David Jones a couple of times a year, shopping in the middle of the week to avoid the crowds. She felt safe in the spacious, quiet department stores. A salesgirl buzzed straight over to her, shining and glossy, almost fizzing with energy. Jill felt snotty and dull in comparison.

'Good morning! Are you having a good day so far?'

The girl was a riot of belts and bangles, piercings and hair fudge. She probably wouldn't sit her Higher School Certificate until next year or the year afterwards. Jill was awed by such confidence in someone so new.

Just looking, thanks, was her automatic response to salespeople, but for some reason she decided to try something on. Maybe it was the music. Or the braces on the girl's teeth, worn like jewellery. Jill admired her self-confidence. And maybe she needed some new clothes.

Forty minutes later, Jill finally made her way to the greengrocers.

She took a different route home, down Maroubra Road and past the police station. She wondered who was in there today and what she would have been working on over the past week had she stayed there. The thought made her think about the movie *Sliding Doors*. If she'd worked at Maroubra as usual over the past six days, she would never have met Gabriel. She had already learned so much from him, and the thought gratified her. Despite her discomfort around him – the ridiculous discomfort of being comfortable – she looked forward to working the rest of the case with him. She resolved again to ask him more about assignments he'd worked in the past and how he'd come to be seconded to the taskforce.

The case had become all about Cutter, she realised, as she ran downhill towards the sea. The brutality of the crimes had led them naturally to focus upon the one man depicted by all the witnesses as the gang leader and the most violent. Trying to find him was their main priority. She wondered whether that was limiting their scope. She knew that the detectives who'd worked the cases before the establishment of the task-force had looked pretty hard at trying to identify other members of the crew. They had one other name at least, Mouse. In the interview with Joss and Isobel tomorrow, she would focus at least some questions on trying to learn more about these other people.

She rifled mentally through other cases, trying to glean something from them that could help with this one. In her experience, home invasions were usually one-off events committed by somebody who knew the occupants of the house and that something of value was kept at that residence. Sometimes, it was a member of the victim's community who'd learned that the homeowner had a safe in which they kept cash from their business, or jewellery they'd inherited. At other times, a punter who'd come good and shouted the wrong person at the local would find their winnings gone by daybreak, often while they slept the night off. And plenty of Harley-Davidson riders had woken to a gun to their head and a demand for their keys in the middle of the night. Jill remembered one incident where the owner had refused, and had been gutshot by a bikie in his living room in front of his wife and kids.

These robberies were different. They appeared to be organised along some other lines. The stolen items of value were typical of any burglary, but there didn't seem to be any other obvious link between the hits. She knew that the previous detectives had investigated any tradies that the victims might have had in common – a plumber or an electrician who might have visited all of the residences and used the chance to scope the house for security and valuables. They hadn't come up with a link. She wondered whether other professions had been considered – even an accountant, a kid's tutor or a gardener could have had a son or a boyfriend, a cousin or a brother who was a criminal and had used their connections to get to the next victim. She added another task to her list: ensuring that all service providers had been meticulously looked at for connections between the victims.

The final stretch home was uphill. Good. Jill imagined the sweat cleaning out the germs in her system. When she reached Maroubra Junction, she decided to stop for the last few items on her shopping list. She bought a chicken from a butcher's shop on Maroubra Road, and a sourdough loaf from the bakery. Walking the rest of the way home, carrying her latest purchases, she thought about the chicken soup she'd decided to make for lunch. Her mum would be proud.

Back in her unit, Jill piled the food onto the benchtop and then went into her bedroom to put her new clothes away. Her brow creased while hanging up the filmy tops and the sundress she had purchased. They looked nothing like the rest of her outfits. She scowled at them, and shut the wardrobe door. Maybe she *would* be wearing Scotty's pretty pendant soon! She stripped off her running gear and took a quick shower. Her nose had cleared a little, but she still felt stuffy; the scented steaminess of the warm water helped a lot.

In a soft tee-shirt, boxer shorts, and squashy socks, Jill returned to her kitchen to cook. She diced carrots, onion and celery, and sweated them in a little olive oil and salt in her biggest stockpot. She added boiling water, a couple of bay leaves and the chicken, looking forward to having the soup with a squeeze of lemon juice in a couple of hours. In the meantime, she cut a hunk of the bread and toasted it, then slathered it with strawberry jam. She took the toast and a pot of green tea out to the balcony.

She stared out to sea, her body humming from the exercise, and zoned out. Within a few moments, however, the case again came to mind. Whatever method the gang had used to target their victims, she thought, it was almost certain that most of them had not seen things going the way they had. In the first robberies, the violence, although terrifying, had mostly been used as a threat to compel compliance. Robbery had clearly been the motive. The motive for the leader now, though, was the violence itself, and if Gabriel was right, cracks in the group would be starting to form. She wondered whether there might be any way they could turn the screws a little more. Maybe put the hovering media to good use, to heighten the fear and paranoia among the group

228

members – get them to turn on themselves. She'd put it to the taskforce tomorrow.

Jill felt the Vitamin D doing her good. She leaned her face into the sunshine and closed her eyes.

29

CHLOE FELT SWEAT at her hairline, but her heartbeat was slowing. God, the guy had scared the shit out of her when she came back around to the front of the basement room. And she had nothing against tattoos, but he was kind of scary-looking.

She debated entering the room. Maybe she should suggest they go up to the house? But she hadn't even met the owner. Would it be rude to just go barging into someone else's house? She couldn't suggest another place to interview him. It's not like she could invite him home for a cup of tea at her house in Seven Hills. And no one back at the network would even dream of giving a cadet an office.

She made up her mind. What could happen, she thought. It's a sunny afternoon in the suburbs and Maryana and her mother are just up the stairs.

Chloe followed Cutter into his bedroom.

When he entered the room behind her, she began to feel even more awkward. Wanting him to feel comfortable enough to open up and speak to her, she was acutely aware in the small room that she stood a head taller than him. She looked for somewhere to sit – there was only the bed. She perched on the very edge and got her notebook out of her bag. The door shut, and her head whipped up. The thud had been a heavy metallic sound – like a vault. Her heartbeat gathered pace again.

'We don't want people listening to us,' he said.

Chloe's eyes darted around the room. A thick curtain covered a small window in the whitewashed wall. It smelled funny in here.

'I'm already disturbed that my name would be mentioned in a criminal investigation,' he continued. 'I don't want Mrs Miceh imagining that I'm an unsavoury tenant. Do you know, if it wasn't for my grandma, I don't think she would even have leased this room to me in the first place.'

Chloe relaxed a little. She pictured the bent old woman in the doorway in Cabramatta, smilingly pushing a piece of fruit and this address into her hand.

'She is a sweetie,' said Chloe. 'How long have you been living here?'

'Just a week or so,' said Henry. 'It's all I can afford at the moment. I have a new job in sales, in the Hills district, so this suits me fine.'

'So, nobody from the police department has contacted you regarding this investigation?' Chloe asked, eager to begin the interview.

'No. But I can't say I'm surprised that they're looking at me.'

She gave him a questioning look.

'I got into trouble as a kid,' he explained. 'Break and enters, stealing. A criminal record is the worst thing, Ms Farrell. The police are very lazy. Crimes happen in a certain area – they go through their database and suddenly there's a cop at your door. It's hard to convince people that you've changed.'

Chloe made a few notes.

'And the tattoos don't help matters,' he said.

No kidding, thought Chloe. Ugh.

'When I was young, I lost my father and my grandfather in a very short period of time,' he said. 'I was particularly close to my grandfather. I think that's why I rebelled.'

Chloe jotted his comments, but wished that he would sit down. He seemed to be standing over her.

'But I've grown up now. I don't do silly little things like that anymore,' he said.

'The police are watching your family home in Cabramatta,' she said. 'Now you know that, what do you think you will do about it?' She readied herself to scribble down his response. 'Will you go to them and ask why they're intruding into your life this way?'

He looked down at her and smiled. Chloe decided that when he'd answered this question, she would stand after all. This whole situation creeped her out.

'No, I don't think so,' he answered. 'You might have gathered that I don't like the police, Ms Farrell. And I don't think they're going to find me out here. My grandmother won't be giving this address to anyone else.'

Chloe rubbed at her left eye. The tic always started when she felt anxious. She moved to stand.

The explosion of movement stunned her more than the blow to her face. Her vision darkened for just a moment, and then returned, orange. Her face was pressed into his bedspread.

'Slut! Stupid slut!'

Chloe bucked with her legs to throw him off, trying to bawl out a scream, but her mouth pressed into the orange fabric, and the scream wouldn't form. All of his weight was on top of her, but Chloe was strong, and she felt his body shifting sideways, sliding off her. Then she felt cold steel pressed into the left side of her neck. She recoiled, jerking her head to the right, and the knife followed, this time biting, deep. She felt warm blood well. She was going to die here. Terror paralysed her.

'That's right, slut. Don't move around, and maybe I won't hurt you.'

He kept the knife to her neck and raised himself off her body. She tried to move a little and he pressed the knife deeper. She stopped moving.

'Stand up now, slut,' he said.

The pressure of the knife forcing her to comply, Chloe stood at the side of the bed, whimpering quietly. She knew that her only hope for seeing her parents again lay in keeping this blade from slicing her throat. She knew now with whom she shared this room. *How could she have been so stupid?* Details of the murder in Capitol Hill came to her, threatening to unhinge her completely. Stop it, she told herself. She needed to stay sane. Do what he told her. She wasn't ready to die yet.

They stood now between the bed and a wardrobe. He pushed her towards the cupboard and for a moment, she imagined that he was going to try to stuff her inside it. She'd never fit. Instead, he reached in with his left hand, his eyes on her the whole time.

Chloe met his eyes once and her knees buckled. His hand whipped out of the wardrobe and caught her arm. He used his right hand to lift her chin with the knife.

'Open your eyes, now,' he said. 'You're not being any fun.'

She forced herself to open her eyes and stare at the floor. If she looked into his demented face again, she wouldn't be able to help screaming, and he would start stabbing her with that huge knife. She knew it.

His left hand held cable. Plastic ties. She'd seen them before in crime scene photos. The restraint of choice for today's killer: cable ties, unable to be broken by the victim without pulling their own hands off. Her thoughts cantered madly. She couldn't let this man bind her. She had to fight now! On the other hand, if he was going to restrain her, he wasn't going to kill her immediately. She might have time to reason with him.

Chloe found her voice, although to her ears it sounded fractured, hysterical. She forced herself not to focus on it, or she'd lose herself to those impulses.

'My b-boyfriend knows I'm here,' she managed. 'He's a cop.'

'Wrong. No. I don't think so.' Grinning, her captor capered a little on the spot, the machete still pointed at her throat. She froze, terrified of the swishing blade. The wound on her neck throbbed, but she sensed the blood had coagulated and she was not bleeding heavily. 'You *said* the police don't know I'm here. You said that, slut. Don't lie to me. Now turn around and give me your hands.'

She hesitated, and he jabbed the knife at her neck again. She whimpered and turned. This man had dismembered a person in Capitol Hill.

Pulling her arms behind her back, he wrapped one hand then the other with the unyielding ties, wrenching her shoulders backwards finally to tighten them.

'Now sit. Here. On the floor.'

Chloe squatted and then dropped to her bottom between the bed and the wardrobe. He'd have to put the knife down to bind her ankles. When he bent over her she'd headbutt – no, kick him – then run for the door.

He seemed to have seen her calculating.

'You can't get out,' he said. 'You have to use the key. And I have that. By the time you get to the door, I'll have filleted you. Did you know you can do that to a person? No, I didn't either, but I've found, recently, that the muscles come away quite cleanly.'

Chloe screamed and screamed.

He ripped his bedspread from his bed and shoved a fistful of the fabric into her mouth. Chloe gagged on the material and tried to dislodge the wad from her airway. She couldn't breathe. He jabbed the tip of the knife under her chin.

'I'm not going to hurt you unless you make me,' he said.

She tried desperately to rein in her blind panic. There were only two choices here. Live or die. This man would kill her now, or she could delay her death and possibly survive this.

'Good,' he said. 'No one can hear you anyway. There's a foot of concrete above us, and these double-brick walls are half buried into the earth. I love it here, don't you?'

He motioned her to lie on her side and he squatted to tie each ankle, and then cable-tied them together.

'Now,' he said. 'I promise not to hurt you, but you need to cooperate. This bit's tricky.'

He stood and reached back into the wardrobe. Chloe panted into the fabric, terrified with each move he made that he would bring forth some object of horror. His hands emerged and he now held a thick wire with a lock, a device resembling something used to secure a bike. He squatted again. He looped the cord through the restraints around her ankles and used it to pull her legs backwards. He then yanked her hands downwards, pulling at the restraints, handling her as though she were an inanimate object. Her shoulders burned and she moaned around the fabric. She heard him click the lock into place. She was shackled into a U-shape, the top half of her body facing the bed.

Immediately, Chloe was engulfed by waves of claustrophobic terror. She was completely immobilised. She tried to roll, but the movement wrenched at her shoulders and thighs. Her neck strained and she struggled to breathe.

'Hogtied,' he said, standing with his hands on his hips, beaming down at her. 'You look good. I've fastened the cable to a bolt in the wall. You'll be staying here for a while.'

He picked up his knife from the bed. 'Shut up,' he said, when Chloe made choking sounds through the fabric in her mouth. 'I'm going to fix a proper gag so you can breathe properly.' He took a scarf from the wardrobe and squatted next to her again. 'Don't scream, slut, or I'll cut you.'

He pulled the bedspread from her jaws, and Chloe spat out the taste, then screamed through sobs. He wrapped the scarf around her mouth. She could at least breathe around the fabric, but the pressure he applied compressed her tongue and chafed at the soft corners of her lips; the knot at the back of her neck cut her circulation.

He sat down on the side of the bed; took a deep breath.

'Now I'm going to show you how I relax,' he said.

Cutter reclined on the bed and lifted his shirt, tended to his wound. The smell filled the room.

Chloe gave into the hysteria that bulged behind her eyes.

30

JILL WAS AWAKE before the alarm sounded at five, but her eyelashes were glued shut. She prised them open carefully, groaned and rolled over. A sea of used tissues littered the ground; one was still crushed in her fist.

She pointed her face into the hot stream of water in the shower and thought again about what she'd ask Joss and Isobel. She figured these were good people caught up in some sort of bad situation, but this was no time for them to be stuffing around. It had been six days since the murder at Capitol Hill, and the taskforce had yet to bring in a person of interest. The media were slamming them on every news update. She knew that Last would want Henry Nguyen brought in today or tomorrow at the latest. They'd had constant covert surveillance on his last known address, and the superintendent had given orders to bring the other suspect, Dang Huynh, in on sight. Joss and his wife might have information that could close the net on these guys.

She pulled on knee-high socks and zipped skinny black jeans into calf-length boots. She tucked a long-sleeved black tee-shirt into her jeans and added a belt and a black jacket. The detectives dressed more casually out in Liverpool than they did at Maroubra and, sunshine or not, there was no way she was going to freeze her arse off out there today. She blow-dried her hair carefully and left it long, warm around her neck, dropped Visine into her red eyes and smeared Vaseline over her lips. She thought she was beginning to feel better.

She stuffed an apple, some industrial-strength cough lollies and a few more tissues into her bag and left.

Gabriel's car was there already, and he crossed the road when Jill parked, smiling at her. He's always so bloody cheerful, she thought, wiping her nose and checking her face in the rear-view mirror before getting out of the car.

Joss opened the door before they knocked, his face a mask.

'Morning, Joss,' said Jill. 'Isobel here? We've got to have a talk.'

He stepped aside wordlessly and led them into the terrace house. Isobel stood by the glass doors next to the kitchen. She wore a terry dressing gown and her hair was still wet. She had an arm across her stomach and worry creased her brow. She glanced at Charlie, seated at the kitchen table, her little hand holding a spoon above a bowl of cornflakes.

'Hello,' said the little girl, scraping her chair away from

the table. She walked over to Jill and held out her hand. 'I'm Charlie Rymill. What's your name?'

Oh how gorgeous! Jill's eyes said to Isobel, who smiled back tremulously.

'Hi, Charlie, I'm Jillian. This is Gabriel. We're friends of your mum and dad.'

'Do you want some cornflakes?'

'Finish your breakfast, honey,' said Isobel, walking over and guiding Charlie back to the table, at the same time that Gabriel said: 'Do you have any Coco Pops?'

'No, we're not allowed,' said the little girl sadly, shaking her head. 'Too much sugar.' Her big blue eyes were multi-faceted marbles.

'Can I put some toast in for you?' asked Isobel tightly, walking into the kitchen. 'I'm making some for us anyway.'

'That would be great, Isobel, thanks,' said Jill, and Gabriel nodded. Jill followed her into the kitchen, and spoke quietly, away from the little ears at the table. 'We know you're on your way to work, but we really need you and Joss to call in late this morning. We have to have your help with this case, and it can't wait.'

Isobel nodded and slotted four thick slices of bread into the toaster.

'Could you put some more in for me when they're done?' she said to Jill. 'I'll just go and make some calls.'

Jill toasted more than half the seeded loaf and took it with a few jars of spreads over to the table. Joss stood staring out into his backyard, immobile, apparently uninterested in the near stranger poking around in his kitchen. He seemed pre-occupied but somewhat less tense than the last time she'd been here.

240

Gabriel had already finished one piece of toast and was speaking to Charlie with his mouth full when Isobel re-entered the room.

'Done,' Isobel said. 'Joss, I left a message for Eric that you might not be in at all today. I did the same with my boss,' she said to Jill.

'Thanks, Isobel.' Jill felt awkward sitting at their table with her piece of toast, interrupting these people's lives. She knew from experience, though, that refusing hospitality on a home visit added to the tension.

Isobel had dried her hair and with that seemed to have collected herself. She brought milk, sugar and mugs to the table. A few minutes later, a big pot of brewed coffee followed and she played gracious host for the next fifteen minutes, but took only a few bites of toast herself. Joss sat with them, but didn't eat a thing.

When Charlie had finished her breakfast, Isobel took her into the loungeroom and switched on the television.

'The Wiggles,' she said when she came back to the kitchen. 'Her favourite DVD. We'll be right for a while.'

'Great,' said Jill, eager now to get to the point. Gabriel sat back in his chair, relaxed, but she knew he was observing everything. 'There's no polite way to say this, Isobel. So I'm just going to say it straight because we really need your help right now. We know you two are holding something back about the night at Andy Wu's.'

Isobel's mouth opened; she looked hunted and guilty. Joss stared straight ahead, his palms flat on the table.

'Thing is,' Jill continued, 'we know the identities of at least two of the people committing these home invasions and we don't have to tell you how terribly dangerous they are. We want one of these men, especially, locked up right now, before he kills someone else. He's not in custody yet, though, and we urgently need to speak with anyone who knows anything about him.'

Jill paused. Music tinkled from the loungeroom, and she could hear what sounded like Charlie dancing. The kitchen was otherwise silent.

'Isobel, you and Joss know a lot about him,' she continued, 'and it's time you told us everything you know about Cutter – Henry Nguyen.'

Isobel jerked a hand to her mouth, her eyes darting to her husband. For a second his posture stiffened, as though he was preparing for sudden movement. Jill did the same. Suddenly, Joss's shoulders dropped and his eyes met her own.

'What do you know?' he asked.

'Well, we know that Isobel called the hotline and told us to investigate Nguyen,' she said. 'It's okay,' Jill glanced at Isobel, who looked as though she was about to cry. 'That tells us you do want to help. We have hard evidence – DNA – connecting Nguyen to one of the crime scenes, and we believe that he has participated in at least six home invasions. We also know, Joss,' she said, turning to him, 'that you knew him well when you were a kid, and we're pretty sure that you recognised him at Andy Wu's home.'

He was watching her closely.

'What we don't know,' said Jill, 'is why you haven't told us that. We don't want to believe that you're trying to protect this guy. Did you know that your wife called the hotline?'

'Of course I knew,' Joss said.

'Then why didn't you tell us everything the other day, Joss? We get it that you're worried for your safety. But why wouldn't you tell us everything you know to help us lock him up faster?'

Joss sighed deeply and raised his eyes to the ceiling. He then lowered his forehead to his hands. Isobel stood and walked to her husband; she touched his neck, tears running now. Jill wondered whether to speak, but Gabriel shook his head silently at her.

When he raised his face, Joss's eyes stared directly into Jill's.

'Look around you, Jill,' he said. 'Everything in this house is my world. I don't want this world to change.' He rubbed at his chin. 'I know that not coming forward was not very honourable, but I fooled myself into thinking that if I just tried to ignore the past, it would stay there. Stupid, really. I've always known that was never going to happen.'

Isobel, still standing at his side, rubbed his shoulder. He placed his own hand over hers and stood. He talked as he paced.

'It seems you know a bit about my life as a kid,' said Joss. 'What you probably don't know is that for the past twenty years I've considered that kid dead. It's like he was never a part of me. I can't relate to anything I did or believed back then. When I got the chance to change my life, I took it and fucking ran.'

Isobel flinched a little and watched her husband closely.

'You're right,' he continued. 'I did know Cutter. I suppose I would have called the group I hung out with at that time my best friends. My mother was out of it and my dad wasn't around. My friends were my family. There was nothing else worth caring about. I just didn't know any different. I know what a real friend is now, and the only one I have in this world is my wife.' He looked at her, his face serious. She smiled encouragingly at him.

'Back then, until I was twelve or thirteen, I didn't really care about my life or whether I was alive or dead. There's not much I can admit to being proud of. Everything was opportunistic. We'd steal anything we could get our hands on. Sometimes so we could eat, sometimes just for the fuck of it. Back then – when you've got nothing else to live for – it was fun. Stealing cars, smash and grabs, police chases . . .'

Joss stood now by the sliding doors, staring into the yard. Jill noticed Gabriel also rising from the table quietly, moving closer to him, wanting to catch every word, but unwilling to break the flow.

'Then something really bad happened,' said Joss, 'just before I went to live with my grandparents.' He looked up and seemed surprised to see Gabriel standing closer to him. 'Me, Cutter, Simon Esterhase and Carl Waterman decided we'd do over Carl's dad's bike shop. We used to call Carl "Fuzzy". He said his dad would get everything back on insurance, and we were dying to get our hands on these new trick bikes in the shop. Mr Waterman wouldn't even let us touch them. I don't know how it happened . . .' Joss paused and started to cough. The cough caught and his face turned red as he struggled to catch his breath. He stared wildly around the kitchen. Isobel was by his side in a moment with a glass of water. He downed it in two swallows, and handed the glass back. Jill felt slightly envious of the silent synchronicity between the pair.

Joss took a couple of deep breaths. 'Sorry,' he said, his voice devoid of emotion. 'Anyway, Fuzzy let us into the shop while his dad was asleep and we took the bikes. We came back after hiding them and knew we had to smash the window so it would look like someone broke in.' He cleared his throat again. 'One of the panels must've speared inwards. Somehow it stabbed Fuzzy in the neck.' Joss was unconsciously holding his own throat, his voice threadlike.

'You didn't actually see the wound being inflicted, then?' Gabriel asked.

Joss shook his head. 'I tried to hold his throat together.' Isobel was at his side, almost touching. 'But, he just, kind of like, drowned.' Tears stood in his eyes. 'He was looking at me, his eyes just . . .' He trailed off.

After a pause, he continued. Emotionless. 'Anyway, he died there while I watched, and then I pissed off. I got taken to my grandmother's after that because my mum got hit by a car. I heard a few months later that Cutter got arrested, but he didn't report me and Esterhase. I thought it was a miracle that I got away with it, a sign that I had to change my life.' He looked up at them, defensive, as though challenging them to doubt him, or to laugh.

He took a seat and began to tear a piece of toast into a pile of crumbs.

Finally, Joss continued. 'You see, where I am today, I don't want people like that anywhere near me. I don't even want to know they exist. When the shit happened at Andy's, I just wanted all of us to get out of there alive. I would've done something to stop them if I could, but there was just no way.'

Isobel nodded.

'And then, just before they left, he looked at me, and I knew it was Cutter. I don't know how, but I knew it was him. I know now that he recognised me too. He followed us a couple of days ago to the movies,' he glanced at his wife. Isobel's hand was at her throat. 'He said some smartarse things. I knew then that we weren't safe and that it was definitely him that night. I told Is I wanted her to move away with Charlie for a while, but she wouldn't go. I knew we had to tell the cops, so she rang you guys.'

'Joss thought that if we did it anonymously,' said Isobel in a quiet, pleading voice, 'that the stuff about Fuzzy would never have to come up. I mainly agreed to do it though because I thought that Joss was mistaken and you guys would look into Nguyen and figure out he wasn't involved.' She looked at her husband apologetically. He laid a hand on her arm and sighed.

'Anyway, I might as well tell you everything now,' he said. His wife looked at him, surprised. 'I've been back to where we used to hang out,' he continued, as Isobel drew in a sharp breath, 'and tried to find out more about him, like where he lives now, so I could pass that on to you.'

'Joss!' Isobel looked angry.

'Anyway, I can tell you he's still hanging out with Simon Esterhase.'

'We're going to want to know everything you discovered out there, Joss,' Gabriel spoke to him for the first time. 'But I'd like you to come out to Liverpool today so that we can record your statement. I don't want to miss a thing you've got to say next. It might be exactly what we need to get the lot of them.'

Jill and Gabriel left Joss and Isobel, arranging for the couple to meet them out at Liverpool at two p.m.

Joss lingered at the doorway as they were leaving.

'Just so we're clear,' he said to them, eyeballing each in

turn, voice low, 'you guys had better get this fucker fast. I told you I'd do whatever I had to do to protect them,' he angled his head back towards the interior of his house. 'And you need to understand that I will.'

Lawrence Last was not in his office when they got back to Liverpool; an urgent meeting with the police commissioner, his assistant told them. Jill shared a sympathetic expression with the uniformed man behind the desk. The taskforce meeting was delayed until Last's return.

Jill and Gabriel spent the next half-hour working on a report to summarise their movements since the last meeting.

They were just wrapping it up when Jill sensed someone behind her, heading their way. She kept her eyes on the computer screen and tried to detect the identity of the visitor from his movements. Derek Reid, she guessed, just before he spoke.

'Don't you two make a cute couple?'

Jill kept typing. Gabriel grunted.

'Come on! Just shit-stirring,' Reid said. 'Got anything new?'

'Not really,' said Gabriel.

'Not that *you'd* share leads anyway, hey, Delahunt?' said Reid.

'We're just finishing up a report, but we won't have anything hard until later this arvo,' said Gabriel. 'We'll fill you in on everything in the next meeting. We've got a couple of vics coming in later today.'

Reid seemed annoyed by Gabriel's neutral tone. He took a step closer to Jill, and because she was still seated, his crotch was now in her face. She stood and glared at him. He laughed at her.

'You wanna get some lunch, Jill?' said Gabriel.

She grabbed her bag from under the desk.

'Aw, how sweet,' grinned Reid. 'Can I come too? Since you've broken your rules about dating cops, Jackson, maybe you should give me a go. I'll make you forget all about Super Spy here.'

'I don't really know what you're talking about, Derek,' said Jill, smiling sweetly, 'but you're going to have to get over anything happening between you and me.' She swung her handbag over her shoulder. 'I don't date body builders. It's a *little* problem I have,' she stared pointedly at his groin, 'with the steroids.'

'Whoa!' Gabriel laughed, and turned to follow Jill as she walked towards the door.

'What's funny, Delahunt?' said Reid, smiling menacingly. 'Why don't you stay here and we can talk about it?'

Gabriel kept walking. 'Forget it, Derek. I don't do cock fights,' he said.

Jill and Gabriel left the room with Reid's parting words: 'Fucking freaks.'

Facing one another across the moulded plastic table, Jill felt an awkward silence between her and Gabriel for the first time since the initial taskforce meeting. The other patrons of the food hall also seemed low on conversation. Overweight kids in school uniform scoffed burgers or pizza for lunch. A young mum seated close to Jill fed her toddler hot chips, the child cawing for them like a hungry seagull. Pairs of people –

a mother and daughter, perhaps, on the left, sisters or friends straight ahead – munched listlessly, exchanging grunts now and then.

Jill felt the muteness stealing over her. When that mode kicked in, she sometimes wondered whether she'd ever speak again. Why did she feel this way now? It couldn't have been Reid's comments – God knows she was used to crap like that. She looked down at the table and noticed that she'd used her milkshake as a barrier between them. This was ridiculous. She forced herself to speak.

'So how did you get posted to this case?' she asked. They'd discussed his past briefly before, but never in any detail.

'Lawrence Last asked for my help,' he said. 'I worked with him a year or so ago on an organised crime thing. I've been attached to police units on a few major cases now.'

'So, why this one?'

'My specialty's interrogation. Because they were coming up with so little trace evidence at the crime scenes, they figured they had to get more out of the witnesses and suspects. Anything to get these fuckers.'

'Makes sense,' she said. 'We're an odd group, this task-force, don't you think? I mean David Tran – what's going on between him and Reid? And I wonder how he got injured – has he said anything to you?'

'Yeah. I'm surprised you haven't been told by someone yet. Everyone out here seems to have an opinion.'

Jill leaned back in her chair while Gabriel continued.

'He's the community liaison officer in the area,' he said. 'First contact for the Vietnamese community. Some of them trust him. Most of them don't. Culturally, it's taboo to speak outside the family about problems. He's seen as a traitor by many of his people because he's operating outside of their rules of silence.'

'Wow. That would be hard.'

'Yep, but it's a double dilemma for David, because he's never been fully accepted by some of the cops either. What did I hear Reid say the other day?' Gabriel took a sip of his drink while he thought. 'Oh yeah, that's it – Tran was called to the desk to speak to someone about some information that could've helped with the case. Reid went with him, so I took a walk over there too. David spoke Vietnamese to this bloke. Reid was like – *You wouldn't think we were in Australia, would you mate?* – some shit like that. Then he had a laugh with the girl behind the desk, um, what was it – *Why don't they save their bloody Chinese for China or wherever they're from?*'

'MENSA candidate, Reid. He's wasted in the cops,' said Jill. 'So what happened to David's leg?'

'Oh yeah, that. Heroin dealers from Cabra. Smashed his thighbone with a hammer.'

'Oh my God!' Jill raised a hand to her mouth.

'Yep. He was off duty. They got him in the toilets in West-field. He'd sent up a few of their best re-sellers.'

'Wow. But David said he was off work HOD.'

'Yeah, Last made sure it was written up as Hurt on Duty. And Last got the fuckers too. Tran I.D.'d the cousin of one of the perps he locked up. So, now they want to kill him.'

'Shit.'

'Yup. For real. That's another reason Last wanted me over here. The organised gang shit is his next big target, once they get on top of the home invasions.'

'So what about you then, Gabe? Are there any deep dark secrets I should know?' Where the *hell* did that come from? Jill felt her cheeks grow hot. She never asked questions like that.

Gabriel sat there, head on an angle, watching her from under the brim of his cap.

'Sorry,' she said. 'I was just stuffing around. You don't have to answer that.'

'No, it's okay,' he said. 'It's just that I'm not usually great at speaking about my past. Specially at this time of year.'

'This is a rough time?'

Gabriel looked at her again, closed his eyes briefly. Finally, he sighed and pushed his food away.

'I joined the Feds with my wife,' he said.

Jill hoped the shock didn't show on her face.

'We met in a psych lecture at uni. We got married and joined the AFP together four years later. Started work on the Monday after the wedding, actually.' He smiled. 'I started the job in organised crime and Abi was assigned to major fraud. Between jobs, we worked our way together through the MOSC program.'

Phew. Jill had heard of the Management of Serious Crime program: it was the most intense major-crime training program in Australian law enforcement.

'Then after September 11, we both got routed to counter-terrorism,' Gabriel continued. 'Three-quarters of us did, to tell you the truth.'

Jill listened. He'd cleared up some of the questions she'd had about him. But where was Gabriel's wife? He seemed to have read her mind as he continued.

251

'Abi and I were together for ten years. She was my world.' A small smile did not reach his eyes; they watched a scene from another time. 'We were still based in Canberra, running surveillance. Just a routine tip-off – a member of the public worried about their neighbour's allegiances. The target was a mufti from Queanbeyan; he'd just visited the subject of another intelligence report. Abi was the eye, following him a few cars back. I was with the rest of the team shadowing her.'

'The eye?' said Jill, and then regretted her utterance. She didn't want Gabriel to stop speaking, and she was afraid of breaking his train of thought.

'Yeah. The eye follows the rabbit – the target. The rest of the team follows the eye and ignores the rabbit. You don't want a fleet of cars trailing some poor prick. We just tail the one vehicle – the eye – and the eye can be rotated; that way we can maintain contact and chop and change positions when we need to.' He paused.

'Go on, Gabe. Sorry I interrupted.' She held her breath.

'Nothing great left to tell you, Jill. Some drunk mother-fucker ran a light and killed my wife. Head on. He made it out alive. Serial offender. Lived to drink and drive another day, I'm afraid.' He reached unconsciously for his napkin and began to shred it, working around the edges in an organised pattern. 'I was first on the scene, thank God.'

Jill leaned forward, as Gabriel's voice had dropped with his eyes to the table.

'We had a few moments,' he said. 'We had a bit of time . . . And then the ambos got there.' He cleared his throat. 'Nothing they could do, though. I'd already tried. Abi and I, we tried, but, the injuries . . .' He looked up. Tears stood in his eyes, and he smiled sadly. 'Five years ago,' he said, 'last Saturday.'

Jill reached a hand towards his, but stopped just before their fingers touched. She could feel the warmth of his skin.

'Saturday,' she said. They'd eaten pasta in his unit. She'd fallen asleep with his cat.

'Yep. First anniversary I didn't spend alone. Thanks.'

Jill knew all about anniversaries. She swallowed at the lump in her throat. They were silent a moment, each thinking about that time of the year when the ghosts crowded closer, clamouring for more attention. This time she let her fingers find his. She covered his hand with her own. What would it feel like, she thought, to find and then lose your soul mate – to feel her dying, leaving you, wanting desperately to stay, but knowing there was nothing you could do? The helplessness, the loss of control; is love worth risking such desolation?

Gabriel gazed at the table. Jill stared at a wet smear on the soft skin next to his eye. She longed to wipe it away. She had her finger poised, ready, but left her hand where it was.

'I bet she was amazing.' Jill wasn't sure whether she spoke aloud. Suddenly, a thought occurred to her. 'Hey,' she said. 'Your cat. You named her "Ten".'

He looked up and smiled. 'Best years of my life.'

An itchy impatience prevented Jill enjoying twilight on her balcony. She sat rocking on a chair, bare feet up on the small table.

It was just over a week since she'd become involved in the case. They'd come a long way – identified the main offender –

but he was still out there, and they couldn't go in hard until they sighted him. Interviewing his friends and associates would drive him to ground.

But this guy was unhinged. He could attack again at any time, with or without his crew. She felt guilty being home so early, but there'd been nothing immediate for the taskforce to do, and Last had sent them home. She'd considered driving around trying to locate him herself, but they had crews from Penrith to Redfern out looking; there was nothing she could do tonight.

The sound of gulls calling blew back on the salty seaweed breeze; the sound left her feeling inexplicably sad. She pictured them, endlessly wheeling over the ocean, crying. She'd never understood people's aversion to seagulls. Beady-eyed greedy devils, scavengers, some called them, pelting them with rocks, tossing cigarette butts at them, pretending to offer chips or bread. Jill could feed them by the hour, ignoring the baleful stares of others who didn't want to share the beach with the birds. She'd grown skilled at aiming the bread so that the crippled gulls got there first – those hopping on one leg, the fishing line that had strangled their other limb still trailing; those with one eye, or a hook gleaming through their cheek or their beak. The fatter birds stared at her, indignant: these rejects were the walking dead. Feeding them is pointless; life is for living. But she saw gratitude in the shiny black eyes of the wounded birds, or she imagined she did.

She scratched compulsively at her ankles with her toes, then stood, walked back into her apartment. Her thoughts turned to the story Gabriel had told her at lunchtime, but she deflected them. They'd spent every day together for the past

254

week. She could spend a night without thinking about him. As usually happened when she thought about Gabriel, Scotty popped into her mind; she imagined him now, laughing eyes smiling down at her. She picked up the phone.

Maybe he feels like a run or something, she thought, dialling.

Idiot. Idiot. The word was now a mantra. Jill mentally repeated it over and over as she smiled self-consciously from her corner of the backyard.

You've gotta come, Scotty had told her. You're not doing anything else. You know my parents. It's just them and my sister. It's nothing, just a barbecue in the backyard.

She clutched a wine glass to her chest, trying to use it as a shield to cover herself in her flimsy new dress. Idiot. What the hell had she put this on for? At least she'd removed the butterfly pendant at the last minute before getting out of the car.

'This is new.' Scotty now stood at her side, barefoot in boardshorts and a white windcheater that highlighted his almost permanent suntan. Her bare arms left her feeling naked.

'Don't start,' she warned.

'Oh. I didn't mean the dress,' he said, 'although now you mention it . . .' He grinned and lightly fingered one of the flimsy straps. She shrugged away, half-smiling, tempted to spin and snap-kick as she usually did when he teased in this manner. That probably would not go down so well at this backyard barbie, nor in this dress.

'I mean the wine,' he said.

'Yeah, well,' she said. 'So?' She took another sip.

'Nothing. I'm glad you're here. So you've almost caught this crazy fucker, huh?'

'Well, we know who a couple of them are. The one we want is Henry Nguyen.'

'Yeah, I heard. Maroubra got updated this morning. The whole city's looking for him.'

Scotty's stepfather, Rob, stood at the barbecue turning the steaks over and over, beer in hand. Scotty's sister's fiancé stood with him, talking and laughing. She could see Scotty's mother and sister, Rhiannon, illuminated behind a flyscreen, spotlit by the kitchen lights. Earlier, standing with them there, trying to help with the salads, she'd felt compelled to pull the blinds, knowing she could be seen but could not see out. Rhiannon, perhaps sensing her discomfort, had pressed a white wine into her hands and shooed her out the door. The wine was ice-cold, and she'd not noticed the first glass going down. She tried to sip more slowly at this second one.

'So, do you like it out there?' Scotty wanted to know.

'I don't know.' Suddenly tired of standing so stiffly, she dropped into the suspended swing seat next to her. Scotty sat down beside her. 'It's not so bad,' she continued. 'Better than I thought it would be.'

'I heard your new partner's a Fed.'

'Been checking up on me, Hutchinson?'

'What was his name again – Gloria? *Gabrielle*? I heard he's a bit, ah, eccentric.'

'Funny. That's the New South Wales Police Force for you, isn't it? Someone doesn't act exactly the same as everyone else and they've got to be a weirdo.' She pushed her feet against the pavers, stopping the movement of the chair. The slight swing of the seat was making her dizzy.

'You're pretty protective of him already,' he said.

'Yeah, well you're being pretty predictable.'

'What does that mean?'

'The whole testosterone thing – mine's bigger than his.' She drained her glass and put it down on the cushion next to her. Scotty picked it up again.

She stood, needing firm ground beneath her. 'I don't want to argue tonight, Scotty. Do you want to go down to the beach before dinner?'

'I'll just get my thongs.'

Scotty unlocked the gate at the rear of the garden and led Jill down the steep, sandy stairway behind the property. Jutting roots from wind-blasted shrubs twisted up through the sand, and she hooked a hand into the waistband of his boardies for balance as they negotiated the shadowy steps.

When they reached the bottom, the bushes gave way onto a sheltered cove. Jill hadn't been down here at night before. The glow from a pale, fat moon washed with every wavelet onto the quiet beach. A couple of anglers, highlighted by moonlight, sat on the rocks to their right. A fragment of their discussion reached Jill as she stepped into the cool sand, carrying her sandals; the distance between them scattered their words in the wind.

The sea air was deliciously cool on her hot cheeks and Jill breathed deeply, padding down to the shoreline. Whipped around by the breeze, she had to keep pushing tendrils of hair from her eyes and mouth. She walked, head down, watching her footprints melt back into the liquid sand at the edge of the ocean. She didn't realise she was smiling.

A shout from the fishermen caused Jill to look up, and she

saw Scotty standing there, staring at her. He held her shoes. Huh. She must've dropped them.

'What're you looking at?' She smiled up at him.

With one long stride, he stood immediately before her.

'You're beautiful.'

So quietly. Did he really say that?

He dropped her sandals by his feet. Jill stood immobile in the sand, acutely aware of every sound and movement. Scotty reached out and caught a wayward strand of hair from her face, wrapped it around a finger.

Jill stopped breathing. Suddenly she knew exactly what she wanted. Scott Hutchinson. Now.

'Scotty.' She reached up and wrapped her hands around his neck, pulled his face down to hers. She closed her eyes, her lips parted.

Nothing happened.

Her eyes snapped open. Scotty's mouth was a whisper from hers, his lips curved in a small smile.

'What are you doing?' he said.

'I would've thought that was obvious,' she answered, trying to pull him still closer.

'You know, Jackson,' his mouth almost touched her own, 'we could've been doing this every night for the past year.'

'So, we're doing it now. Shh. Too much talking.'

'Except tonight you've been drinking.'

She dropped her hands, stepped backwards. Suddenly freezing, she wrapped her arms around her body.

'You think I'm drunk?' she said.

'Look, Jill, not drunk, but . . . wait!'

She snatched up her sandals and strode through the sand.

'I don't want it to be an excuse,' he called after her, 'a

258

mistake. I don't want you to regret this tomorrow and freeze me out. Would you frigging wait a second – you're going the wrong way!'

What was the right way? Humiliated tears rolled down her cheeks. She felt ridiculous and so exposed in this dress. She would never get stuff like this right.

31

EXTRA POLITE. SHE hated it when they were especially civil to one another.

For her part, Isobel had to be courteous in order to censor the screaming shrew who wanted to tear strips from her husband. How could he go to Cabramatta to look for that psychopath? What else, she wondered, have you been doing that I don't know about? Why did you ever hang around that freak in the first place? Why didn't you kill him when we were at Andy's? Instead, she asked, 'Can I get you a drink of something, hon?' She'd just tucked Charlie in for the night.

'No, that's okay, babe,' he said, mid-lift on a shoulder press using his hand weights. She knew he hated to talk when he was in the middle of a set. Hence her question right now.

'I'll get something later,' he added, his deltoids distended, a vein bulging in his neck.

I'm sure you will, she thought. It usually took three reminders to get Joss to take out the recycling. He'd taken the bottles out four nights in a row now. The hundred-litre recycling bin was full of his empties.

At the mirror in their bathroom, she carefully cleansed her face, pretending not to notice the new creases of worry around her eyes. She toned and moisturised, then brushed her teeth. Please God let them catch him, please God let them catch him. A mental hymn in tune with the rhythm of the electric toothbrush. She gargled the same song.

Tidying the bathroom a little, Isobel thought about the night ahead. She knew she'd find it difficult to sleep – replaying their interview at the police station, Joss's answers, the warnings of the detectives. She wondered whether she should take Charlie up to north Queensland. Probably. But what about Joss? Despite the fact that he'd managed to open up to the police, could she trust him to behave rationally down here alone? And she knew he wouldn't come with her. The inner tussle already tightening her stomach, she reached for the yellow pills at the back of the medicine drawer. Left over from minor surgery, the opiates would get her at least a few hours of dead sleep. She swallowed two with a handful of water from the tap, grimacing when one stuck on the way down.

She pulled on shortie pyjamas and climbed into bed. Twenty minutes later, she was snoring through a magazine on her face.

A hand over her mouth. The blood blasted from her toes to her crown in the split-second before she recognised Joss's face

261

above her own. His eyes hard, unrelenting. Telling her: *they
are here*. No fucking around. It's fight or die.

All without words.

Our baby, his eyes said next. I'm going to get her.

He took his hand from her mouth. Gave her the bat.
Remember the lessons.

With the thought of her baby in that man's hands, the
strength that ran through Isobel's body left her wanting to
bite, tear flesh with her teeth. She positioned herself behind
the door. The bat felt spongy in her hands; she felt she could
snap it in two. Already furious with the fuckers for taking so
long to get to her, she practised seeing the blood spray from a
head, wiping it quickly from her eyes to swing again.

When the massacre had first started, Joss had been careful to
step around the bodies. Even when the mounds at Kibeho had
grown so wide that there was nowhere else to walk than over
the dead and dying, he would try to avoid treading on a hand
or a leg on his way to pull another breathing person out of
the pile. By the end of the third day, however, he marched
over dead faces, strode through brains, stepped straight onto
balls. There was no other way to get around.

Now, Joss moved silently through the darkness of his
home, ignoring the hands grappling at his ankles, moving
through the body parts. His own hand was finally whole
again, holding his knife. He heard it laughing and he smiled
back at it, his teeth flashing in the dark.

I'm coming, Cutter.

*

Leaning against a counter in Joss's kitchen, Cutter stared at his diluted reflection in the glass of a cabinet. While he listened to the quiet movements above him, he allowed himself some time to think about what he was going to do to Mouse. He couldn't believe the fucker wouldn't come tonight, that he didn't know his fate for turning Cutter down.

He selected a toothpick from a tiny bowl on the counter next to him, and worked at some food caught in his teeth. As usual, when using a toothpick, he couldn't resist the urge to press the sharp thing deep into the softest crevice of the gum, the agony mushrooming a feeling he equated to what love must feel like. He sucked happily at the metallic tang of his blood.

Studying the now slimy wooden splinter in his hand, it occurred to him that he should use the needles on Mouse. Perfect. He sucked the toothpick dry before placing it on the bench. Lately, he couldn't get enough of that taste.

He needed to hurry now. He walked into the loungeroom carrying the twelve-litre container in one hand and the machete in the other. He slashed a few times at the couch in the centre of the room and began sloshing the accelerant over the furniture.

Esterhase could see no way out of it. He felt sick, his limbs rubbery. He'd been pissing his shit out for over a week. Everything he ate turned to water. And his gut ached. He rubbed it unconsciously as he stood silently in the upstairs hallway of the house in Balmain.

Cutter had explained about Joss. Esterhase still felt disbelief. He hadn't even recognised him when they'd done over that house in Green Valley. But Joss was only part of the problem. Man, the whole thing was so fucked up. If he killed Cutter, this prick Joss still knew too much. And if he didn't do this job with Cutter, the cunt would completely schiz and he'd be next. Mouse had better be packing for Vietnam right now, he thought. Cutter had just smiled when he told him Huynh wouldn't be coming. Esterhase had nearly shit his pants just looking at him.

He breathed in the dark, his heart hammering. Too many things could go wrong. Who knew when Mouse would break, or when Cutter would get them all caught. He had to do this job tonight, and then he was getting the fuck out of the state. Shit, maybe he'd even go to New Zealand.

Esterhase stood in the dark thinking about what he had to do tonight. He bent forward slightly as the fist in his gut squeezed at his innards.

Isobel had thought it impossible for her heart rate to increase further until she heard the furtive footsteps stop outside the room. She'd spent a few moments agonising over the possibility that Joss could return quietly to the bedroom and she might hit him by mistake, but she knew now as certainly as if there were no door between them that the person standing out there was not her husband.

The corridor outside the double doors was black; the light in the bedroom with her, slightly brighter. She stared so hard at the rind of darkness that she thought she was imagining it when the door finally began to move. Terror wrestled with rage; her senses focused, and she squeezed the bat harder. Ready.

The scream of a siren split the air and Isobel recognised their fire alarm a heartbeat before the door flew open and her nightmare barged in. While the siren shrieked, the dance between her and the masked man seemed silent, slow.

I'm sorry Joss, she said internally. I let him get closer than a metre.

Somehow, the man had got hold of the end of the bat. He raised the knife above his head. Isobel could almost feel the pain in her shoulder where she imagined it would slice into her. Her daughter's blue eyes danced in her vision and she sobbed goodbye. Then, with the strength of a grief beyond anything she had ever experienced, she drove the bat forward into the chest of the man in front of her, propelling him three feet across the room. She felt the movement of his weapon as it fell past her ear. She considered picking it up, but, bent double, he was already preparing to move forward again.

Instead, she went to meet him.

Isobel lifted the bat above her shoulder and kept her eye on the ball, just as her brothers had taught her. She swung, the bat slamming into his temple, the thud shuddering up her arms and into her neck, causing her to bite her tongue.

With the fire alarm sobbing in her ears and blood from her tongue on her lips, Isobel spoke quietly to the man unconscious in her bedroom. She ignored the smoke swirling around her feet and his body.

'You leave my family alone,' she told him. 'You leave us alone.'

He didn't move, but she kept the bat close, and bent down to him. The fire alarms bawled for attention: it seemed as though there had never been silence. She was aware of a heat somewhere behind the doors, but she had to know. Carefully

at first, and then scratching, clawing, she ripped at the balaclava covering the face in front of her.

The skin at his temple was already beginning to bulge.
Somehow, she knew that his brains were leaking out of a
fracture in his skull. The long dark hair curled into the
hollows of his neck, like snakes nesting comfortably with
the spider tattoos.

He had carried the other children through the carnage,
crying, just like this, crooked in his right arm. Joss couldn't
hear his daughter's sobs over the sirens, but he felt them, wet,
against his shoulder. The alarms deafened him, just as the
mortars had, but he was well practised at relying on his other
senses. He stayed close to the wall, moving slowly, ignoring
the bodies at his feet – back from Charlie's room to the
bedroom, to Isobel.

The balaclava walked out of the smoke.

And they faced each other.

He manoeuvred Charlie a little higher. Her legs clung to
him, terrified. Inconsolable at being woken from her sleep by
this noise, she buried her face deeper into his neck. She didn't
see the shock in the masked man's eyes when he saw that his
opponent carried a little girl.

Joss smiled at him. The sight seemed to confound the man
further. The enemy shifted his machete in his hand.

Joss knew somehow, with certainty, that this was not
Cutter. This fact heightened his impatience. He willed the
man to act.

The enemy signalled to Joss to raise his hands. Joss
walked forward, quickly, still grinning, watching the other's

eyes widen with anger, disbelief, watching him raise the machete, wave it, a warning.

Joss kept his left hand pressed tight against his leg until they stood eye to eye. He watched the other's internal dialogue – this guy's crazy! Should I do something? He's holding a kid! The fucking house is on fire!

Joss studied the eyes even more closely when he plunged his knife into the masked man's diaphragm. As awareness dilated the enemy's pupils, Joss angled his body sideways a little, turning Charlie's body towards the wall. The blade of his knife buried in the other man's gut, Joss felt his opponent's heart beat in his hand. He stared intimately into the other man's eyes and pulled the knife upwards.

When he felt the flames climbing the stairs, Joss reclaimed his knife and wiped it on his leg. Charlie's body now shook with coughing. Joss's eyes streamed in the smoke.

He walked into his bedroom, heard the mortars falling, and listened to the howls of the orgiastic Tutsis drunk on the blood of the Hutus in the camp. He stepped over another body, and looked around for his wife. His saw the open window and crossed the room quickly. In the light from the half-moon, he saw that Isobel waited.

Joss handed their daughter through the window, and climbed out to join her on the roof.

32

JILL SHUT THE bedroom door, but she imagined she could still hear the woman rocking out there, back and forth, by the bay window. It reminded her of a circus tiger pacing its cage – the obsessive movements of a beast driven mad by captivity. She'd spoken to many sufferers of schizophrenia, and some told her that the medications made them feel just like that, imprisoned in a chemical cage in their mind. She focused on the room in front of her to distract herself from Joss's mother. Perhaps Mrs Preston-Jones was fortunate to be oblivious to the trouble her son faced.

Gabriel sat on a tapestry-covered chair at one side of the queen-sized bed. Joss and Isobel sat on the bed on either side of their little girl, Charlie, who was asleep, lightly sedated, under the covers. They all still reeked of burned wood. Images of the charcoaled bodies from the morgue this morning wafted through Jill's mind with the scent. Superintendent Last had called Jill just before dawn from the crime scene, the family's terrace in Balmain.

'This thing's gone to hell,' he told her over the speakerphone while she walked through her bedroom, still in darkness, gathering clothing. 'Your victims, Preston-Jones and Rymill . . .'

'Are they okay?' Jill could hear the fire brigade sirens in the background.

'. . . are on their way to the Prince Alfred Hospital.' He obviously hadn't heard her. 'Smoke inhalation, nothing too bad. Their house burned down.'

'Okay,' said Jill. So what was Last doing there?

'There's a couple of bodies in there, Jill. Preston-Jones admitted to killing two men who broke into their home tonight. He says it's our boys – the same men that committed the home invasion at the Wu property.'

Jill sat on the edge of her bed, raised a hand to her mouth. 'And is it?' she said.

'Looks like it, Jill. The description fits. The local boys called me when they got Preston-Jones's story.'

'So what happened?' she asked.

'I haven't yet personally spoken to Preston-Jones. I've been told that he and his wife escaped with their child by climbing onto the roof. Neighbours called the fire brigade, but their house burned out. The Inspector here tells me there was almost certainly some sort of accelerant used. The fireys couldn't get anywhere near it until it was all over.'

'Have you seen the bodies?' Jill wanted to know.

'They're on their way out now. The Inspector tells me that formal identification won't be possible tonight. It smells like a barbecue out here, Jill.'

She winced. That smell. She knew that many in the emergency services could not eat pork because of the scent memory. A burned human body smells just like roast pig. She'd once worked with a cop in Wollongong who vowed never again to attend a barbecue after a triple-fatal house fire in Corrimal.

'I've already spoken with Gabriel,' said Last. 'Sorry to do this to you, Jill, but I'll need both of you out at Glebe as soon as possible. I'd like you to meet the truck when it arrives with the bodies.'

That had been hours ago, Jill thought, and it was still only just past mid-morning. She and Gabriel had travelled straight from the morgue to the hospital, but had been told that Joss was back at Balmain police station and that Isobel and Charlie had come to this house in Mosman.

Springing Joss from Balmain station had not been easy. The Inspector had come in early for the show. The Balmain crew wanted in on the glory. They all knew the story would go global: *Victim kills machete slayer, saves family from burning home!*

She and Gabriel had waited until Joss had given his first recorded interview of the events and then booked him out, the political powers of the taskforce outweighing the pissed-off Balmain command. Last wanted Gabriel to do the full interrogation. They'd yet to decide whether charges would be laid.

Jill looked at Joss, now lying curled around Charlie, and figured further questioning would have to wait. His eyes were heavy-lidded and blinked more slowly by the moment. Isobel, pale-faced, stared at a wall. Shock, thought Jill. It's best to let these people sleep a while. She caught Gabriel's eye, gestured with her head to the door. He stood.

'We're going to let you guys rest for a bit,' said Gabriel.

Joss looked up blankly. Isobel didn't move. 'We're going to stay out here if that's okay with you, Joss?'

Not that you have any choice, Jill thought.

'Of course,' croaked the man from the bed, and coughed. 'And thank you.'

Gabriel followed her from the room and closed the door. Jill bypassed the sitting room, and found a homecare nurse drinking coffee in the breakfast area off the kitchen. The woman stood when they entered.

'Please,' said Jill. 'Don't let us bother you.'

The woman picked up her cup and left the room anyway, glancing back nervously from the doorway.

'Probably all over the news by now,' said Gabriel, walking into the kitchen.

'Ah, you think?' said Jill.

'Yeah, it would be,' he said, missing her sarcasm. 'She's probably been watching it all morning.' He nodded at the doorway the nurse had just exited.

Jill smiled tiredly. 'You making coffee?'

'Yup. Want one?'

'Definitely.' She opened the fridge. 'You think they'd mind if we fixed ourselves something to eat? I'm starving.'

'Well, we'd be feeding him if we were back at Balmain doing the interview. What's in there?'

Jill found a Tupperware container filled with shaved ham and another with finely sliced Swiss cheese. She grabbed a loaf of bread and a jar of hot English mustard and closed the refrigerator door. There was a tomato and an avocado in a bowl on a benchtop.

'Toasted or plain?' she asked him, spotting a sandwich press near the kettle.

'Might as well go the whole hog.' Gabriel clicked the switch to turn on the appliance.

They took their food out to a sun-saturated, wrought-iron outdoor setting in the backyard. Jill moved an overflowing ashtray from the table, her nose screwed up in distaste.

'So, you reckon we'll have to charge him?' she said, after several bites of the sandwich.

'Yep,' said Gabriel, chewing.

Jill leaned back in her chair. The sprawling gardens, although now overgrown, had obviously been professionally maintained at some stage in the past. The drone of a leaf blower on a neighbouring property couldn't drown out the manic activity of bees in the blossoms around her. She licked at a burgeoning cold sore on her lip. It thrummed under the skin – all that was left of her cold.

At one o'clock, they decided they could not let Joss and Isobel sleep any longer. Last had already called twice, wanting to know if they'd recorded the interview yet. Gabriel set his equipment up in one of the formal lounges on the lower floor. It was unorthodox to do the interview outside a police station, but Jill had not wanted Charlie to be moved around unnecessarily.

By six p.m., Jill was making her way home, exhausted. Joss and Isobel had given them the same story. They'd woken to a sound outside their bedroom, and then the fire alarm had sounded. Joss had gone out with a baseball bat to investigate, and had encountered a man with a knife. The alarm must have allowed Joss to approach the offender undetected, and he'd managed to wrestle the man to the ground, turning his knife against him. He'd rushed back to the bedroom and found the second offender, caved his head in with the bat.

Isobel had rescued Charlie. Before they went out to the roof, the couple had removed the mask of the man in the bedroom, and had identified an Asian male, mid-thirties, with spider tattoos on his neck.

As they'd stood out the front of the quiet home in Mosman before leaving, Jill had noted the stress signals she'd detected while the couple were speaking. Gabriel had been non-committal. They were both in shock, and the cues could be confusing at such times, he pointed out.

Jill wound her windows down while driving towards the ocean. She let the early evening breeze play through the car, tangling her hair.

Thank God, she thought, driving past the surf club at Maroubra Beach. Cutter's dead.

Now he understood what it felt like.

Constable Andrew Montgomery sat dripping from his shower in the small gym beneath Liverpool police station. He towelled off the top half of his body and reached for his mobile, tried Chloe's number again. If *he* got this many missed call messages from a girl this early in a relationship, it set off a wacko alarm, and he began putting as much space between him and her as possible. Problem was, he'd never felt this way about a girl before Chloe, and now he kind of understood the compulsion to ring again and again.

Nothing. No answer.

He stood from the bench and finished drying himself, made his way to his locker and reached for his uniform. He'd finished half of his double shift, and had another hour's break before signing back on for the nightshift. Most of his mates were pissed off with the extended hours. Ordinarily, Andrew would have been more than happy – the overtime pay got him closer to his US–Canada skiing holiday. Two years' planning and saving, the trip had been the first thing on his mind every morning until he'd met Chloe Farrell. He smiled at himself in the mirror, straightening his collar, thinking of her.

The smile faltered. He wondered again why she hadn't called. He knew he wanted to see her every day, and he thought she'd felt the same. He'd let Sunday pass, certain each call he received would be from her. He'd never waited for a call from a girl before and he somehow liked the anxious anticipation of having to wait for something he really wanted. By Monday morning, though, he was over the game and ready to concede defeat. He called her. He'd been trying every couple of hours since, and now here he was, Tuesday night. No word.

All of the possible explanations sucked. He couldn't figure out whether it would hurt more that she just didn't care enough to have returned the call, or whether she'd got what she wanted from him for now and didn't need him at the moment. Actually, that would be worse, he thought – that Chloe had deliberately targeted him only to glean some information on the home invasion case.

He took his shoes over to the bench again and sat, leaned his face into his hands and rubbed at his temples. He felt stupid for giving her the little information he had; he'd never done anything like that before. He mentally chewed through their conversations again. All he'd really told her was that there'd been an apparently important anonymous phone call and that the caller had identified someone called Henry. It had just been a tease. Nothing she could actually use – just something to attract her interest, make those eyes light up. She couldn't actually do anything with those details, could she? He'd scanned the news the last couple of days and there was no sign that she'd reported the scraps of information.

Another possibility for Chloe's silence nagged at him and again he pushed it away as ridiculous. Chloe couldn't actually have used that information to try to find Henry herself, could she? I mean, *we* couldn't even find Nguyen, he reasoned with himself. How would she have had a hope when she didn't know his address or even his surname?

Andrew Montgomery decided he'd sign on early. He grabbed his holster and notebook from his locker and made his way towards the stairs. At the doorway, he suddenly paused and reached into his top pocket.

He chewed at the skin around his thumb and pressed the phone against his ear.

33

JILL TOOK THE call while dressing for work. 'Tonight?' she said into the phone. 'Why tonight?'

'Your sister's going away on another shoot,' her mother replied. 'As usual, she waited until the last minute to tell us. She's going to Italy this time and thinks it may be one of the last big overseas shoots she does. She thinks they're about to send her out to pasture.' Jill knew Cassie was paranoid about her age: thought she was lucky to still be modelling at thirty.

'Okay, I guess I can come,' said Jill, holding the handset under her chin and trying to towel off at the same time. 'Where are we going?'

'East Ocean in Chinatown.'

'Yum. That's a bit a hike for you guys, isn't it?'

'Actually, it's quite exciting. You'll never believe what your father's done now.'

'What?' asked Jill. Her father wasn't big on spontaneity or surprises.

'He's booked us a suite at the casino. We're going there after dinner.'

'Wow. What's the occasion?' Jill nervously ran through a checklist of anniversary dates and birthdays – nothing she could think of.

'No reason. Can you believe it? Last night I told him about the dinner plans and he said he'd arrange for us to stay in the city.' Frances sounded thrilled.

Jill smiled widely. It was great to see her parents relaxing a little. Even though she'd been only twelve, and traumatised, when she had returned home after the abduction, she had recognised the changes in her parents. There had been times early on when it seemed they went weeks without even speaking to one another. Sitting on her bed now, holding the phone, Jill felt another subtle adjustment in her tension levels, as if another piece of ice had sloughed away from the glacier that had been her heart for so many years. Her family seemed to be healing, finally.

'That's great, Ma. So, who's coming?'

'Tim and Robyn, Avery and Lily.' Jill hadn't seen her brother and his family for a month or so, and she was pleased to hear their names. 'Cassie, of course,' her mum continued, 'and she's bringing her new friend. They've been seeing each other for quite a while, apparently, so that should be interesting.'

After the call, Jill hurriedly finished getting dressed for work. She figured that the pressure on the case would lessen with the news that two of the offenders were dead. Police and community relief would be massive when they announced that one of the deceased was the ringleader – Cutter. Still, she didn't want to be late to the taskforce meeting today. There could be word back from the coroner, more details from the crime scene, or word on whether Joss would have to face formal charges. And there were still two offenders in the wind.

Despite the remaining heavy workload, she wondered whether the taskforce would be dismantled now that Henry Nguyen had been killed. As soon as the 'sexiness' of a murderer was taken out of the equation, media interest and political pressure, in that order, would diminish, and competing workloads from other cases would begin to pull the taskforce apart. She wondered how she felt about that. She had expected to be delighted and relieved; she'd been thinking she would put in for a transfer closer to home, even try to get back to Maroubra, not that that would be easy. On the other hand, she had been enjoying working with Lawrence Last. She wondered whether he would request her help on another case.

And then there was Gabriel. So different to Scotty. Jill wasn't sure exactly how she felt about their partnership coming to an end, but suddenly the morning didn't seem quite so bright.

She gathered up her handbag and briefcase, and left for work.

At just after seven p.m. Jill left the departmental car undercover in a parking station on George Street and walked down to Chinatown. She pulled a ruffled black cardigan over her white shirt as she walked. The evenings were still a little cool, especially in the city. She waited at the lights on Hay Street while other pedestrians walked straight in front of cars, ignoring the horns and expletives of motorists still trying to get home. She shook her head as two giggling girls, both on mobiles, caused a dark Mercedes to slam on the brakes. She hated driving through this intersection.

As she climbed the stairs to the restaurant, the noise from the street gave way to Japanese harp music. She spotted her family sitting at a circular table near the window overlooking the streetlights below. Spicy scents followed her as she walked past a trickling fountain and candlelit tables to reach them.

'Hi everyone,' she said, smiling.

Jill's mum rose to give her a hug and four-year-old Lily leapt from her seat before her mum, Robyn, could stop her.

'You're sitting here, Aunty Jill! Mum, you said she would sit here.'

'Yes, Lily, it's okay, settle down now.'

Jill made her way around the table; her sister, Cassie, stood when she reached her.

'Hey, big sis,' she said, kissing Jill on both cheeks. Cassie's lips were berry-red with wine, her cheeks flushed.

'Hey, Cass,' Jill replied, wishing she'd had time to change out of her work clothes. Cassie wore black, a sheath of slinky fabric falling to the floor, leaving her arms and shoulders bare. A heavy silver band circled her throat. She looked beautiful, but very thin.

'Jill, this is Aidan,' said Cassie, and the man next to her stood and offered his hand. He wore a casually crumpled suit, his shirt open at the throat. He brushed a long dark fringe from his eyes and smiled at her.

'Pop ordered lobster,' called Avery, her nephew, from across the table, waving a menu. Avery sat next to her father, who was wearing his good suit. 'It says on here "market prices", but the waiter told us they're a hundred bucks each and Pop ordered two!'

Jill's father told Avery to keep his voice down, but everyone smiled.

A waiter came past with wine, water and juice for the table and asked Jill whether she'd like to order a drink.

'I'll be fine with what's here for the moment, thanks,' she told him, watching Cassie helping herself to the wine before the waiter could pour it for her.

The plates seemed to multiply on the table, bowl after bowl of sticky, steaming food. Jill tried dishes she'd never tasted before – abalone, sea-urchin roe – and others, some of which she wasn't certain she wanted to know the main ingredients.

'Dad, what's got into you?' laughed Jill, selecting a piece of marinated tofu with her chopsticks. 'You've never ordered like this before.'

'No. Aidan helped with the ordering tonight,' her father stated, staring dubiously at a jellied dish in front of him. Aidan and Cassie laughed loudly together, the area around Cassie's plate clear of the mess that surrounded everyone else's. The waiter arrived with another bottle of wine and took it straight to their side of the table. Jill's mother caught her eye.

'How was it out there today, darling?' Frances asked.

'Not bad. Pretty good, actually. Liverpool's kind of growing on me.'

'Maybe that's because the case is nearly over,' her mum said. 'Does it still look as though it'll be wrapped up soon?'

'Yeah, it looks that way,' said Jill.

Her mother smiled. 'Do you think they'll send you back to Maroubra?'

'I doubt it,' Jill answered. 'But they could send me anywhere.' Her mobile was ringing. Jill reached for her handbag. 'Sorry, ma, just hang on a second.'

'Jackson,' she said into the phone.

It was Gabriel.

'Sorry to interrupt your evening, Jill,' he said. 'I just got off the phone with Last. The coroner's got a report on the bodies. He wants us to go over to Glebe and get a wrap-up.'

'Tonight?' Jill sighed, looking around the table at her family. Her mother watched her.

'Yep. The pressure's on to let the public know that Nguyen's dead. They want it released to the media before the morning.'

'Okay. I'm out to dinner with my family. I'll be over there in half an hour.'

'Don't hurry too much, Jill. The coroner's still tying everything up. Forensics are faxing over some findings to add to his report.'

'I'll see you when I get there, then.'

She hung up.

Frances Jackson was already standing. Jill didn't think it would be long before this party broke up altogether anyway. Her father had been frowning for the past fifteen minutes. Cassie and Aidan's conversation was garnering them stares and raised eyebrows from nearby tables; they laughed and argued, oblivious.

She made her apologies and left the restaurant.

*

Jill made it to Glebe in fifteen minutes, parking out the front of the building on Parramatta Road. She reattached her gunbelt and showed her badge to gain entry to the Coroner's Court. At the office of the state coroner, David Mobbs, she gave her name, asking the PA if he was available. There was no sign yet of Gabriel.

'I'm sorry, Sergeant Jackson. He's not ready for you yet,' the woman said from behind a glass partition. Her face was haggard, her hair a mess. Jill guessed they would've been working around the clock since the bodies came in early on Tuesday morning. 'If you just hang on a moment, I'll try to get some idea of the wait.'

The woman made a brief phone call and turned back towards Jill.

'Going to be up to an hour, I'm afraid,' she said.

Jill thanked her and made her way back to the front of the building. A departmental vehicle pulled in behind hers, and she walked out to meet Gabriel.

'Maybe another hour,' she said to him by way of greeting. 'Want to go get a coffee? It stinks in there.'

They walked around the corner and into a side street with a brightly lit café. They were the sole customers, and the pimply waiter alternated between watching them and the plasma screen behind the counter showing a Bollywood movie. After ordering, Jill moved to a Formica table at the back of the room, and they took a seat under glaring fluorescent lights. The coffee was barely passable.

'So, do you still reckon Joss will be charged?' said Jill.

'Probably,' said Gabriel. 'But the charges will likely be dropped before it gets to court.'

'That's what I think,' said Jill. 'When all the evidence

comes through linking the men in the house to the home invasion gang, it'll be ruled self-defence, and he'll get off.' She sipped the coffee slowly; it may as well have been warm water. She grimaced. 'I don't think anything will come of the incident with the death of his childhood friend, either, do you?'

'Nah,' said Gabriel. 'Too long ago, extenuating circumstances – the kid killed was involved in the robbery of his father's shop.'

'Joss has been worried about that for a long time.'

'Mmm. I've actually been wondering whether this boy Fuzzy – Carl Waterman – was Cutter's first kill.'

'I know. The thought's crossed my mind as well. I guess we'll never know now.' She pushed the cup away from her and leaned back in the uncomfortable seat. 'Bizarre, the way Joss's life caught up with him, isn't it?' she said. 'It's like you try to push away parts of yourself that you don't want to know anymore, but they always come back to be dealt with.'

'There's one part of his childhood that won't be coming back for more.'

'Cutter,' she said.

'Uh huh.'

She was quiet for a moment, and then found herself saying, 'Gabriel, I really appreciated you opening up the other day about your wife and your past.' She suddenly wanted him to know this. It could be that they would be separated by work very soon. 'In fact,' she said, 'I've really enjoyed working with you over the last two weeks. I've learned a lot.'

'Thanks. We've had fun.'

Her brow wrinkled a little. She didn't know whether she'd really describe the experience that way, but she kept going.

'I was terrified about coming out to Liverpool, to be honest,' she said. 'I have a hard time getting to know new people. You made it easy.'

'It was easy because we're both in the same boat,' he said. 'People usually find me weird.'

'So I'm weird? Thanks! '

'Yep, a bit.'

'Anyway,' Jill shook her head and laughed. 'We were talking about the past never really staying buried, and I guess I've also been through some things that make it hard for me to open up.' She coughed; her cheeks felt hot under the lights. Such conversations left her feeling as though she was walking through shadowy waters over rolling logs. She feared that at any moment she'd dislocate a knee or step into a sinkhole and never emerge again. 'Um, yeah,' she said, 'I just thought I'd say that I appreciated you being so open and easy to get along with.' There, she thought. That would do.

'You said that,' he said. 'So. What'd you go through that makes it hard for you to open up?'

Just like that. He just came out and asked things. God! She swallowed. Thought about what to say. Stared at him, then at the table. Unrolled the wax strip around the top edge of her cardboard coffee cup. This was when her words were going to fail her. She couldn't think of a thing to say. He waited, patiently.

'I got kidnapped when I was twelve,' she said. Fuck.

He sat quietly, attentive, his face neutral. Maybe it was that, she thought later. No horror or great concern, no reaching over the table to touch or comfort her. No expressions of anger and indignation about how someone could do that to a child. She found herself speaking again, in a rush.

'I was at a sports carnival,' she said. 'I was hanging out at the back fence with my two best friends. They were smoking. I was gonna try it. First time. There was a gap in the fence. It was surrounded by trees. We just slipped through.' She took a sip from her ruined cup. It was empty, but this barely registered.

'There was a guy,' she continued. 'I didn't see anything. I was coming through the gap in the fence backwards and I just got grabbed and lifted up. They put something over my head. I started screaming. I heard my friends screaming too, but he ran with me back to the car. He threw me in and the car drove off. There was another one driving.'

Jill stared unseeingly at the countertop. She was back in the car.

'He tied the thing tighter around my head and then he put his feet on me. He must've put me on the floor of the car. They had me three days, although when I got back, I thought I'd been gone, like, two weeks or something. They kept me in a basement. I was blindfolded. Alone, when they weren't with me.'

Well not really alone. Jill thought briefly about the white-eyed girl – a dissociated part of herself that had separated from her consciousness when the pain and fear had become unbearable. 'They burned me,' she said in a small voice. 'Raped me. I didn't even know what sex was.' Her voice trailed off.

'They dropped me off at a school oval,' she continued, finally, in a tiny voice. 'I was naked. Still blindfolded. I often wonder who found me, and if they're okay now. I can't remember any of that last bit. There are lots of blanks.' She looked up at him. 'I suppose I should be grateful for that.' She laughed, harshly. 'Stuff still comes back in nightmares, though,' she said. 'I guess that's what I meant when I said the past keeps coming back.'

'That's fucked,' he said. 'Sorry.' Then, 'Did they catch them?'

'Nup. Not then,' she said. 'The younger one killed the older one when he got senile and started telling anyone who would listen about the sick shit they used to do to kids. They were part of an organised ring.'

And I killed the other one six months ago. She thought it, but didn't speak the words. The knowledge registered feelings of relief, satisfaction, horror. She stared at her hands.

Jill's mobile sounded, and she fumbled reaching for it.

'Jackson,' she said; then, 'Okay. Be right over.' She put the phone back in her jacket pocket. Gabriel was already standing.

'They're ready?' he asked.

'Yep.' She found her legs wobbly when she stood. 'Forensics have faxed over a copy of their findings to Mobbs. His report's being printed now.'

Fifteen minutes later, Jill's passenger door wasn't yet shut when Gabriel hooked a U-turn in front of the traffic on Parramatta Road. Tyres shrieked. She held on. He hit the siren.

'It wasn't him.' Jill said it again, third time.

'He's going to go and get them, Jill. Try to get them on the phone.'

The coroner's report had revealed that the burned bodies in the home of Joss Preston-Jones and Isobel Rymill belonged to two men named Simon Esterhase and Guo Qi Xu, AKA

Tatts. Each had a substantial criminal record. They were both known associates of Henry Nguyen. Cutter.

A comparison of the organic material found at the Rice and Capitol Hill crime scenes had specifically ruled out that Nguyen was one of the dead men.

The phone rang unanswered at the Mosman residence.

34

PERFECT TIMING AS usual, Mother, thought Joss, driving through the night back to Mosman from Rozelle Hospital. He'd made the trip countless times throughout his adolescence – his grandfather doing the driving in the early days, then his grandmother. Finally, before leaving for the army, he would use the trip as practice for his driver's licence. His mother had made the trip many more times without them, in an ambulance, after hours of screaming obscenities, often naked, sometimes in front of their affronted North Shore neighbours.

Tonight, Joss's wife and child made the trip with him. He figured that his family's arrival and the disruption to his mother's routine had caused her fragile chemical stability to crumble yet again.

He stole a glance at Isobel's pale profile, and gripped the

steering wheel tighter. It wasn't as though their presence in the Mosman house could have disturbed his mother too terribly. Isobel had said barely anything since they had climbed from the roof of their burning home on Monday night, two days ago. Even Charlie was quiet, listless.

Thinking back to that night, Joss could almost smell the smoke in his daughter's hair. When he'd handed Charlie to Isobel on the roof, the night air and the urgency of the situation had roused his sensibilities. Leaving Isobel clutching a wide-eyed and shuddering Charlie, he had worked quickly, the sound of the flames now audible over the noise of their smoke alarm. He had lowered the ladder to the ground and gone back for Charlie. He had prised his daughter from his wife's grip at the edge of the roof, and again clinging to her with one arm, had instructed Isobel to follow him. On the ground safely, they walked in single file towards the front of the house. A huddle of neighbours now stood in the street, mobile phones to their ears, panic painted on their faces in the streetlights.

Joss had pulled his blank-faced wife into the shadows near the Wilkinson's terrace next door, motioning her to squat with him behind the large council wheelie bins. Urgently, he'd asked Isobel what had happened when he'd left the room, and she had recounted, as dry and factual as a police officer testifying in court, what had happened in the bedroom. His relief when she had described the dead man's features had brought him to sobs. But the emotion behind the tears quickly gave way to grief for his wife. She had that night become a member of a terrible club, and it was his fault. He knew too well that killing another human being left a terrible legacy.

When he'd heard emergency services approaching their street, Joss had made Isobel narrate, three times, an alternative story: that he had killed both men in the house. When the details of her account were consistent, he had taken her hand and Charlie's, and walked with them through the smoke and out into the street.

Now, in the driver's seat, Joss steered with one hand; the other rubbed at his forehead. Either Isobel would come to believe the tale he'd constructed that night or she wouldn't. Regardless, the weight of the repression, or the horror of the truth, would burden her. His poisoned past had infected his innocent girls. He could never forgive himself. They'd probably have a better life without him.

A gentle rain smeared the world outside the car. Joss wished they could stay in here forever, that he could just drive with his family to another place, another time, where none of this had happened, and his girls were shiny and smiling again. He glanced into the rear-view mirror. The shoosh of the tyres on the night-wet road had lulled Charlie into a fitful sleep. Isobel's forehead rested on the passenger window, her breath a frosty ghost on the glass. What did she see out there with that thousand-mile stare, he wondered.

Joss accelerated carefully. He hunched forward over the wheel, staring intently through the drizzle. Nearly there. He had to get back to the house in Mosman. The ghouls in his mind were impatient, and the bourbon was waiting.

It's taking forever to get there, thought Jill.

Night roadworks had snarled the traffic, and Gabe kept the siren on until they hit Mosman.

When they finally arrived, Jill climbed carefully out of the car. The dirt-tang of the rain on the road filled her nostrils, all senses acute. Joss's phone had rung out five times on the trip over, and her neck was taut with tension. If Cutter was coming after this family, she thought, it could well be tonight. She and Gabriel had been out here until late last night finalising the statements. The police presence would've kept him away yesterday. In the car, speeding over here, Jill had tried to reason that it was more likely that Nguyen had done a runner – figured his luck had run out and gone to ground. But the intensity of Gabriel next to her as he negotiated the vehicle through the city traffic had chased the thought from her mind.

Gabriel believed Cutter was coming here.

She took several deep breaths to flood her bloodstream with oxygen and moved around the car to his side.

The mansion squatted in the darkness. If there was any moon, tonight it was obscured by the mist that hung above them. The drizzle had stopped for now, but it draped, poised, waiting to fall.

Jill led Gabriel in through the heavy iron gates, her radio in hand. The overgrown vegetation around them shifted and breathed in the dark; the garden of a madwoman. There were hiding spots everywhere, and Jill kept her other hand near her gun. The house ahead lay completely silent, but she'd expected that. There were obviously no nursing staff on tonight. The nurse, or Joss or Isobel, would've answered the phone if they were in there. If they'd been able to. She swallowed the thought, and moved closer to the house.

On the threshold of the ornate entryway, Gabriel touched her elbow, pointed with two fingers to his eyes, and then to the right of the house. Jill nodded and walked left; Gabriel moved to the right. She debated whether to call for backup. She'd wait, she decided, until they'd determined whether the perimeter was secure. She hooked her radio back onto her gunbelt, took her gun from its holster and unclipped her torch.

Most of the gravel path that must've once surrounded the house had been reclaimed by the garden; the sound of her footfalls was absorbed by wet vegetation. Jill smelled rot with each step.

She'd not reached the back of the sprawling house when her tread crunched. Broken glass glinted at her feet in the torchlight. She directed the beam upwards. The small white-framed window probably opened onto a laundry or small study; the glass had been shattered, and the window hung ajar.

Jill signalled Gabriel's radio with her own, and stepped away from the window, into the grass. She made a quiet call for police assistance and waited for her partner. She watched him jog silently from around the back of the building.

'I've called for backup,' she whispered, playing the torch beam over the window and back down to the glass below to show him what she'd found.

He nodded.

It was not difficult to gain a toehold in the red brick wall for the one step-up needed to reach the window. The frame was clear of glass. Jill pulled herself in after Gabriel. As she'd guessed, the room was a laundry. A tiny one. These houses were all designed by men, Jill couldn't help but think, in the days when a male would never wash a shirt or cook a meal. She and Gabriel stood face to face in the darkness. Their breathing was the only sound she could hear.

'We should do this together,' he whispered.

'No time,' she said. The blood-spattered walls from the house in Capitol Hill filled her vision, and she felt compelled to move quickly. What if he's in here? What if they're still alive?

She couldn't decide whether the look Gabriel gave her was of relief or doubt, but he nodded, and they moved out of the room.

'I'll take downstairs,' he whispered.

Jill kept her back to the wall as she made her way to the grand staircase in the centre of the loungeroom. Cutter had no firearm offences on his sheet, but that meant nothing – he had access to the nine guns from the Capitol Hill robbery. She ran lightly up the stairs with her heart in her mouth, bolted to the cover of a wall and squatted in a crouch.

That window could've been broken ages ago, she told herself, as she slid along the cold plaster wall. No one really looked after this place. She used the reasoning to temper the panic that always built when she couldn't see anything.

The hallway that led away from the stairs was window-less, and the darkness was built of shadows and blacker voids behind them that could conceal anything.

They'd kept her blindfolded in the basement when she was twelve, and she knew that terror grew so quickly in the absence of light that it could push all vestiges of sanity from the mind. She waited for the numbness to kick in. The sensor that tripped when she experienced any emotion too strongly should have engaged by now. But her anxiety continued to climb.

Jill decided to take control of her feelings by tuning in carefully to all of her other senses. The house creaked and moaned in the quiet way that old houses complained as they aged.

She steeled herself to enter the doorway on her left. The master bedroom, she remembered, pushing the door backwards with her left hand and then following her gun into the room. She swept through quickly, back flat against the walls when possible, listening for breathing or movement in the dark. Nothing.

Back in the hallway, Jill froze. *There.* A sound, behind her. Footsteps. She squatted, and then crawled back towards the noise. Peering over the balustrade of the balcony, she spotted Gabriel patrolling. She let go of her breath. He'd heard her too, and signalled. She moved back into the hallway, and made her way into the second room. A bathroom. Tiny. She checked the possible hiding places and made her way to the third room along the hallway. Joss's room, she remembered, as she pushed the door back.

Jill heard the woof of the knife as it sliced through the darkness, but didn't feel it when it bit into her gun hand. Pain or not, her gun clattered to the ground, and she screamed into the mask in front of her. Panic detonated behind her eyes as she struggled to get her left hand up to strike, but he had the momentum and he used it to pull her to him, towards the knife. When she stopped screaming to breathe, she thought she heard him giggle. She pulled backwards with everything she had, but he had hold of her jacket.

Every millisecond of the next few moments seemed to register. She saw his eyes widen and at the same instant, she detected movement behind her. He heaved her towards him with the force that still reverberated from his original strike, and smacked his forearm across her throat.

Gabriel stood in the doorway. His gun pointed at them.

Cutter chortled in her ear and she felt his arms and chest tense to pull the machete sideways, to slice her throat. She absorbed his madness, and the physical power that accompanied it, through the skin of his arm on her neck.

Gabriel's eyes met hers.

Yes, she told him, without a word.

Then there was just white. No sound.

The blast blew them backwards and Jill flew through the air with Cutter, landing merged with him on the floor at the base of the bed. Her cheek rested against his neck. Above his nose was purple-red, wet. His right eye and the top of his skull were pulverised.

Her mouth filled with the smell of singed wool, cordite, and vaporised blood.

Jill's hearing returned in stutters. She listened to Cutter living and dying with each breath. The death rattle.

She couldn't move. She lay there breathing in this man's soul as it left his body. She felt close to him, part of him, dying there with him. Her mouth on his neck, she whispered into the blood. Not long now, she told him.

But Cutter first had something to say.

Because they made no sense, and she'd never been certain that she had actually heard them, Jill had never repeated the words to anyone.

'Coming, Grandfather.'

'Thanks,' Jill managed in the back of the ambulance.

'Sorry,' said Gabriel.

She couldn't hear him, couldn't hear anything at the

moment actually, as the deafness had returned, but she'd seen him mouth the word. She nodded and tried to touch her face. The medical attendant pushed her hand away. The bullet had been so close that her cheek was seared. The ambo sprayed something cold on her skin that felt wonderful.

'Tell me you're a great shot,' she said to Gabriel. She couldn't hear herself. She was probably shouting.

He smiled at her, reached forward and gently smoothed her fringe from her forehead.

'I'm a great shot,' she saw him say.

Gabriel's hand continued down the length of her hair and onto her shoulder, then stopped. Emotions scudded across his dark eyes like a storm across a night sky. She saw grief, guilt, hope. A question.

She reached up and found his hand, held it tight and closed her eyes. She rested her injured hand on her chest.

Underneath, the butterfly pendant seemed to tremble against her heart.

35

OCCASIONALLY CHLOE HEARD someone sobbing. Felt a little sorry for the girl. At least, it sounded like a girl. You never can tell, she thought sleepily, it sounds kinda muffled. Hands bound behind her back, ankles shackled to the bolt in the brick wall, Chloe Farrell no longer recognised the moans as her own. The gag in her mouth had long ago dried her saliva; her throat rasped raw from screaming through the cloth, but this discomfort and the spasms from her contorted muscles now failed to register. The thirst and pain had pushed her to an altered state of consciousness, a nowhere land, which she accepted, matter-of-factly, as the waiting room for death. After four nights bound and gagged on the floor in Cutter's subterranean room, squashed between his bed and a wardrobe, Chloe was comfortable in the silent softness of her mind.

She was careful, however, to stay away from the edges of this dreamlike state. If she let her mind wander too freely it found the memories – the consciousness of what had happened to her. The images stabbed into the protective bubble surrounding her psyche and filled it with blood.

When the memory played, the recording didn't stop until it had gone right through. Forced to watch it all, what the man had done to his stomach on the bed above her, Chloe had at first tried screaming to herself to run instead of entering the room with Henry Nguyen. Now, she just waited until the memory played out and the muffled nothingness returned.

He'd be back, he had told her, four nights ago.

On the floor, bound to the double-brick wall, the girl whimpered and sobbed. In her mind, far away, Chloe Farrell tuned out the sound and waited to die.

Maryana Miceh couldn't figure out why Mummy had been crying all morning. Probably Daddy said something mean again, she thought. She and Uncle Ken had been watching the boring news all morning. Maryana hadn't even been allowed to watch *Hi-5*. She had thought that her mum would have liked watching *Hi-5* better, because the news just made her cry harder. When she asked Uncle Ken what was wrong, he told her everything was going to be fine, and picked her up and squashed her in a hug. She told him to put her down because his whiskers were scratchy.

When she'd tried to see what they were so interested in on television, Uncle Ken had led her away. Then he had scrooched down to her height and put his hands on her shoulders. He went all serious and she had wanted to smack him because he looked like he was going to cry too. Uncle Ken never cried and he shouldn't start now, while Mummy was so upset. But all he told her was that Henry wouldn't be renting with them any more. Maryana had felt mean and happy at the same time, because she really didn't like Henry. She knew that was un-Christian, because he had always been nice to her and because he had a sore stomach, but she couldn't help it, and she had smiled. Then it had occurred to her that this was probably a Bad Thing. Probably that's why Mummy keeps crying, she thought. We need the money from the rent.

Maryana wondered what would happen to Henry's room now. Maybe she and Eva could use it for playing again. She had been nowhere near the room since she'd seen that man's sore tummy. Now, knowing he wasn't coming back, she ran down into the backyard and squinted through the crack in the wall. Henry had left all his stuff in there. Maybe he didn't want it anymore. That wardrobe looked pretty old. Kneeling on the grass peering in, Maryana thought about the money. Maybe we could have a fete like they did at school last month, she thought. She had heard Mrs Marshall telling Mr Jacoby that they'd made shitloads. That sounded like a lot.

Maryana stood back up. It was hot today. Probably soon they'd be allowed to go swimming.

What was that? She jumped at the sound, dropping back to her knees in the grass.

Again!

Someone's crying in there!

Maryana Miceh ran as fast as she could up to the kitchen, and she could run pretty fast. She'd beaten Jasmine Hard-castle in cross-country last week.

Epilogue

SWEAT STUNG HIS eyes and he used the hand holding his knife to wipe his brow. The scrub here was the thickest he'd encountered, and he hacked at some tangled vines draped like a monstrous spider's web between two trees, blocking his path. Joss had come at this clearing from a different approach yesterday. But he knew it was around here, somewhere.

Shirtless, he tucked his knife back into the equipment belt slung low around his hips. For the tenth time in as many minutes, he pushed dirty blond hair out of his eyes. Maybe he should cut it all off again, he thought.

Just when he was beginning to worry that he'd gone completely off course, Joss found the area he'd been searching for and pulled an axe from his belt. He set to work chopping branches from the fallen tree, the timber dry and covered in papery bark, perfect for firewood.

He didn't stop until there was way too much to carry back. He doubled over, hands on hips, and caught his breath, staring at the sandy soil around his feet; he studied a rivulet of sweat slipping over an ankle and into his sneaker. Fitter than he'd been in a long while, he recovered quickly and straightened, then set to gathering all the wood he could carry into a sling he'd brought for the purpose.

Striding from the scrub that bordered the isolated beach, Joss was forced to squeeze his eyes tight when the brilliance threatened to overload his senses. He opened them again, blinking, and made his way towards the camp. The colours were amazing. The perfect white of the sand and impossible turquoise of the ocean ahead; the honey-tan of Charlie, now five, shovelling sand into her little yellow bucket; and the molten-red of his wife's bikini. She lifted her huge sunglasses and winked at him, a small smile on her lips.

Once he'd stacked the firewood near the tent and the embers of last night's campfire, he kicked off his shoes and walked back through powdered sand. He dropped onto his towel next to his family, and grabbed the bottle of water next to Isobel. As he drank, an image of cold beer flicked up, a mental advertisement, but he quickly changed the channel. He leaned back in the sun, his mind again shifting through scenes of life before today.

There was no way he'd ever have consented to go to rehab until he'd reached the point where he simply had no resistance left. That night, pulling up behind the detective's vehicle at the house in Mosman two minutes before the troops arrived, he'd left Isobel and Charlie in the car. Finding Cutter missing part of his head on the floor of his old bedroom was just too much.

That had been seven months ago. He'd spent three of them in an inpatient unit with around thirty other thirsty vets. He'd left some new friends and old habits at the hospital, along with a couple of the worst memories. He'd also left the person he'd become closer to than anyone else in his life, other than the two people with whom he now shared the beach. Carrie, his therapist. In her office at the hospital, she'd done combat duty with him, walked through his memories, exploring, in exhaustive detail, the experiences he feared had almost pushed him into the madlands his poor mother had inhabited.

Carrie had been at his mum's funeral last month, Isobel holding onto her tearfully before they left. Isobel and Carrie had also done a tour of duty together, during individual and family therapy sessions.

He'd left the bill for the treatment to Veterans' Affairs.

Not that money was an issue now really. He could be retired today if he felt like it. He'd never have believed the house in Mosman would have sold for so much.

But taking the winter off to holiday in the Top End would do fine. He smiled lazily, watching Charlie scratch an itch on her pink zinc-covered nose, the action sticking sand to her face. She scratched again, and more sand smudged into the pink cream.

She'd start school next year, they'd decided. And he'd go back to the insurance company. As much time as you need, the partners had insisted, sending a monthly bouquet of flowers out to him at the hospital. He'd given them to the nurses before the other guys had seen them.

Isobel told him that his work colleagues had telephoned her and offered their support, expressing their shock when they'd learned he'd served the country in Rwanda. Great, he'd thought more than once since then; they were the type of guys who'd want war stories every lunchtime, but wouldn't eat with him again if he told them the real deal.

Charlie stood from her sandcastles and moved around to the left side of his chair; she carried her bucket with her everywhere. Her nose was now completely covered in pink sand, and she swiped a tentative finger at it every couple of moments, gluing on some more.

'Um, do you want to go for a swim, Daddy?' she said. 'I'm hot.'

'Yep. Me too,' he smiled at her. 'But maybe you should go and show your mum your face before we go swimming. You've gotta do something about your nose.'

She gave him a look of quiet indignation, then half-dragged and half-rolled herself across his stomach, the most direct route to her mother.

'Mummy,' she said, standing proudly, pot-bellied in her yellow bikini, her bucket by her side, 'Could you please fix my nose? I'm not decent.'

Dr Leah Giarratano has had a long career as a clinical psychologist. An expert in psychological trauma, sex offences and psychopathology, she has had many years' experience working with victims and psychopaths. She has worked in psychiatric hospitals, with the Australian Defence Force, and in corrective services with offenders who suffer severe personality disorders. She has assessed and treated survivors of just about every imaginable psychological trauma, including hostages; war veterans; rape, assault, and accident victims; and has worked with police, fire and ambulance officers.